Meridian

TATTERED & TORN

AURELIA T. EVANS

ENTWINED PUBLISHING

Tattered & Torn
ISBN # 978-1-80250-254-1
©Copyright Aurelia T. Evans 2025
Cover Art by Kelly Martin ©Copyright June 2025
Interior text design by Entwined Publishing
Published by Eternal, an Entwined Publishing imprint

Published in 2025 by Entwined Publishing, United Kingdom.

Entwined Publishing is a division of Totally Entwined Group Limited.

TATTERED & TORN

Book six in the Meridian series

She's fallen from heaven, but has she fallen from grace?

When she hits the stairs of the Archimedes Public Library of Meridian, battered and naked, she doesn't know who she is, how she ended up there, or why her shoulders hurt so much.

Police detectives and demon hunters Noah Dunn and Andrea Black immediately recognize her as an angel. The only problem is that, with her wings ripped from her and her memory hazy at best, there's no way to determine whether she's an angel turned human or entirely fallen from grace.

For now, Jane Doe is just trying to get used to being human. Until she figures out what she's doing in a spiritual battleground like Meridian, she agrees to lend her empathic powers to the detectives' aid.

They especially need her now, as the summer heats up and the street kids they protect start to go feral...or missing.

Prologue

On an unseasonably cool evening in September — a Tuesday — a meteor entered Earth's atmosphere, scorched the dimming sky with a blue glow for fifteen seconds, then burned out over Meridian, Texas, before it could hit the ground.

This, in itself, was not unusual.

Objects from space enter Earth's atmosphere all the time without anyone seeing them, especially during the day. However, this celestial event occurred when the sky was dark enough and the meteor itself large enough to last long enough to notice. A number of security cameras also caught the event.

In this case, only a handful of people actually noticed it, and because it didn't last long enough to capture on their phones, most of them promptly forgot. No one posted asking about whether someone else had seen that flash in the sky or some UFO. No one reported it to news outlets. No meteorologist thought it was important enough to mention during the evening news.

The event lasted fifteen seconds, in a brilliant bright sapphire, and died without fanfare.

* * * *

The head librarian of Archimedes Public Library — three stories of books, a rare book collection, several rows of DVDs that echoed Blockbusters of old, and a children's section that doubled as a play-date space, a mix of the magical and modern that made her proud to be a book bearer — switched off the last light in her office. She folded her jacket and scarf over her arm in case the false fall weather was too chilly for her from the building to her car.

After locking the grand wooden double doors behind her, Beth gripped the railing to descend the two dozen stairs down to the street. On wet days, the stairs were a bit more difficult and she would use the zigzagging accessibility ramp to ease her way down, but tonight she was feeling particularly lively, and she was looking forward to a date with an older gentleman at one of her favorite restaurants.

He'd texted her to let her know that he'd already arrived at the restaurant and was ordering some wine for when she arrived. This was their third date, and although she hadn't been looking forward to returning to the dating world, she was quite enjoying being courted. Her apartment still smelled good from the roses he'd bought for her last time. And, since this was their third date, she might just let him try to kiss her.

Young people usually thought the third date was the sex date, but she and Gerard weren't going that fast — although she certainly wasn't planning to wait six months like with her first boyfriend, back before texting and golden-age dating apps. There was something exhausting and exhilarating about trying again, though, in the new world, with its new ways.

Beth had lived in Meridian all her life. A few years ago, she'd transferred from the old public library to the Archimedes, which the notoriously solitary Mr. Vega had built for the city. She'd watched Meridian turn from a nothing waystation on the way to Fort Worth to a bustling city to rival Dallas. She hadn't known whether she'd like it as buildings stole the horizon and it began its inevitable sprawl into suburbs, but she was still here, her family was here, and it wasn't terrible at all.

Her shoe hit an uneven place on a concrete stair. Beth clung to the brass railing to keep from falling.

The Archimedes was such a new build, even by Meridian's standards, that there was no reason why the concrete should already have been so uneven from the annual freeze and melt—which seemed to destroy streets and sidewalks solely for the devil to laugh at the inevitable skinned knees, black eyes, and tire blowouts.

Streetlights hadn't quite caught up to the earlier evening darkness, and Beth's eyes weren't so good at night anymore. She found her flashlight app and switched it on to see what that dark blob in the slightly darker blob on the stairs could possibly be. No one had run in to tell her that something terrible had happened during open hours. And she might have bad night eyes and needed to wear special glasses to drive, but she would have noticed if there had been an earthquake, even a minor one.

The flashlight switched on—blinding at first, but her eyes eventually adjusted.

Beth stumbled back a few steps with a gasp. A shriek strangled in her throat behind the hand she brought to her freshly lipsticked mouth.

"Oh my God, you poor dear. Oh my."

She fumbled to get to the actual phone part of her phone to call the emergency services.

"Hello? Hello? Yes, I'm at the Archimedes Public Library. My name is Beth Holding. I'm the head librarian. There's an unconscious woman on the front steps. The concrete is all broken around her, and it looks like she's knocked out and bleeding. No, she's not dead. I may not be a doctor, young man, but I can see her breathing. No, I haven't touched her. I don't want to hurt her any more than she already is. Oh, she looks like she's been beaten pretty badly, or maybe it was a fall? I can't imagine how or why. Just get paramedics down here quickly. Oh, dear. Can I cover her with my jacket? She's not wearing a stitch. Okay, I can hear sirens."

Beth crept carefully down the steps and unfolded her jacket to shake it out like a blanket and cover the poor girl's nakedness. She was bleeding from multiple places on her bare body, but not terribly. Just by eye under the flashlight, Beth couldn't tell if she had any broken bones.

"Just hold on, sweetheart," Beth whispered to the girl. "Just hold on. See? Help is on the way. I'll pray for your healing."

Red and blue lights flashed against the looming hulk of the library above. Beth ran down to meet the paramedics, who pulled out a gurney but rushed with a spine board up to where the woman lay halfway up the stairs.

When Beth turned back to watch them, shining her light where they were working, she thought it was such a curious thing. Where the concrete damage spread from a central point under the girl, the cracks looked just like wings.

Chapter One

The first thing she knew was darkness and pain.

She sensed even then that it wasn't really the first thing, that the real first thing had been so far away from darkness and pain that these things were especially terrifying now. But it was just a sense, not a complete thought.

Pain and darkness first. Then terror.

She wasn't sure she'd ever felt any of these things before, but they felt like all that there was.

Then she opened her eyes, and there was light. Even though it was only from fluorescent tubes between wormy ceiling tiles, the light chased away some of the terror.

She sighed, although everything still hurt, including her ribs, which made breathing ache like a bruise. She didn't think things like breathing and blinking were supposed to be so hard and she didn't think light was supposed to be so bright, but she *was* breathing, she *was* blinking, and there *was* light. All of these things were good. The hurt, not so much. But she breathed and blinked again and again, until she could flex her diaphragm and make a sound during an exhale.

Rustling compelled her to turn her head with an involuntary groan away from the fluorescent lights. A flimsy blue curtain surrounded her bed, about two feet away on every side. Blue sheets covered the partially reclined hospital bed. A thicker textured blanket over them kept her legs warm, which was good, because everything not covered by the sheets was cold. The hospital gown she wore was as flimsy as the curtains, inadequate against the aggressive chill.

To her right was a vital signs monitor. It was silent, but the changing numbers of her temperature, oxygenation, and the jumping line of her heartbeat briefly fascinated her.

Her heartbeat. Somehow, that seemed significant and marvelous. She watched it for what seemed like a long time and not long at all before turning her head the other way.

She groaned again. Her neck didn't like it when she moved. Her head didn't like it much, either. In fact, her entire body told her to lie still and maybe close her eyes again, now that she knew the dark wasn't all-encompassing.

But on the other side of her was a man, straightening in his chair. Underneath his gray trench coat, he wore a sports shirt and light chinos — both rumpled and wrinkled — and a loosened tie.

"Hello, ma'am. Can you hear me?"

"Where am I?" Her voice was weak, soft. It surprised her coming out of her own throat, although she couldn't remember how else it was supposed to sound.

He looked confused and a little frustrated until she realized she hadn't spoken in the same language that he'd spoken to her. She blinked a few times, moving her tongue around in her mouth as though in adjustment, then repeated herself.

"Oh, good. My Spanish is passable, but I don't know a lick of French."

"Sorry."

He shook his head to indicate it wasn't important. "You're in the Meridian Mercy Hospital. Did you know you were in Meridian, Texas?"

She tried to shake her head like him but winced. When she blinked, she saw in her thoughts an image of Texas, but she didn't know where Meridian would be on it, why she would be in Texas, or where she'd come from.

"You were unresponsive when the paramedics picked you up," the man said. "I'm going to ask you some questions now, if that's okay, ma'am."

She didn't reply, because she wasn't sure if it was okay or not.

He pulled a notebook out of his pocket and leaned forward, his elbows on his knees as he poised a pen. "Can you tell me your name?"

She blinked so hard that her forehead hurt. She was pretty sure the first question was supposed to be the easiest one.

"It's okay. We'll move on. Do you know what day it is?"

She couldn't tell in her curtained room whether it was day or night, much less what day it was. Did he mean day of the week or the date? Didn't matter. She didn't know, either.

She wasn't sure how, if she didn't know what day or date it was, she knew what each of the days and dates it could be. It was like all the information was there on the pantry shelf, but she wasn't the one who'd bought it, and there were things hidden around a corner that would elucidate everything else, but she couldn't reach them.

Something was wrong. Something was wrong in her head. Maybe that was why it hurt so much. As though someone had crawled into her skull and mugged her memories. How could she know what mugging was when she couldn't remember whether she'd been mugged or where she'd learned what mugging was in the first place?

"Hey, hey, it's okay. Do you know who the president is?"

President. President. A president was a kind of leader. *Take me to your leader.* Heads on coins. Heads on bills. Heads on busts. She thought of these things but had no context of herself with them. Did she have coins? Bills? Busts? No. She had a head of her own. She had hands. Who was president again? She thought she knew, but she couldn't find it.

"It's okay, ma'am. Calm down."

She was breathing hard and fast, even though it ached to do both. "It's not okay. It's *not* okay. You don't think it's okay, either. You're frustrated. Do you think I can't answer or that I won't answer?"

"Ma'am, it's okay. Calm down and it'll be easier to think of things. The harder you try, your whole head might blow." He smiled to defuse her panic but clicked his pen several times over. She'd given him nothing to write.

"Why can't I answer your questions?" She flexed her hands under the sheets, which was when she realized that the white bandages on her arms weren't part of the hospital gown. "What happened to me? Do we know each other?"

"We don't know each other." The man shifted his pen to his notebook hand. He rested his right on hers, with the sheets and blanket between them. "I'm Detective Noah Dunn. Me and my partner have been watching over you off and on for a few days, waiting for you to wake up. As to what happened to you, we were hoping you could tell us."

"Is everything supposed to hurt this much?"

"You wouldn't be in the hospital if it was," Dunn said. "You've been healing quickly — unusually quickly — but you had a lot to heal from. The swelling's gone down a lot, and it doesn't look like you broke any bones. Some people might call that a miracle."

"Doesn't feel like a miracle."

He laughed. "No, I don't suppose it does. But you were found on broken concrete without clothes or identification or any record from surrounding video of how you ended up there. One moment everything was normal. There was what seems like some kind of electronic glitch in all the cameras in the area, and then you're there, *boom*, like Wile E. Coyote losing the battle with gravity. Anyway, if it feels like you ran into a brick wall, it's because that's not far from the truth. I guess we're here to ask you if you remember anything to clarify the confusion. Don't get me wrong. Strange things happen in Meridian every day, but that doesn't mean we stop asking the questions."

"I can't answer them. I don't remember what happened."

"What do you remember?"

He took his pen in his right hand again. When she flexed her fingers once more, her knuckles pushed against the blankets. Wincing with each angle change of her elbows, she pulled her hands out from under the sheets. They were covered with smaller individual bandages. She moved each of her fingers, fascinated by the way they listened to her even though they didn't feel like hers — maybe because of all the bandages and injuries.

"They looked like oven mitts when you first came in. The doctors thought you'd broken every bone in your body, but most of your injuries turned out to be superficial, although not exactly mild. I believe the total was five hundred forty-three stitches, give or take a hundred."

"Is that bad?"

"Does it feel bad?"

"Yes."

"The doctor said you might experience some amnesia about the event, because the CT indicated a concussion, although not a terrible one. We weren't expecting amnesia quite this...complete."

"You're frustrated."

"It's okay, ma'am."

"Why do you keep saying that? It's not okay. You don't think it's okay. You think I'm faking it or confused or crazy. I am confused, and I don't know if I'm crazy, but I'm not faking it."

"Ma'am..."

"Stop calling me that. It's wrong. It's wrong. All of this is wrong. My arms. I need to see my arms. I need to see my body. Something's terribly wrong. And it's not okay. Stop pretending you think this is okay."

"Well, the more you tell me it's not okay and that I'm frustrated, the more frustrated I am, so it's kind of a self-fulfilling prophecy," the man said, irritation finally creeping into his tone.

But he wasn't rough when he set his notebook and pen aside to cover both her hands with his to keep her from scratching at the edges of the bandages.

"As long as we don't know who you are, there's only so much I can call you. We have you listed as a Jane Doe for now. There've been no missing persons reports that match your description. You have no tattoos or piercings, and if you have any distinguishing birthmarks or scars or anything else, we've been waiting for all the hematomas and lacerations to heal and the swelling to go down enough to see them. And for you to wake up, of course. Am I frustrated that you can't tell me anything? Yes. But I'm not frustrated *at you*. All right? And if I'm suspicious, I'm afraid it's a hazard of the trade. We'll get to the bottom of this, ma'am."

"Detective?"

"Yes, ma'am."

"If you have to call me anything, call me Jane, although I don't like that, either. It's like these bandages. Like it doesn't fit or move right."

Dunn searched her face as though looking for clues, but he couldn't seem to find any. "Okay. If you don't mind, I'd like to call my colleague. She's nearby, just doing some work while I watch over you. With your permission, she'd like to be present while your doctor assesses your progress and gives us an estimation of when you can be released. If you're well enough to stand, she would like to take some pictures of your injuries and see if she can record distinguishing marks as well to update our report and make combing through missing persons easier."

"Just her?" she said. "You won't be there?"

"It's not procedure for a man to be in the room while a woman is being photographed for evidentiary purposes."

"Why?"

"Because being naked with a stranger makes people feel vulnerable enough without adding the awkwardness and the sometimes threatening power dynamic of the opposite sex. It also eliminates the potential for sexual harassment lawsuits."

She followed the path of the bandages on her arms to the thin hospital gown. The gown was mostly flat over her chest, but she had bandages there, too, all over her body. They obscured her shape, more like a ragdoll than a person, but that wasn't the only reason she was familiar yet unfamiliar at the same time.

"I want out of these bandages."

"One thing at a time. You might not be in a good state to even stand if your head still hurts. Are these lights hurting your eyes?"

"Yes."

"We should definitely get a doctor in here. And if you don't mind my saying, m— Jane, you still have a catheter in. So I'm going to fetch my partner, who will fetch your nurse, who will fetch a doctor. The nurse is an old friend of ours, the doctor an old acquaintance."

"Okay."

Dunn left her alone in the small curtained room, but as he left, he gave her a glimpse of the world beyond those curtains. The curtained room was part of a much larger room, albeit a quiet one, and although the lights were bright right over her, they weren't on everywhere in the larger room. Beyond her little room murmured conversation both casual and confidential, but there was shouting in another part of the floor, or maybe underneath it. The fluorescents buzzed above and around her, with the moans of the dreaming and suffering, grunts of effort, sobs that brought tears to her eyes.

She didn't prefer the darkness and pain. She preferred the nothing from before she'd realized she was in either one. But now that she was awake and aware, she couldn't convince herself to fall back asleep. Even so, she rested her eyes until the rustle and clatter of the curtain rings compelled her to open them again. She winced once more from the light.

Noah led in three very different women. The first was in jeans and a plain tucked-in shirt under a three-quarters peacoat. Like Noah, she carried a gun in a hip holster, which was revealed when her jacket swayed open. The second had curly red hair and wore pink scrubs. She was shorter than Andrea, and curvier. The third wore a white coat, red blouse, and black slacks.

"Jane, this is Andrea Black, my partner. The nurse is Poppy. She's been taking care of you during the nightshifts. Dr. Hanover here sutured most of your lacerations and has been keeping up with your assessments."

"You really have been making amazing progress," Dr. Hanover said, "what some might call preternatural. It's the difference between a few weeks of suture maintenance and many, many months of physical therapy. I know you don't feel normal now, but everything you're experiencing, including your amnesia, is not unusual or cause for immediate concern. However, I'd like to take you in for another scan to see the progress of your concussion. Then we'll see about those bandages you're not enjoying."

* * * *

After what felt like too much poking, prodding, pulling, pricking, and loud, loud, loud noises during the imaging tests, Jane just wanted to go back to her room-within-a-room and maybe have something to cover her head against the light, which seemed to be everywhere.

"It's going to take the radiologist a few hours to get back to us on the scans, although just from my cursory glance, it looks like the hematoma is entirely healed, which is amazing improvement in such a short time," Dr. Hanover said. "Trauma-based retrograde amnesia is trickier business. It may not even have anything to do with the concussion at all. Your brain could simply be protecting you."

"Protecting me?"

"The brain is a funny organ. It plays memory tricks. Its usual razzle-dazzle is remembering things that never happened, mixing up details, sometimes creating or removing them. Unless you've got a special brain hard-wired to retain information, memory's a shiftable and undependable thing, but it's all most of us have got. Contrary to popular belief, traumatic events tend to brand themselves into people's memories, but there's a significant enough fraction who lose that traumatic event instead. We can't control it, and you may never access it again, but it can also reemerge when you least expect it."

"Should I be encouraged or worried?" Jane asked.

"That's between you and your therapist, I'm afraid."

"I don't have clothes. What makes you think I have a therapist?"

The doctor smiled. "Andrea and Noah aren't going to just throw you to the wolves. There are places you can stay until you can get back on your feet. Some of those places have counsellors and access to anonymous support groups. Are you hungry? We've been feeding you intravenously, but we can rustle you up something from the cafeteria. Body repair requires plenty of protein and carbs."

She was hungry—at least, that's what she thought those low cramps centered in her upper abdomen were—but she didn't want to eat. She wanted answers.

"Poppy, why don't you get our guest something to eat? Now, let's see if we can't remove this IV and the catheter. Noah, Andrea, if you'll excuse us…"

Noah and Andrea started out through the curtain.

"No. Why do they have to go?" Jane asked.

"For your privacy. The catheter isn't much fun coming out, and going to the bathroom afterward is sometimes difficult. But after all the intravenous fluids you've been getting, you'll want to go to the bathroom in the next few hours. Poppy can help you with that, whether in the bedpan or the patient-access bathrooms down the way."

"We'll be right outside," Noah said. "We'll come have dinner with you."

"Splendid. Now, shoo."

Then it was just her and the doctor alone, who seemed capable, if chatty, as she removed the IV needle from Jane's hand. The doctor left in the IV on her arm connected to the low-dose morphine drip. Next, the doctor folded back the sheets and blanket and, after asking permission, lifted the hospital gown, giving Jane a good look at her mummy legs and feet as well. When she moved those mounds of bandaged knees, they panged so hard that the headache she'd been fighting panged right back in answer.

The doctor patted her thigh. "Try not to push yourself to do too much too soon. No matter how quickly you're healing, it's still a process, and the best of these processes is rest. Let me move you the way I need to."

Jane tried not to whimper or kick out at the doctor as she removed the incontinence underwear, mercifully clean, then the catheter.

"No blood where it shouldn't be so far," the doctor said. "Another good sign. Was that too unpleasant?"

Jane shook her head.

"Good. Now, use this emergency button on your bed when you need the bathroom. It goes directly to the nurses' station."

For the life of her, Jane couldn't remember how to go to the bathroom, although it seemed like one of those things that a person should know, that she wouldn't even have to think about. Maybe, when the time came, she wouldn't.

When she was settled again, the doctor put her oximeter back on to update her vitals.

"It really is amazing how much you've improved since you arrived. We feared for your life at first, but they should study your body's reparative abilities. Noah and Andrea always bring in the weird ones. Between you, me, and the wall, I think they like working with me because I don't make a fuss about the weirdness. Bodies in general are strange and varied, and it's unethical for me to make a spectacle of you just because things work a little different for you than me. If I wanted more attention, I'd write more articles, wouldn't I?"

Jane didn't know what the doctor was talking about, but she learned more from everything she heard, even when it didn't make sense. So Jane liked that the doctor chattered like this, although she suspected it was intended more as a distraction from the things that the doctor was doing to test the movability of her joints and Jane's reaction. The bandages impeded her motion some, but she did what she could while waiting for the detectives to return with food, because like the bathroom, she felt like she should remember what ice cream and spaghetti tasted like. She knew what these things looked like — like pictures in a children's book — but she couldn't recall anything ever being in her mouth.

As a result of the doctor's chattering, Jane calmed. Even her pain had receded a little. At the very least, it wasn't insurmountable. She didn't know who she was or what she was doing in a place where she didn't think she was supposed to be, but the people who surrounded her were nice enough.

Andrea and Noah returned with a disposable plastic tray of what limited cafeteria food was available overnight. Andrea set the tray up on the hospital bed table while Noah opened a bag of plastic cutlery.

Jane stared at the collection of components for a while, trying to figure out how to hold the fork and knife, although she didn't think she was supposed to need the knife for what was provided. No, she needed the spoon for the mashed potatoes and gravy, the fork for the green beans. She could use her hands for the cheeseburger, which was what the bun was for.

Once Jane determined that was the order and arrangement of things, Dr. Hanover made a note in the file that she hung at the end of the bed. "I need to work with some other patients, but if you do well with food, we'll look into how your exceptional healing has treated your stitches."

* * * *

Noah and Andrea were enthralled by her while she ate dinner. They'd bought themselves something so she wouldn't have to eat alone, just some day-old croissants from the café, but long after they'd finished, Jane continued to exclaim over every bite of food. It didn't matter that just the act of chewing made her head hurt. The food itself seemed to help with the headache, as did the water she drank with a straw once she figured out the combination of mechanics required.

Jane couldn't speak to the quality of the food. The sight of it was less than thrilling, as though elements of the burger weren't quite real, others too dry. The green beans, in contrast, were a little too wet, swimming in water from the steam bath and some butter. Nevertheless, as she applied herself to the process of eating—more complex than anticipated, but once she figured it out, required less thought—she felt as though she tasted everything and experienced its texture for the first time, and every bit of it was the most amazing thing she'd ever had.

"Hungry?" Andrea said.

Jane nodded, although the cramping sensation in her upper abdomen had calmed down. She wiped her mouth with the paper napkin provided. "Detectives, I know you have questions for me. I'm sorry I can't answer them. But I have questions for you."

Noah sat back in the chair where he'd been when she'd awakened. Andrea sat on the foot of the bed.

"Dr. Hanover says my case is a weird one and that you specialize in weird cases. I was that weird case well before I woke up, unable to remember what happened or anything at all. Why are you still here? I'm not going anywhere, and I don't think I'm dangerous. Did I do something wrong?"

Noah and Andrea shared another glance. They were about the same age, casual in each other's company, and the way they danced around each other and communicated without speaking—a kind of shorthand, primitive telepathy—suggested they'd been partners for a long time.

"We're here because of the mystery around the accident. We don't know how you got hurt, nor what hurt you or what hurt the concrete under you more," Noah said. "We don't know if it was an accident or if you were attacked. Although you were naked, there were no signs of sexual assault, but that doesn't mean someone didn't want to hurt you."

"And from the mystery of your arrival, more mysteries compound," Andrea added. "Who you are. Where you came from. Why you appeared to have broken bones at the scene, but by the time you arrived at Mercy, X-rays showed no breaks. Why you're healing at an accelerated rate. And we're still hoping your memory returns so at least some of these questions can be answered. You're not our only priority, but you're certainly not something we see every day."

"Well, she hasn't thrown up what she ate, so let's consider that a success. I'll go tell Poppy," Noah said, leaving before Jane could ask him what they were hiding from her.

And they were hiding something.

Their secrets made her suspicious. Of their motives. Of their kindness. Of their lingering. But regardless of her suspicions, she was completely dependent on them. She was able to move but hadn't yet tried to walk. She'd been able to eat but still suffered stinging and stabbing sensations in her jaw, in her head, and had needed to pause to work out what a fork was for.

If she were somehow able to get up, she still couldn't run. If she were able to run, anything on the way could stop her because she simply wouldn't know how to use it fast enough.

And where would she run to? What would she be running from? Until she had some kind of foundation, she had no choice but to stay, and they had no choice, it seemed, but to stay with her.

At least they *were* kind, superficial or transactional though it might have been. Andrea smiled at her, although she didn't say anything as she studied Jane with a slightly worried expression.

"I'm not a complete mystery, am I?" Jane said. "The two of you are looking for something, something the doctor doesn't know to look for. What is it?"

"We won't know unless we find it," Andrea replied.

Jane rested back on her pillow. Without something or someone engaging her, she realized she was quite tired. Unconsciousness she understood. It was simply nothingness. She didn't understand this feeling of weight in her head that wasn't headache, nor why doing so little had exhausted her. Perhaps it was from the constant confusion, trying to figure *everything* out, and her frustration, which mirrored that of the two police detectives. Both they and her own mind were withholding from her, leaving her lost in a jigsaw puzzle body that didn't feel like her own.

At least she'd learned that cheeseburgers tasted good, and she could eat a whole bowl of mashed potatoes with white gravy. If what she'd eaten wasn't considered the pinnacle of haute cuisine, how much better was better food?

To that thought, she slipped into sleep and woke to Noah in his chair and Andrea in another chair that she must have found while waiting. As soon as Andrea realized Jane was awake, she snapped at Noah to look up from his phone, then pushed herself out of the chair to fetch someone.

"How long was I asleep?" Jane asked.

Noah stood to stretch his legs. "Not long. Recovery, even accelerated — or maybe *because* it's accelerated — is draining. I've been there myself."

"You've been where?"

"In a hospital bed, restless as hell but falling asleep at the drop of a hat. And if you don't mind my saying, when I was last in a hospital bed, I might have been gored, but I didn't look as bad as you did when you first arrived at Mercy. You want answers. I want answers, too. But accelerated healing or not, you can't rush it." He touched the bandages on her arm lightly.

The place he touched warmed, and that warmth spread, and not from the heat in his body.

He blinked, then jerked his hand away as though he'd touched something hot.

Poppy came back in and deputized Noah to help her push the hospital bed out again, this time into an empty examination room. There, Poppy helped her shift from the bed to the paper-covered vinyl table to see if she could sit up on her own. Jane found she could sit, but she immediately started shaking. Noah pulled off the blanket from the hospital bed to wrap around her shoulders. Jane smiled weakly as he wheeled the bed back out into the hall to give everyone more room.

Dr. Hanover came in with the records while Poppy was taking more vitals, as the bandages allowed.

"Looks like you're doing so well," Dr. Hanover said, checking the last vitals against Poppy's. "Now, Noah's going to toddle on out of here while Poppy helps me with your bandages and Andrea takes photographs. Does that sound all right to you?"

"Can Noah stay?"

Dr. Hanover and Andrea shared a similar glance as Andrea and Noah before.

"Why do you want him to stay?" Dr. Hanover asked.

"Whatever pictures Andrea takes he's going to see anyway."

"That's true," Andrea said. "But it's not—"

"Procedure. With a woman. Is that what I am?" Jane held up her hands again. "Somehow, that doesn't seem right. Either way, he'll see me. Wouldn't you rather speak — or not speak — to each other in the same room rather than repeat it later?"

"I'll need for you to make a statement to that effect," Andrea said slowly. "But if she approves, I guess there's no reason why he can't stay. Are *you* okay with that, Noah?"

He nodded, also slowly, as though to give Jane the opportunity to rescind. "I'll stand right over here. I'm not going anywhere."

Chapter Two

Over the course of working as a cop in the city of Meridian, Noah had learned never to be surprised by anything, or at least not to be surprised by being surprised.

He honestly didn't know how anyone lived in this town thinking it was normal, but people had their own coping mechanisms — like whatever blocked Jane Doe's memories, because he didn't think a concussion had anything to do with it.

Sure, every anomaly in her amnesia could be dismissed as medically valid, if unusual. But this was Meridian, and the circumstances of the incident that had brought her to Mercy were far from medically explicable. He was absolutely certain paramedics recognized broken bones when they saw them. That by the time she'd gotten an X-ray she didn't have a single crack didn't mean the paramedics had misdiagnosed. Weeks' worth of swelling had receded in days to the point that the woman's basic structure had become more apparent, like a person emerging from a slab of amorphous marble.

The uncanniness of her healing was no more apparent than when Dr. Hanover and Poppy started peeling Jane Doe's bandages from her hands and arms. Upon the removal of the adhesive bandages on Jane's hands, Dr. Hanover paused.

There were people like the good doctor all over the city who weren't in complete denial about the weirdness in Meridian, although far from being entirely enlightened, Dr. Hanover was simply the kind who didn't question it. Still, on occasion, she blinked.

She blinked now, trying to make sense of the sutures crisscrossing complete scars or nearly healed scabs edged with new pink skin. Finally, she held Jane Doe's hand out for Andrea to photograph, palm up, then down.

Andrea, too, seemed shaken. She'd always been more sensitive to Meridian's strange than Noah, probably because she'd grown up in a fairly quiet suburb. She had some kind of hard string in the back of her mind that sometimes twanged in the direction of the supernatural — not a full-blown lighthouse in the darkness, but she had a glimmer. Noah trusted that instinct implicitly.

Noah didn't have anything like it himself, but he had experience, and his family had moved him to Meridian almost as soon as it had improbably sprung up out of the prairie desert for what seemed like no reason at all — like a mirage, or perhaps inspired by one.

Noah was more unsettled by the fact Andrea was shaken than that the woman had healed so fast that she looked like she'd been stitched for no reason at all. Maybe Andrea hadn't fully believed they'd found what Noah had thought they'd found.

It was almost funny. They lived in a city where cryptids, monsters, and demons lived, where stone angels and gargoyles moved and sometimes flew, where they rousted a new demonic cult every week, but Andrea was having trouble with a newly fallen angel. For Noah, there was no mistaking it. He'd had the librarian send him the picture she'd taken of Jane Doe on the steps. One of the paramedics had grabbed a shot of it as well before they'd left.

Even if he didn't have those pictures, he had the library's security video. It had glitched out for five whole seconds, a few seconds before and after impact, but it showed enough.

And even if he didn't have that, Public Works hadn't repaired the steps yet. Noah and Andrea had put caution tape, hobbyhorses, and cones around it and covered the imprint of wings with tarp so it wouldn't become another 'Jesus in a grilled cheese sandwich' selfie moment. The last thing incidences like this—and Jane Doe—needed were attention.

Unlike Dr. Hanover, who tiptoed on the edges of understanding for her own sanity, Poppy was firmly part of the Meridian frontlines with the two detectives. She'd been a nightshift nurse long enough to witness Meridian's dark side firsthand, and she'd almost been killed by a vampire five years ago. Noah and Andrea had been the ones to find her before a pestilence demon had pulled her into a gutter, which meant she'd since trusted them enough to send cases their way. She didn't flinch as she continued to unwind the bandages on the Jane Doe's arms, revealing more stretches of largely healed skin.

"I don't know how I'm going to explain this away," Dr. Hanover said as Andrea took multiple flash photographs of Jane Doe's arms, which looked less like she'd been in a terrible impact accident a few nights ago and more like she'd been a Frankensteined experiment a few months ago.

Jane herself seemed just as quietly fascinated by her own arms as everyone else, almost unblinking, as though she kept forgetting she needed to, then blinking several times in succession to make up for it.

The bandages, which had covered most of her skin like clothing, had also caused the illusion of bulk. Without them, she was alarmingly thin, her skin nearly translucent, as though from a wasting disease, which put the way she'd eaten the cafeteria food into some perspective, although she wasn't quite to the point that her bones seemed overly large in comparison, like some people who had lost a great deal of weight too quickly or beyond the structure of their frame. Noah could think of no reason why an angel, fallen or not, would or could be malnourished.

Most angels and demons kept information about the Great Beyond secret from mortals on the physical plane. They didn't agree on much, but they agreed about that. People were obsessed with heaven, hell, the karmic wheel after death. However, the spiritual plane didn't actually seem to be that relevant to the physical plane, not when the spiritual entities seemed so damn aflutter to get physical. It was funny, really, looking at it from the outside — everyone on the other side fighting to get in and everyone in the world fighting to get out.

The question passed back and forth between himself and his partner — Why was this one fighting to get in?

He was inclined to believe she really did have amnesia. Most stone angels and gargoyles didn't talk to him — and the demons talked too much, though you couldn't trust what they said — but from what little he'd gleaned, the transition from heaven to earth was a tad bumpy. He got jetlag flying from DFW to LaGuardia to visit his sister. He almost always drove when he and Andrea worked together because otherwise he got carsick just traveling around one city. Jane Doe had traveled much farther.

He and Andrea hadn't even really confirmed what she was yet. They'd almost been afraid to. They knew it happened, of course. There was that biblical reference to the dragon sweeping his tail and knocking a third of the angels down, but Noah didn't know how he felt about the Book of Revelation or whether he could ever hope to make heads or tails of John's acid trip. All he knew was that Meridian had been the site of many fallen angels, although by no means the only location where they fell. Maybe John the Divine's revelation was fast and loose with timelines, like Genesis, and his revelation meant that a third of the angels would fall over time.

Irrelevant? Perhaps to him, especially since it seemed like not all fallen angels became demons, and he'd never read that one in his Sunday school lessons. Cemeteries and building edges were filled with those who'd remained angels, just turned to stone.

Sure, they could be demons in disguise pretending to be angels, but that would mean that Christian spiritualist Angela Cabrera was a wolf in sheep's clothing and that her rumored tension with the darker occultist and alleged Satanist Bartholomew Vega was a sham.

No one had actually confirmed which kind of Satanist Vega was—if he was one at all—but from Noah's experience, Vega's energy in Meridian was cold, cruel, and the runes and spells built into his architectural influence upon Meridian were part of the reason why the city was such a demon magnet.

Cabrera's work was also everywhere, even on Vega buildings, and her primary work had a much different energy. Noah wasn't all that much of an 'energy' person, but someone behind him made his neck hairs prickle, children's choirs creeped him out, as did any kind of public chanting, and Cabrera's pieces didn't do any of that to him. What she built into her art was far more benign, and he'd worked in concert with gargoyles before.

Meridian had definitely had its share of nephilim either way, with atypical records of meteors and meteorites in the area going back fifty years and as recently as a year ago — not counting Jane Doe's arrival on the steps of the Archimedes.

Most records had the falls either burning up before they hit the earth or, if they made impact, hitting in less populated areas — on the outskirts, in the forest, or outside Meridian entirely. In all Noah's time working for the Meridian Police Department, he couldn't recall a single fallen angel ending up in the hospital from her injuries. Maybe they all arrived like that, though, and she'd just been brought in for those injuries because she'd fallen in the middle of the city rather than outside. Maybe the others only crawled in when their Humpty Dumpties were all put back together again.

He'd never met a nephil right after their arrival, or one who didn't know what they were or who wouldn't know yet whether they were angel or demon. It was an interesting opportunity to witness a process no one else had ever personally experienced before — or if they had, they hadn't put it in writing. And if she was an incipient demon, they could possibly nip her plans in the bud before she had time to reach full power.

That was his and Andrea's working theory, anyway, or at least it had been when they'd viewed the librarian's picture of Jane Doe from before she'd been removed from the Archimedes steps. Meeting Jane Doe in person while she'd been still in a coma, broken, bandaged all over, had shamed their usual spiritual bullshitting. She was a real person—or at least that's what she looked like. Pitiful. Pathetic. Even fragile. The demons of this world were often indistinguishable from people, but even the ones who successfully hid behind a human appearance couldn't completely conceal their nature from people who knew what to look for, especially when those people had an All-Seeing Eye tattooed somewhere on their body.

She'd looked like a woman who'd been on the wrong side of a domestic, which he'd seen a lot as a beat cop. These days, he saw cult sacrifice, eviscerations, even massacres, the kinds of cruelties that happened when you mixed monsters and demons with humans—and it wasn't always the monsters and demons doing the evil.

But there was something so fucking intimate about just one woman looking like someone who should love her had beaten her black and blue until her welts had split.

It certainly made him a little sick to his stomach about God, if God was the one responsible for this. Or maybe falling was like diving from a high cliff into water that only looked like it was deep—reckless irresponsibility on the part of the one who jumped.

Noah had a lot of questions. But living on the fence between natural and supernatural meant getting used to a world with questions and not a lot of easy answers.

When he and Andrea had originally come to Jane, they'd wanted to stop evil before it started. Now, he just wanted to know who she was and that she was okay, at least for now.

Physically, she appeared to be doing more than okay. Poppy and Dr. Hanover were working on her foot and leg bandages now. Same story here—same skinny limbs, same scars and scabs, same veiny skin, like she desperately needed a week of sun and far more substantial cheeseburgers than she'd just consumed. Other than having what Noah considered unusually long toes, she seemed...human—a little weird, but neither ethereal nor powerful. If anything, she seemed *more* fragile, diminished. And without the bandages, she was colder, pulling the blanket over her shoulders.

"I know you're cold," Dr. Hanover said, "but we have to remove your hospital gown to get at the bandages underneath, and for Andrea to get the pictures, you'll need to put the blanket down. Don't worry, we'll get you another blanket, a warm one, right after we're finished."

Jane frowned, but she shrugged the blanket off again and crossed her arms over her chest to hold what heat inside she could.

Dr. Hanover and Poppy continued up Jane's thighs, lifting the hospital gown up to the disposable underwear she'd been given. Although she'd expressed that she didn't mind Noah there while she was undressed and inspected, she seemed self-conscious about being seen, with the dazed bewilderment of youth—although if she was nephilim, how young could she be?

"Extraordinary," Dr. Hanover muttered when she was through unwrapping the limbs. "If I were more ambitious, I would insist on additional blood and imaging tests over the next few weeks, but I've been instructed by Billing to let you leave as soon as you're able, and barring a transfer to Mattea Psych, you look like you should be able to very soon. There's no apparent physical reason why you couldn't. You've only been unconscious for a few days, not long enough for atrophy to set in, although you might be weak and have some muscle pain. Can you try to stand for me?"

Poppy held Jane's hand and wrapped an arm around her shoulders to help her slide off the table. When Jane placed her bare feet on the linoleum floor, she curled her toes away from the cool vinyl, then let her feet press flat. She was shaking again, as much from weakness as sensitivity to the cold. She leaned against the table, but with Poppy steadying her, Jane eventually stood on her own.

"Fantastic," Dr. Hanover said. "Given how things have healed, you might not even need PT. You'll just want to make sure you do some standing and walking every day to remind your legs that they know how to do these things. Now, I'm going to remove the hospital gown. Are you *sure* you're okay with Detective Dunn staying?"

"Yes. It's okay."

As upset as she'd become when she couldn't remember who she was or what had happened—and he'd been upset, too, but he was usually good at hiding it, so it had just frustrated him more that she'd kept telling him that he was upset—she was calm now. As though finding her feet had given her a foundation to depend upon.

She was taller than he'd thought, although her long, thin limbs should have been a clue. She still covered herself in front as Poppy untied Jane's hospital gown and spread it away from her back.

Andrea did her best not to react, but it was hard not to wince whenever they saw the wicked gashes left behind on nephilim, angel or demon—like branches broken from a tree during a storm, except with exposed white of bone and the desiccated brown of once-red flesh. It was as harsh and arresting as seeing someone whose arm had been ripped off.

There were also a few birthmarks underneath, harder to notice when they were so insignificant in comparison to the gashes. Three large moles clustered over the jut of her right hip. They didn't look like anything in particular, and he didn't think they were of spiritual concern—just another way in which her celestial body had become human, with birthmarks, moles, freckles, divots, and bumps. Unmistakably real, starkly so, especially in the way she defied all Classical models of angels as soft but dense sculpted beings. She looked like a hard storm breeze would cast her on the draft like dandelion fluff.

Neither Poppy nor Dr. Hanover remarked on the wing gashes, because neither had the All-Seeing Eye. The camera, indifferent and neutral to good and evil, would capture their image, but a person would still need the Eye to see it. Noah didn't ask why it worked that way. He just needed a record of what had once been wings, although seeing how fast a nephil healed was worthy of note as well. They still had the Polaroids that Poppy had taken for the initial medical records and because she'd known that Noah and Andrea would want to see them as well, in case they ended up needing it for a report. And sometimes they really did write reports about the things they encountered, depending on how public-facing those encounters were. They would probably need them for this Jane Doe, since the librarian had been a witness and there was a medical paper trail.

Poppy gently helped Jane remove the hospital gown entirely. Most of the adhesive bandages on her trunk had been on her back, since that's where she'd landed, and the gauze bandages had been removed before taking the pictures of her back, so there was little left of note when she stood in the room with just the briefs on, except that her arms chill-bumped all the way down and her nipples had tightened against the cold. She held her arms out like Andrea told her to and stared at the wall, unperturbed beyond the temperature.

Demons didn't mind displaying their bodies, but it had never occurred to Noah that angels wouldn't have any scruples about that, either. Noah supposed heaven didn't much need clothing, any more than Eden at its origin.

However, when Jane put her arms down at Andrea's permission, she gazed down at herself, at the long stretch from breasts to hips. She touched the dip of flesh under her ribs, inspected the nub of her navel, covered her small, almost negligible breasts with her hands, all with something approaching confusion. Then she let Poppy help her back into her hospital gown, and Noah could breathe again, now that he could inspect her from where he stood without any concern that he would be accused of some form of institutional impropriety. Poppy then undid the bandages all over her head, neck, and hair.

Dr. Hanover inspected the areas of the scalp where she'd sutured and shook her head. "It really is amazing. I'll remove these first so you can give your hair a nice wash. If you keep standing steadily, you can probably even take a shower after we're finished. Poppy will help, if you need her. It's not like you have to worry about wound care anymore," she added dryly.

Jane had thin, almost invisible eyebrows, but her short hair was wavy and thick, the black of a grackle instead of a raven. It was greasy and messy and tangled, but Noah thought it would soften the harshness of her cheekbones and jawline.

Jane looked back at him. "Did you get what you needed?"

"I think so," Noah replied. "Andrea?"

"Just one more, of your face."

Jane didn't smile. Although her eyes were a muddy hazel, the light from the flash brought out the gold and green for a moment.

"You can sit down again, unless you'd like to remain standing, while I start removing these superfluous stitches. Although if you don't sit, I might have to get a stepstool just to reach the ones on your head."

Jane climbed back onto the table and lowered her head so that Dr. Hanover could start her work of making her appear a little less like the Frankenstein monster's bride. Removing the stitches made its own difference. What scabs and scars remained looked like wounds that were never that serious to begin with. Jane had to lie down on her back, then roll over on her belly, for the rest. It was a lot of stitches but quick work.

Dr. Hanover helped her sit up again. "You've done so well. Tell me, now that the bandages are off and the stitches removed, how do you feel? Any pain?"

"My head still hurts."

"How would you describe that pain?"

"I thought I did."

Dr. Hanover grinned. "Sharp, stabbing, burning, throbbing? Is it on one side of your head, the top of your head, the back, where the neck starts? Is it pressure on your forehead, your cheeks, your teeth, your temples? There are all kinds of headaches."

"I feel like something's pressing to get into my head on every side, and on the inside to get out."

"Good description. Do you hurt anywhere else?"

"I hurt everywhere else. Like…everything's a bruise. But I don't seem to have many anymore, do I?"

"Does this hurt, specifically where I'm pressing? Does it cause pain to radiate outward or refer elsewhere?" Dr. Hanover pushed several pressure points.

"No. It's tender, but not worse."

"Based on what I'm seeing and feeling, you're in excellent physical shape, although I would recommend speaking with your general physician or a nutritionist to determine if you're consuming enough calories or getting enough sunshine. Honestly, if I didn't know better, I'd wonder if you'd been kept hostage in someone's house for a few years. So, as your doctor, I prescribe lots of sunshine and calorie-dense foods, if you're one of those people who simply doesn't like to eat or forgets to. Now, would you like to return to your bed while we process you out of the hospital, or would you like Poppy to take you to the bathroom for a shower? I always feel much better after a nice warm shower. Or, if warm water makes you ache more, a cool shower can be refreshing as well."

"I think I would like that shower. Thank you."

"Very good. I'm going to talk to these nice detectives for a bit."

Poppy led Jane out barefoot into the hall. Jane winced with each step.

Andrea put her camera back in its case. "What're your thoughts, Doc?"

"I'm thinking that woman ain't human," Dr. Hanover said. "But that's neither here nor there, medically."

"DNA tests would show that she is, so for your purposes, she's just an accelerated healer," Noah said. "That's not what we mean."

"Well, I'm afraid I've reached the end of my expertise," Dr. Hanover said. "The pain she's still

41

experiencing might be any number of things beyond my purview in emergency medicine. If she's an accelerated healer, it might be autoimmune. It could also be psychosomatic from her trauma, as I suspect the amnesia is. Physically, she's the equivalent of a child who fell off the tall slide at a playground, but you and I both know she experienced much more than that. Because she's without insurance, there's no reason to keep her here unless you transfer her to Mattea for evaluation, but between you, me, and the table, she's not mentally ill. She just needs rest to let her healing mind catch up with her body. Does she have a place to stay? Preferably somewhere quiet."

"There are a couple of women's shelters we can bring her to in the morning," Andrea replied. "We might just take her to an IHOP or something to fill the time. She seemed really hungry while she was eating."

"And skinny as hell. We can probably pass her off as a potential abuse victim to our respective bosses," Noah added.

Their sergeant gave Noah and Andrea extra leeway to do their particular work. She was like Dr. Hanover—she knew there was something for her to know, but it made her life less chaotic if she didn't know it. Most of their cases never saw the inside of a courtroom and therefore didn't require the same meticulous documentation.

What they did wasn't quite vigilante justice. It just took place in what one might call an 'extralegal' world. There weren't laws, much less prisons, that could hold most demons if they didn't want to be held, and how did one cite a pestilence demon for doing what it was designed to do?

Really, he and Andrea were more liaisons to the city's supernatural underbelly than they were police detectives—a too-small, overworked faction designed to protect the natural where it overlapped with the supernatural. First responders, but more a mixture of firefighters and social workers. With guns that held bullets dipped in holy water.

Although their nightly routine more closely resembled that of beat cops, they'd each been made detective to give them more flexibility in what cases they took and more authority to step in if an incident seemed more in their lane, as well as to give other officers someone to privately confide in regarding whatever weird they'd stumbled upon without having to embarrass themselves in front of other cops.

"I'm heading to my office to finish up her file," Dr. Hanover said. "I'll be back in about thirty to forty-five minutes. She probably won't even have any goddamn scars by the time she's checked out."

The doctor shook her head as she left the exam room. Andrea and Noah stayed behind.

"Women's shelter?" Noah asked as soon as the door closed. "You want to put her in a women's shelter? It may work for the forms, but she *wasn't* abused, Andrea. She fell from grace. On purpose."

"That doesn't make her a bad person, and right now, she doesn't know any different. I'd be less worried about her there than at one of the halfway houses. Someone might mistake her for a junkie and offer her something she doesn't know to refuse. You want to be responsible for her getting hooked on meth or heroin after only a few days on Earth?"

"We've never heard of nephilim forgetting who they are after they fall."

"Maybe a lot of them forget who they were and just go about their lives like people in fugue states, starting from scratch. It's not like we'd know."

"I think if she's healing this fast, whatever's blocking her memory is going to heal, too," Noah said. "We've met too many gargoyles, demons, and angels who know exactly what they are to think that this amnesia is normal."

"So what do *you* want to do?" Andrea asked. "Throw her in the creek and see if she floats?"

"I think we just need to keep an eye on her for a few days. She can stay with you—"

"No way. I've got custody this week. If you want to keep an eye on her, she stays with you."

"That's not protocol—"

"My *kids* are in the house, Noah. She clearly doesn't mind being alone with you, and I'*m* not worried you're going to be an asshole about it. You were the first person she saw when she woke up. She imprinted."

"She's not a duck."

"She kept looking at you during the photographs, during the stitch removal, whenever the doctor would ask her things. She's not, like, infatuated, but she trusts you. You're trustworthy, even to vulnerable women, you blandly attractive man."

Noah punched Andrea's arm, neither quite playfully nor hard. Andrea laughed, leaning against the wall with her arms crossed.

It was a running joke between them that he was like his car—shiny, well-kept, well-built, serviceable, but just dated enough that no one remembered it was ever there. He was square-jawed and broad-shouldered, blond hair turned to ash from age but not yet silver or gray, skin perhaps not as tanned as it would be if he were on dayshift instead of night, and he kept himself more or less in shape to do the work to the best of his ability.

Andrea was the striking one, with darker features and a killer body she hadn't been able to hide in a beat cop's uniform. She worked out much more than Noah did, and she could deadlift more than he could. She was the one people remembered, even though Noah was the one they looked to for confirmation and the final word—which annoyed Andrea to no end.

He didn't radiate 'cop' when he was off-duty. Take off his gun, his badge, and his jacket, and he could walk into any office in the world and be perceived as one of them. Give him work boots, he could join any construction crew in the world. Give him flannel, he could convince anyone he was a farmer. He was One of Those Faces—pleasant to be around and easy to leave. It was how he went through life and how life went through him. Most of the people he dealt with, other than Andrea, were too caught up in their problems to really *see* him as anything but an obstacle, a means to an end, or a tool in their toolbox.

He'd been the first thing Jane Doe had seen, and although she hadn't been looking at him the whole time during the doctor's examination and stitches removal—it may have seemed so from Andrea's position, but Jane had mostly stared at the wall next to him—he'd felt included in her immediate periphery. She'd oriented herself toward him like a sunflower to sunlight.

He and Andrea had left in shifts to do their nightly work, but he'd spent a great deal of the last few nights just watching her, catching up on paperwork, but doing so in the closed-off world of her coma as she emerged from the bumps, bruises, blood, and swelling. She'd been an uncharacteristically quiet point in a chaotically turning world.

He didn't know what to make of her, whether she was angel or demon, whether she'd aimed for Earth or hell. He was wary of her vulnerability, skeptical of her fragility, but she still *felt* vulnerable, *felt* fragile.

She wasn't the first person in his line of work that he'd wanted so badly to save.

"I'll ask what she prefers," Noah finally said. "If she's okay staying with me, she can. If she wants to go to a halfway house or a shelter, she can go there."

"Oh, so we're leaving it up to the unknown quantity."

"It wouldn't be the first time one of our subjects' motives were ambiguous. Or ambivalent," Noah said.

"Doesn't mean it isn't dangerous, especially when we invite them into our own home."

"At least we have some control there."

Andrea shrugged her camera bag onto her shoulder. "See, that's the difference between you and me. You go through life thinking you have control. I never assume I have control."

Chapter Three

After Noah unlocked the front door of his townhouse, he entered first to switch on the lights as Jane followed him in.

She had successfully showered at the hospital, with some instruction on how to use the various travel-size toiletries given, and Nurse Poppy had made sure that she could use the bathroom without issues. Each process was somehow both familiar and new, but she already better understood the contained cycles of her body.

The ache of hunger, the ache of fullness, the ache of urgency, the ache of wariness... These seemed to be daily trials and tribulations. That the body held so many aches and pains that made her muscles stiffen and throb and left her with a pressure headache seemed out of the ordinary, but Dr. Hanover had only instructed Noah and Andrea to make sure she was eating and give her an NSAID after she ate next if she was still hurting. If she were an average person, she would have been given at least a few days' worth of painkillers upon release, but if she were an average person, she would have still been unconscious and would have required stitches for a lot longer. Dr. Hanover didn't anticipate Jane would need additional opioids, given that she'd already been on a low dose and hadn't been so uncomfortable that she'd asked for more.

Before Jane left the hospital, Andrea had visited the nearest store. She'd had to guess Jane's sizes, and her long legs were a little too long for the pants that Andrea had chosen, but she'd been able to walk out of the hospital in something other than a hospital gown.

After taking her to IHOP and watching her demolish a stack of blueberry pancakes, hashbrowns, and a glass of orange juice, they'd asked her what she wanted to do until she figured out who she was—or if she didn't figure it out, until they found someplace for her to choose who she was going to be.

She'd quite enjoyed blueberry pancakes, especially the way blueberries burst over her tongue and the maple syrup sang in her mouth. Orange juice had made her teeth ache in a better way than her head did. She thought the juice had also helped that headache to subside somewhat.

However, as soon as she'd left the hospital on the way to that restaurant, she'd looked back and marveled at just how big the hospital building was—a series of buildings, actually, more like a campus than its own entity. Noah and Andrea had led her to one car in a sea of cars that, as soon as Andrea had helped strap her into the back seat, took them into a roaring river of more cars that led to other buildings—some broad swaths and others towers stretching into an inky black sky devoid of stars because of all the stars that the buildings and the streets made for themselves.

The world was so much bigger than the curtained room, adding to the pressure around her head, although the bandages had been removed and her hair was loose and air dried. And this was while the sun was down and most people were asleep and she couldn't see as much. When the sun rose, there would be so much *more*.

"So this is where I crash after my shift. Andrea and I work mostly seven to seven, give or take a couple hours, and we sleep during the day, meaning right about now. I wake up at about three in the afternoon. I was thinking we could stop by the scene of the incident this afternoon to see if it jogs your memory. I don't think that works in anything but the movies, but at the very least, it won't hurt."

"Whatever you think is best," Jane replied. "I wouldn't know where to go even if I wanted to do anything different."

Noah grabbed some bottled waters from the fridge and handed her one, then raided his small pantry for snacks, although Andrea had bought her some of those, too, nestled among the other toiletries and clothing options she'd been given.

Jane followed him upstairs. The hall led to three small bedrooms. Noah brought her to the far one opposite the other two.

"There's no easy or diplomatic way to say this, but because Andrea and I sometimes bring people into our homes who we're not sure we can trust, there's a latch lock and a padlock on the outside of the door. It sounds extreme if you don't know who some of our guests are. Now, I don't think we need to use the padlock, but I would feel better if I didn't have to worry about you wandering around while I sleep. This room has its own small en suite bathroom, a television, and everything, and here we have fresh water and snacks. You shouldn't need anything else while I'm dead to the world across the hall. I say 'dead to the world.' If you try to, say, break down the door, I will wake up, and I'll be armed, so that's not advisable. Does it bother you in any way that I need to lock you in?"

"That's not normal, is it?" Another glance at the other two rooms, which had a shared bathroom between them, indicated there were no locks on the outside of those. Just this one.

"No, it's not. But it's for your safety and mine. Just while I sleep. I'll get up, shower, then let you out. You shouldn't need anything other than what's in there. Would you like to see?"

Yes, I would like to see your prison. Just because she couldn't remember yesterday didn't mean she was born then.

She had a feeling that some kind of confinement would have been her lot, no matter which option she'd chosen. She'd cracked concrete without cracking herself. For all Noah knew—for all *she* knew—she was a dangerous person, which was doubtlessly the reason for locking her in. That didn't mean her feathers weren't ruffled from being treated as though she was dangerous by default when all she'd done so far was wake up.

She pushed open the door. The room was bigger than the makeshift room of curtains, outfitted with a bigger bed softened by multiple pillows. A television was mounted above a dresser, which was where Noah put the snacks. A heavily curtained window was next to the entrance of a much sparer bathroom than the communal one where she'd showered with Poppy's help.

The more curious elements of the room were painted or carved into the corners and crown molding, around the window. She didn't know what any of the symbols meant, but they whispered to her like tree leaves in a breeze.

"Really, if you need anything or if you remember anything immediately important, you can open the door a little ways and holler. I don't use a white noise machine or earplugs or anything. I'll hear you. Is this okay for the next six, seven hours?"

"I don't like being shut in," she said, crossing her arms against new goosebumps. Those arms looked like she'd had some kind of bad childhood accident— certainly not one from a few days ago. Now that she'd seen her healing for herself, she understood that she wasn't just lucky. Something else was going on, and perhaps that something else was the reason why she was being locked into her room. If she couldn't know what that something else was, maybe she *needed* to be, no matter how she didn't like it. "I've been shut in for a few days now, haven't I? In my own head. In the bandages."

"I'm sorry. I forgot you don't like the cold. I do keep it kind of cool in my house, because I sleep better that way and Texas is hot enough without my little piece of it being hot, too. But there's the comforter, and there are more blankets in the dresser there. I could get you one of my jackets."

"Andrea bought me a heating pad. She said it would be good for some of the pain, too."

"Good. There's a strip under the nightstand you can plug it in to. Here's the remote for the television." He gave her a brief tutorial on how it worked. "There aren't any blackout shades in here like in my room, but the curtains are pretty thick, if you want to catch some sleep, too."

"I'll be okay," Jane said. His tired anxiety was making her antsy, as though something crawled around under the clothes Andrea had bought for her. "I'm not thrilled by the lock, but I would like some quiet."

She rested a hand on his shoulder to settle his worry. It happened again, a spark not of static but of warmth instead—a sensation she couldn't explain, beyond even her unconscious recognition. It only intensified when he covered her hand with his. The warmth spread further, some of it hers, some of it his, pleasant as soft light, as the hot water of a shower, as the texture of the shirt Andrea had chosen.

"It's too late to say good night, so good morning." His voice had deepened slightly, as though that warmth where they were connected had reached his throat. "Remember, call me if you need anything. But for both of our sakes, let it be something you *need*. I'm cranky when I wake up." He grinned to show that he probably wouldn't take it out on her.

"Good morning, then."

He locked her door, then Jane heard him shut his. She could tell he didn't take long to fall asleep. She was sleepy from the heavy pancakes, but her mind was still waking up, turning on tiny lightbulb by lightbulb. His falling asleep tried to pull her down with him, but once he untethered from consciousness, she was less prone to the suggestion.

The first thing she did was remove her clothes. While shut away, she took the opportunity to inspect herself, rather than some doctor or cop calling their observations the final word.

She pinched her skin, observed it under the light from the fan over her bed, observed it in darkness under the comforter she'd folded back. When the cool air—cooler every minute from him turning down the A/C—brought shivers to her once again, she cocooned herself under the comforter. She liked her body against these cool sheets, though — smooth and soft, a less crisp texture than the ones at the hospital.

Warmly ensconced in bed, she played with the remote until she found an animal show that fascinated her with vibrant colors, which had not been a hallmark of her world thus far. The night turned everything to shades of gray, and a hospital consisted of the blandest white, cream, beige, brown, and blue.

Jane watched animals until she fell asleep to the calming voice of the narrator.

Before she was ready, she woke to Noah's hand on her covered shoulder. She groaned, her limbs stiff, and held the comforter tight around her. But when Noah smiled, she couldn't refuse him, because that smile was genuine and relaxed and amused, and not in the same somewhat stunned way he'd been amused while she'd eaten.

The smile collapsed into alarm that panged through her chest when she unwound herself from the blankets. Noah immediately turned around, looking away, and Jane remembered that other people acted uncomfortable when she was comfortable with her nakedness. Even though he'd already seen her, it wasn't permitted for him to see again without both permission on her part and willingness on his.

She rummaged through the bag of clothes and pulled on a different configuration, just to see how she felt about new things. The jeans were a little baggy on her and still not long enough. The T-shirt was also soft but a little thicker. It covered more of her and bore an image from some kind of comic book or action movie. She knew about both but couldn't narrow it down beyond that.

When Noah turned around again, he snorted.

"Andrea sure does have a sense of humor. Which is…mean of her because you can't appreciate it. She just wanted me to laugh at you in Scarlet Witch merch. But don't worry, she didn't make you the butt of the joke."

"What's the butt of the joke, then?"

"Me, I think. It looks like she had to get your clothes from the juniors' section. Hungry again?"

She nodded.

"All right. Brush your teeth and take another ibuprofen, just in case. I'll be waiting for you downstairs. Was being cooped up too difficult?"

"No. I slept for most of it and watched document-aries."

Noah checked where she'd left off. "Just making sure they were actual documentaries, not animated or scripted TV shows. So you can tell the difference between fact and fiction. That makes things a little easier."

* * * *

They drove in a different car than they'd driven to Noah's townhouse. Shinier, with curvier lines. He took her to a restaurant where they ate in the car with the windows down. She exclaimed at everything she consumed, from the cherry limeade to the Texas toast grilled cheese, tater tots, and popcorn chicken. Noah had black coffee and a sandwich, but as with the blueberry pancakes, he seemed perfectly content to feed on her enjoyment.

The cramps in her stomach calmed down, so she thought those in particular were basic hunger. But oh, how she delighted at every bite—as though it was the first time she'd ever had food, although that didn't make any sense. How could she know what all this food was without having eaten any of it?

She sipped on another cherry limeade as Noah drove them away from the restaurant.

"You've had some rest, some quiet, some sleep, some food, and your bandages and stitches have all been removed. Do you feel any better at all?" Noah asked.

"Yes. Less hungry. I can move my body better. But I still hurt in my limbs, in my head, more now than when you woke me up, and I don't know why."

"Does it hurt like a knife? Like scraping your knee?"

She shook her head to test if she could. The headache allowed her to do that now without throbbing worse. "No. Like my headache. Pressure in, pressure out, but in my arms and legs and back and abdomen and shoulders, in my ribs when I breathe. My joints aren't so stiff now without the bandages, but it's still an effort."

"I'm sorry to hear that. Do you know if you had this pain prior to the incident?"

"I don't... I don't think so. It seems new."

"If it wasn't caused by the incident, it's possible the pain started before. Kind of reminds me of my sister, who has lupus. But all bodies have their quirks. Dr. Hanover might be right that your accelerated healing itself could be causing the pain. Your whole immune response could be in overdrive. Which means it may retreat when you don't have any more healing left to do. We can hope, right?"

She was right that there was so much more to the world in the daytime. She could see so many more buildings, so many more cars, so many more people. It was inconceivable to her that there could just be so many of everything, a constant bustle of activity assaulting her from every side. But the window was cool against her forehead, the cherry limeade pleasant on her tongue, and Noah switched some music on low volume for her benefit while he listened to his police scanner but didn't respond to it. She didn't understand what they were saying, which somehow made it better.

"Noah, do you know who I am?"

"I thought I was the one asking that of you."

"You seem to know the answer you want me to give."

He pulled into another parking lot, this one without drive-in menus. "We have an idea," he confessed. "But we don't want to influence you to give an answer that isn't true. We don't know your name. Missing persons files still haven't given us anything. But we have an idea of why you're here. Does that answer your question?"

"Who do you think I am?"

"It's not what you want to hear, but I can't tell you that. Because it ultimately remains to be seen. You're going to have to tell us."

"You shouldn't know more about me than I know about me."

"I don't think that will be the case for very much longer."

"You think what you're about to show me will help."

"We hope so."

"Where's Andrea?"

"Running some errands and picking up her kids from school."

"She has kids?"

"Two. Daughter and son. Previous marriage. Didn't work out."

"Why not?"

"They both had issues." Noah turned off the car, then muttered, "The fact they both watched the waitresses walking away from the table probably had something to do with it."

"What was that?"

"Nothing. We're here. The library's up there. The steps we found you on are where that yellow caution tape and blue tarp are. Are you ready for this? We don't have to do this today. We don't have to do it at all. Public Works will eventually get around to repairing the steps. It'll be like it never happened, at least here."

"I would like to see." She opened her car door.

"We'll be brief. Schools are getting out, so there'll be more foot traffic soon."

Noah led her to the library steps. She crouched at the base of them and looked up the length of the stairs, wondering if any of it would seem familiar. It didn't. A cold dread trickled down the back of her neck as she followed the concrete up to the impressive stone façade of the building, to the gargoyles and angels guarding its roof.

She couldn't say where that dread came from or if it was even her own, but she bit her tongue, then her lip, then her cheek, trying to keep the earth from moving beneath her.

As soon as Noah determined she probably wasn't going to break down, he ran up the steps to pull the blocks, hobbyhorses, and cones away, wrapping tape around his hand as he went. When he took off his jacket halfway through, she was briefly distracted by his thighs pressing against his pants, his shoulder blades pressing against his shirt. That was significant, the blades working in and out, in and out, but every time she got close to what that significance was, it fluttered away like flies from a slow hand.

Then the sight was as pleasant as sour cherry, lime, and ice on her tongue.

Noah straightened as though startled by something. He glanced back at her, but she didn't say anything, so he resumed his work, finally pulling the tarp aside to show the damage done to the concrete where she'd been found.

Impact.

She looked up at the sky, but there was nothing there—not a tree, not a skyscraper, just clouds. If she'd fallen from a plane or helicopter, she would have either died or, regardless of accelerated healing, been broken all over. She could have been doing other things up there, perhaps—parasailing, base-jumping—but she didn't feel like a daredevil, and would she have been doing any of these things without clothes on? It was warm on the ground, but it would have been cooler in the sky, and she didn't like cold.

She walked up the steps to the broken concrete. Funny. The break patterns looked just like the shape of wings.

Then it wasn't funny at all, and she tripped, falling forward into the craggy matrix of stone and adhesive.

"Whoa... Jane, are you okay?"

No, that's not right. That's not right. "That's not my name."

Noah let the tarp fall and draped his jacket on one of the horses. He didn't offer to help her up, because she wasn't trying to get out.

She crawled to the center. Turned around. The concrete hurt, but it was a different kind of hurt from the rest of her, and if she was careful, it didn't have to hurt too badly. She just needed to see. Not as others saw it, but as she would have seen it after the incident. Accident. *Impact.*

"Tara." She pronounced it with a broader A. "My name is Tara. And I think... Did I fall?"

Noah's lips thinned, which emphasized the geometric quality of his face, but he nodded.

She stared up at the sky. The clouds. At nothing. But there was more beyond that, wasn't there? Whole galaxies, a whole universes beyond the clouds, beyond the tight cold-hot of protective atmosphere around the planet. There was so much more than even just the nothing of space. More than the screaming face of a barren moon.

Impact. From a fall. "From where?"

Noah just looked up with her. "It'll come to you."

"How could I survive?"

"Hard to say. But you did. So do others."

"There are others like me?"

"We think so."

She spread her arms as though they belonged to the wings in the broken concrete. Her shoulders hurt, and the thing she wanted to do more than anything in the world was cry, so she did.

People were starting to notice, surrounding the broken place and broken person inside it with curiosity. Noah flashed his badge to anyone who came too close and told them to move along, just police business. He received some disapproving looks — perhaps because he was a big, strong detective standing over a weeping woman — but when the swell of curiosity passed, he crouched next to the broken concrete, then cautiously crawled in to lie down next to her, staring up at the sky.

That only made her cry harder. Noah pushed himself up awkwardly, grunting from the corners of concrete pressing into his body, but he stared down at her with increasing concern. The suspicion that had been pernicious in the set of his eyebrows loosened. His mild blue eyes showed the early swim of tears of his own. If he was self-conscious about that or about resting in rubble with a crying woman, he kept it hidden. Then he cautiously insinuated his arm under her neck to give her something less sharp and uncomfortable to rest upon.

Tara—that felt so much more honest than Jane to her—pressed her hands against the pangs in her chest that made her afraid her heart would stop or her ribs would split open to match the wing-breaks beneath her. She turned on the rubble to press her face into his shirt, not because she was ashamed but because the sorrow spilling out was too big for her to hold alone.

Noah closed his arms around her in response. He was careful how he held her, but he didn't refuse or push her away, just let her sob on his chest as though her heart was breaking, although it somehow continued to beat.

"I think I lost something, something so important," she said into his shirt. "How far did I fall?"

"Pretty far," he replied quietly.

And that was when she knew, or at least understood.

She didn't remember everything. She wasn't meant to, where she was now. In her head, in her body, there were things that weren't supposed to be there but were, that were supposed to be there but were no longer.

She moved her shoulders and missed her wings. Not even the lingering taste of cherry limeade was enough to make up for the loss of what she was.

She'd fallen for a reason. Angels with the will to choose had to choose to fall. She just didn't know what she'd chosen. She couldn't remember what she'd seen on Earth that had brought her down, what had been worth the loss of her wings and the peace of not being able to feel, not like *this*—prickles of gravel and rubble, itchiness in the last scars from the fall, headache, but also the flavor of a sugary drink, heaviness in her stomach from food. She hadn't had this tenderness in her breasts, certainly hadn't had a navel, and everything between her legs had been smooth and without complication. She'd had a body, as physical as it had been metaphysical, and she'd felt things, but she hadn't *felt* in such a fully physical way. Metaphysicality in this world was wrapped in an assault of emotions and sensations that concealed it like a piece of sand in the largest giant clam. At its best, it would grow to the size of a pearl, but there were still all those layers of flesh between to distract from the irritation.

And am I ever going to stop crying? Although Noah's arm and chest were comfortable, the rest of what she lay upon was emphatically not. Her wings were gone, snapped off and lost on the way down. She might never have them ever again, depending on why she was here. But she felt no malice, no anger, no fury, nothing to explain why she would have fallen — out of resistance or rebellion. Just this overwhelming sadness.

The tears did eventually stop, if only because it seemed like she'd cried every last bit of moisture from her body.

The other side of having a body that felt things and produced its own humors was that her face was a mess, her nose was dripping and draining into her mouth, and she'd soaked all that mess onto Noah's chest.

"It's okay. It sometimes seems like it won't stop until it does." He swiped at his face and sniffed back what appeared to be his own tears — and some red-faced, red-nosed, red-cheeked, red-eyed confusion along with them. "I have tissues in the car. I also have another shirt."

"Why are faces like this?"

Noah laughed as he continued to sniff back his tears — such a beautiful, honest sound that it pierced through her misery like sun through the clouds. She sat up in the rubble, wincing from the concrete pressing into her legs and buttocks. Noah would have helped her, but he struggled to stand as well. They both managed to find their footing in front of each wing.

"I know why I'm crying," Tara said. "Why are you?"

"That's an excellent question. You just seemed so miserable, the very picture of sadness — real sadness, real loss. It reminded me of when my mother died. Seeing my father break down...and my sister... I'm used to laughter being contagious, not tears. Not like that. I guess I'm just invested. Did you get the answers *you* were looking for?"

"The ones that matter."

"Fancy a jaunt to my work to meet with Andrea so we can figure out where to go from here?"

"Yes. Yes, I'd like to leave."

She still couldn't remember the moment of impact, but she remembered how excruciating the fall-scorch had been, the ripping away of her wings, and she remembered a moment after she'd hit the ground, pain as blinding as the light of her that had been extinguished.

The sooner the steps could be repaired like new, the better. She'd hardly want to be reminded of such terrible failure.

Chapter Four

In the car, Noah fetched a box of tissues from the trunk, then dug through his bag of spare clothes for a shirt.

While she blew her nose and made herself presentable, he blew his nose, too, genuinely surprised by the punch of emotion that her crying had evoked — not just its strength but purity — when he could usually push feelings down or aside.

Grief was an ambush emotion. In the early months after his mother's death, he'd sometimes had to excuse himself. Not as bad as his sister, but mourning had had its way with him for a while. These days, he didn't suffer the same attacks. When grief came for him, they were much more subdued — overcast melancholy instead of an outpouring. But seeing Jane — *No, Tara.* Seeing Tara break down had brought him right back to those days.

It hadn't been so much that he'd felt the same kind of mourning. How upset she'd been had reminded him of what it had been like, the same intensity in her, in him.

Unlike his sister, however, Tara had reached out for comfort without a thought, without self-consciousness or an assumption that she needed to bear it alone. Maybe that was what had plucked those old strings, because his sister had suffered for so long in silence. Despite her husband, her children, her father, and her brother, she'd chosen to handle it — or not handle it — alone until she couldn't anymore, and her husband had insisted that she start seeing someone because she was scaring him.

Noah had scared himself, getting misty in the middle of public library steps, attracting way too much attention. The moment Jane had finally come out the other side of her abject sorrow was as much a relief to him as it must have been to her.

Although, despite concrete trying to dig a hole up the crack of his ass, it had actually been quite pleasant holding her, having her trust him enough to do so, even though he was a stranger. Then again, she simply didn't have the hangups other people did about bodies, intimacy — probably because she'd never had a body like this one. It also explained why she seemed to love food so enthusiastically. It was refreshing, endearing. It made him want to trust her, to view her as utterly ingenuous.

That was dangerous. Whether she was angel or demon, she wasn't a human being. Not really. He couldn't assume that she had a human being's motives. Angels were usually on the righteous side of a fight, but that didn't mean they acted within the confines of man's law or that they were fluffy little Christmas decorations.

Not all of them were soldiers—any more than people were—but they had such a defined moral compass that they could cause grievous harm to others if they thought an action was worth the risk, which could put them at odds with police. Sometimes they raged against that injustice, and perhaps they should, but he was a cop, not an angel.

If Tara was fallen well beyond merely losing her wings, then she was even more dangerous, because she might only *seem* ingenuous, and these things that endeared her to him might simply be a ruse to make him trust her, protect her, so that she could lead him around like her own personal golden retriever with a badge.

He unbuttoned his shirt, then pulled it and his undershirt off. He felt her gaze before he saw her staring. He dared not let himself think she was also a little intrigued. He was already entirely too entangled with this woman. The last thing he needed was to *imprint*, as Andrea had put it.

It wouldn't be the first time he'd wanted to save someone who he maybe couldn't save, nor the first time he'd put himself in a position to be manipulated by someone he viewed as vulnerable.

Which was why he had to be suspicious, even if he didn't like to be.

He pulled on his blue T-shirt as quickly as he could, then threw his jacket in the back seat and slipped behind the steering wheel again to drive them to the station.

Tara tucked herself into her seat with her knees up near her chest, pressed into the corner, drinking the rest of what was probably a watered-down cherry limeade. He'd get into automobile safety with her another time. If she wasn't trying to drum up sympathy, he needed to let her process what she'd remembered, because it wasn't just new information. It changed her entire sense of self. A few hours ago, she'd been a woman with strange healing powers who couldn't remember who she was. Now, she was an angel, fallen, and she remembered enough.

It wasn't his job to comfort her or make her safe. It was his job to dot every 'i' and cross every 't' in the report he had to make to justify City Works' repairs and scratch out the 'Jane Doe' on his report on the potential accident or assault. It was his job to make sure she integrated into Meridian society as seamlessly as possible, angel or demon. Once she was out there in the city, what she did was her decision. All he had to do was impress upon her not to do anything that ended up making it his decision.

"This is where you work?" Tara said as she followed him up to the building.

"On occasion."

The main Meridian Police Department building was a mixture of old and new, built off of the original sheriff's department from prior to Meridian's urban explosion. The interior had been renovated in the seventies and again in the nineties yet never seemed completely modern, and their HVAC system always seemed thirty years out of date.

It was as intimidating as the Archimedes Library but lacked its majesty, instead squatting like a toad at the top of an overly intricate set of stairs coming in from multiple sides. The ceilings were either too low or too high, the floor either linoleum or terrazzo tile, a patchwork of identities and ideas without one cohesive whole, and none of the departments were too keen about the others.

For instance, although Noah and Andrea technically worked in the Special Investigations Department, their office was nestled in Homicide, because SID didn't have private offices and Homicide did. Plus, their investigations tended to overlap. Homicide hated having them there and put mocking signs up on their office door all the time, calling them the X-Files or Crackpot Division, but the one that seemed to stick — which was why they left the sticky note up all the time now — was Q Division. With the inclusive pride flag Andrea flew in her pencil holder, they were sometimes also called Queer Division, but because Noah wasn't insulted by that, neither he nor Andrea let any of the mockery bother them.

Especially since homicide detectives usually bit the bullet and brought them in on cases when needed. If they'd *really* wanted Q Division out, they would have been a lot more effective at chasing them away. Q Division was more like the annoying pet they just couldn't bring themselves to get rid of because the pet brought slippers to their bed and the newspaper in every morning.

On good days, when they'd been particularly useful for a while, other detectives viewed them almost with fondness. Then Noah and Andrea would sabotage a case to keep a crime from being brought to the district attorney when it seemed perfectly black and white to everyone else, and they'd go back to hating them again.

It was a vicious cycle and the reason why their office had several locks, although the window glass wasn't bulletproof.

Tara asked to go to the bathroom, so they had to take a detour, but his office was within sight of the end of the hall, so he pointed out where to go and headed there himself because it looked like Andrea was already in. He wanted to brief her before Tara joined them.

As soon as he closed the door behind him, Noah swept past Andrea's desk toward his and said, "She doesn't remember everything, but she remembers enough. She knows she's not from here. And her name is Tara."

"No last name?"

"Nephilim don't exactly come from loving parents, so no. We're going to have to get her an identity."

"We're going to help a demon get an identity?"

"We're going to help a fallen angel get an identity, yes."

"You can't be this naïve."

"She needs an ID so we can close out her case, period. It doesn't matter whether she gets one from us or out there when her demon friends take her under their wing. And if she's not a demon, she won't have friends who can get these things for her."

Andrea leaned back in her chair, chewing on the end of her pen. "You like her."

"I want to do my job in such a way that helps rather than hinders her, regardless of whether she's evil or not, so naturally I must like her because she has a pretty face and is sweet when she cries?"

"You said it, not me," Andrea said, holding her hands up.

"Fine. If you don't want to do it my way, *you* can cover her paperwork and I can deal with City Works."

Andrea grinned. "Well, now, let's not be too hasty. Did she do all right last night? And at the library?"

"She did fine during the night. She broke down at the library."

"That explains it."

"I don't want to help her because she cried."

"You keep telling yourself that."

"You would have cried, too."

"Wait, you cried?"

"I didn't say that." Noah spun around in his own chair before settling behind his desk. "It was moving, and seeing the broken wings for myself... Pictures don't do it justice. She reacted like she'd just realized she'd had a double amputation, because that's exactly what happened. So cut her some slack, all right? Whether she's good or evil, that seemed genuine, at least. We can't just treat her like an inevitable demon. We have to treat her like both angel and demon at the same time. Schrödinger's fallen angel."

"Fancy."

"You need to raise your standards."

"And you need a bouncer for yours. Oh, look, your damsel in distress cometh."

"She's your damsel in distress, too," he hissed back at her while Tara wove between desks.

Most of the detectives out in the bullpen didn't spare her more than a glance, except homicide detective Reeves, who followed her progress with interest both prurient and suspicious. Fortunately, he didn't do anything but look, or else Noah would've had to worsen interdepartmental relations even more. But Tara looked like she knew exactly where she was going, so no one stopped her.

She entered their office, careful as she closed the door behind her, because the blinds shook and knocked against the door. Andrea stood up and closed all the blinds on three sides so evening sunlight could pour into the little room but no one inside the building could see them. Unless they outright shouted, they'd remain largely unheard and undisturbed.

When Andrea turned back to Tara, whatever blithe, pithy comment she'd intended to say died on her lips. Tara stood there in one of the few empty spaces in the office that wasn't at risk of a box or pile of manila folders falling on her. She was without flaw, no scar, no scab, although her wing gashes would still be there under her T-shirt.

Tara looked at Noah, since he'd already acclimated to an angel who knew she was an angel. "So what now?"

"Depends," Andrea replied, "on what you came down here for."

Tara picked through the mess until she made it to the chair next to Noah's desk. She turned it around so that she was next to Noah but facing Andrea. "I don't remember what it was. I don't think we're supposed to remember much."

"I think you're supposed to know what the fuck you're doing here, though," Andrea said.

"I'll figure out what I'm doing here eventually. Other than eating. Which is almost worth the price of admission."

"Hell, dude, we haven't even broken out the Ben & Jerry's."

"I don't know what that means."

"It's a particularly tasty pint of ice cream you can get at your local grocery store," Andrea replied. "Later. But you were the one who came in here and asked what comes next. And that depends. Do you have friends here to set up your new life for you, or are you all on your own? Do you want a job? An education? Or are you just here to wreak some havoc? We don't know what comes next for you until you know what you want to do. What's next for Noah and me? That identity, so we can close out your Jane Doe file. Signing off on the City Works report as an unfortunate accident. Keeping an eye on you. But keeping an eye on you where? If you're a demon, you go walking off into the sunset without our help. If you're just a fallen angel, you end up in a halfway house. We can't even make a case for emergency placement in a women's shelter at this point."

"Because I'm not a woman?" Tara asked quietly.

"Because you don't look like you've ever been hurt in your life, and you don't look scared anymore. You don't need either of those things to be the victim of abuse, of course, but I'm not putting you in that kind of shelter when someone else needs it more than you do. Do you have a general objection to being called a woman? I ask because you've said that several times. Is it just that you're an angel, or is there more?"

Tara looked down at herself. "The matter of man or woman was irrelevant to me before," she said slowly. "Now...I suppose I favor one rather than the other, but it still doesn't feel right. Woman."

"Well, there's the option of going with man or X, but both could potentially attract unwanted attention around here. You can identify as whatever off the official record. Maybe when you've been here long enough, you can make a case for amending the information. But for now, does it bother you too much to be labeled on the record as a woman?"

Tara touched the screen print on her T-shirt. She wasn't wearing a bra. What was underneath wasn't substantial enough for that to matter much, but because women's clothes tended to be thinner, it was abundantly obvious to Noah that she had breasts and that she was cold. He held out his jacket to her without a word—not for modesty but warmth. She accepted it with warmth of her own.

"It doesn't bother me," she replied. She swam in Noah's jacket, but the arms were long enough. "It just feels like a lie."

"So does the picture on my driver's license," Andrea said. "But in all seriousness, if you need it to be something else…"

"No. I suppose I should get used to this."

"Well, the bright side is that you can make that mean whatever you want, and like I said, you can theoretically update the information later through less shady channels. So, we've got a five-foot-eleven female with hazel eyes. First name Tara." Andrea scribbled on her legal pad. "Do you have a last name where you're from? If not, we can extrapolate from what you are and what you did—your heavenly occupation, as it were. It's where we got a lot of our surnames, too. Or we can just go random. Random is easiest. Then our ID guy isn't constrained by certain variables. It's illegal as hell, so please don't repeat anything I'm saying in here out there."

"Of course. But my name is Tara. Now that I remember my name again, I won't relinquish it. I had no second name, and I can't recall an occupation."

"Well then, I think we've got enough information to have an ID made for you," Andrea said. "Next thing we need to know is your intentions."

"Excuse me?"

Andrea was typically kind, but she didn't mince words or make any attempt to soften the aggression of her clipped tone. "Why are you here? The winged don't fall for no reason."

Tara looked down at her long fingers as she picked at her nails. "I'm sorry I'm not much help to anyone right now, including myself. I wish there were a less traumatic way of getting from there to here. I wish I knew all the things I knew there. I wish my body would stop grumbling and aching and fussing. Is it always like this? I was better in the car, but now…" She rubbed at her upper arms, then at her legs, more massage than mere friction.

"Sorry to say that the grumbling is permanent. You'll probably get used to it," Noah replied. "I think the aching and pressure you feel is something else, though. It was better in the car?"

She nodded. "And in the shower. And at your home, but that may have just been from the heating pad between warm sheets."

"The simplest answer is that you probably just need to be warmer," Andrea said. "You and I can do some proper shopping later. What I bought wasn't meant to be the extent of your wardrobe, just to get you through a few days in something other than a hospital gown. Do your arms feel better in Noah's jacket?"

"Some. Not a lot."

"Why don't we try this weekend when I'm off? I normally can't stand shopping, but if you behave yourself until then, my daughter might have a few things to say. She's only eight, but she has some fervid fashionista opinions. She won't let you leave the house if you're going to embarrass her."

Tara had been wan since the library, but she smiled, full, broad, and bright, and for the first time since she'd awakened, Noah thought everything was going to be all right.

"I wouldn't refuse."

"Here's the thing, though. If you don't know what you're going to do and we don't know what you're going to do, that limits how we can proceed. We should probably process you into one of the halfway houses we partner with, but I can already tell that option isn't sitting well with Clark Kent over here." Andrea leaned toward Tara with a conspiratorial wink. "He loves to save the day but doesn't like the paperwork afterward. Victim logistics aren't the sexy part of the job."

"You know, I'm right here. I can hear you," Noah said. "Working on paperwork and everything. God forbid I don't like throwing people to the wolves when we're finished with them."

"Halfway houses sound scary, but they're just places with a bathroom and a roof over your head and meals until you can get back on your feet," Andrea explained. "The ones we funnel people through are good for men, women, and children, with an emphasis on safety of everyone, so *I'm* not worried about you there like he is. They also help find job openings in the city…although we'll have to do some assessments on what kind of education we want to lie about you having. To be honest, you're our first fresh nephil. We don't really know what angels do after falling when they want to stay angelic. We know what the demons do, but they end up getting to their feet pretty quickly."

"Yet, suspecting that I might choose a different pair of wings, you still offer to take me shopping with your daughter," Tara said.

"Well, it's obviously conditional. If you try to suck out my soul before then, you're on your own."

"That's not on my agenda. But conditions may change at any time."

"Great, now she jokes."

"What makes you think I'm joking?" Tara appeared perfectly serious, then let a small grin creep through. "What use would I have for your soul?"

"That's what I keep telling demons trying to sacrifice me to their master after I free their younger sacrifices and they try to make do with me. I'm, like, really? You think Baal's going for these stretch marks? Unless he wants to be wine o'clock buddies, I don't know what he's getting out of that."

She surprised Tara into a laugh that sounded more like coughing while she tried to figure out how she was supposed to do it. Finally, she just let her amusement drive her instead of the other way around, and it became a sweet laugh, more similar to her crying. "It isn't funny. Why is it funny?"

"Because, angel, irreverence is release," Andrea said. "Most angels and demons and the people playing with their fire take themselves entirely too seriously. If they just removed the sticks out of their asses, maybe Meridian wouldn't be such a Hellmouth. But just because I joke about it now and then doesn't mean I'm sloppy. If you try to even marginally corrupt my daughter, I'll use my unregistered spare to put a bullet in your head."

"What does marginal corruption look like these days?" Noah asked. "Are you going to go mama bear on her if she offers your child a piece of candy?"

"Okay, maybe flagrant corruption," Andrea said.

"Are the two of you always like this?" Tara asked, but she seemed pleased, slouched and relaxed in the jacket, even though the chair by Noah's desk wasn't the most comfortable.

"No. But watching over you, waiting for you to wake up, has been very restful, which is not typical for us at all," he replied. "If we seem overly casual, it's because things have been uncharacteristically quiet."

"Why'd you have to go and say that?" Andrea threw her stapler remover at his head.

He caught it, but the teeth gave him a good bite in return.

"If most angels and demons tend to resolve their fall on their own, why watch over me at all?" Tara asked. "Surely the hospital has procedures for a Jane Doe."

"Yeah. They contact the police," Andrea said. "You would have ended up in the system either way. The original detectives didn't mind losing the paperwork. Amnesia's nice and romantic for a soap opera. Not quite so much in real life. At least we have the means to work inside and outside the system to help you — to a point, of course. Things won't always be so quiet for us, especially now that the genius over here *said* it's been quiet. And we really should get back on our patrols."

"What do you patrol?" Tara asked.

"The kind of thing we can't put in paperwork," Noah said.

"What the fuck is going on out there?" Andrea stood at her desk and reached for the blinds to open them.

Their office's privacy meant that it was difficult to hear anything going on outside the office except the occasional clamor, either of camaraderie or the kind of chaos that accompanied homicide arrests, distressed families, and being in the department next to Assault. The temporary holding cells between the two departments made the area slightly rowdier than the average small-town drunk tank, so it was nice they couldn't hear most of it.

Noah turned around in his chair to undo the blinds behind him as well. Homicide looked quiet, which meant the ruckus was probably in holding or Assault.

Andrea opened the blinds over the door, then stepped out, her hand on her service weapon. The irreverent, insouciant cop was gone in favor of the consummate professional she became when the occasion called for it. She was at her best when underestimated. Noah might not have even noticed that something was wrong if her little sixth sense hadn't been silently strummed. That intuition of hers had saved his and other people's lives several times over.

"Stay here and stay down," Noah said to Tara, who was rubbing at her legs again, agitated as she stared out into the bullpen. "The glass isn't protective."

His hand on the butt of his service weapon, too, he followed Andrea out of the office and into Homicide.

After that, it was a matter of following the shouting.

The hubbub from other officers, big-bellied bellows and authoritarian sharpness, wasn't unusual, but the screams made his skin crawl cold. They were full-throated and wretched and interspersed with howls and exclamations of outraged pain, like angry jaguars.

Two men in holding banged on the bars, shouting for the kids to shut the hell up. Noah understood their annoyance—holding was echoey, and if the screams were piercing to him in Homicide, they must have been worse inside the cells—but adding to the cacophony wouldn't help much. The men, however, were shut in, harmless for now.

Noah pushed into Assault behind Andrea, who had released her weapon but stood at wit's end at the entrance.

The horror of the shrieking and yowling didn't begin to cover the chaos of the unfolding scene, which included children—too young to even be called juvenile delinquents—biting, scratching, and clawing at each other and at every adult trying to break them apart and hold them back.

With a large adult for every child, they should have been able to keep the average angry child at bay. Angry children often acted within reason and logic—childish reason and logic, but reason and logic nonetheless. They would fight dirty but settled quickly when they realized they couldn't land a hit with their arms held behind their back. Even troublemakers tended to shy away from the threat of greater trouble. They didn't want to go to jail, and they certainly didn't want to be taken home to face their mother.

Had these children been foaming at the mouth, Noah would have called the hospital and the CDC to let them know about an outbreak of rabies. Had these children been decaying, he would have declared a zombie apocalypse. He didn't know who to call for children who appeared entirely feral, blood on their mouths and under their nails, splattered over their clothes, scratches on their faces and hands, hellbent on attacking each other with the ardency of an uninhibited blood feud.

Given the unfettered hatred in their eyes, maybe he needed to call a freaking chaplain. MPD had a total of five chaplains, three variants of Christian, one Muslim, and one Jewish. Exorcism wasn't in any MPD handbook, but the Roman Rituals were on Noah's office bookshelf, just in case.

The children weren't just kicking, biting, and clawing at each other. They did the same to the officers and detectives trying to hold them. None of the police directly engaged with children had their guns out. Some on the outside like Noah and Andrea did, but all but one had lowered their firearm.

Andrea edged around the chaos and put her hand on the one officer's raised gun. "Are you fucking crazy? You're going to shoot a kid or a cop."

"Well, what the fuck are we supposed to do? Read *Mother Goose* to them?"

"What happened?" Noah asked.

"This! This happened. At Mansfeld Elementary during recess," the officer said. "They just kept getting worse and worse."

"Why'd they bring a bunch of inexplicably violent kids to MPD and not Mattea?"

"I don't know," the officer snapped. "To scare 'em straight or something? Maybe they assumed it was a playground turf war and they could broker a treaty. It wasn't my fucking idea!"

Noah leaned over so only Andrea could hear. "Magic?"

"Simplest answer is drugs."

"Does that feel right to you?"

"No."

The uniformed officers in the middle of the fray started taking out batons and tasers. The tasers didn't do anything but make the kids more violent. One of them lunged after the officer who tased him and closed his teeth over the man's jaw, then pulled a chunk of his face off. The boy didn't even have all his teeth. A little girl aimed directly for another officer's family jewels but collapsed when a different officer struck her across the face with a baton.

Noah knew this was going to go really bad for everyone involved if it continued, but he didn't know how to enter the fight without becoming part of the violence. The only thing he could think of to do was pull the officers off the children rather than the other way around. Once Andrea figured out what he was doing, she worked to do the same. The children just wanted to fight each other. Bad as that was, you weren't supposed to get between two dogs fighting. You let them fight until Animal Control could get the goddamn tranquilizer gun.

Noah wasn't positive a sedative would even slow them down if a taser just made them madder, but it was worth a try.

"Get multiple ambulances here," he shouted at the officer who needed a task to distract him from his trigger finger. "Have the hospital contact Mattea about over a dozen inexplicably violent children — children, not teenagers. Possibly drugged."

The officer nodded while others helped those who Noah and Andrea dragged out of the melee. Once they were no longer trying to stop the kids from attacking each other, the children wanted nothing to do with the adults.

If the cause was drugs, it would wear off or the kids would get tired. If it was magic, who the fuck knew what it would make the kids do or for how long, because magic didn't always metabolize. It might not end at all without physically removing a cursed object or applying a counterspell — and he and Andrea had to know the original spell to do that. On top of that, if they were to bring out something that needed to be burned in ritual offering, they'd never hear the end of it, even if it worked.

"What now?" Andrea shouted over children screaming and police yelling into their radios and phones.

"One kid at a time," Noah finally said. "Four men to one child, zip-tie them to the window bars, and so on. Most of them are too small for cuffs."

"Four people to one child?" one of the Assault detectives said, panting but incredulous.

"One for each limb. Unless you want to go back to one on one and see what doing the same thing and expecting a different outcome gets you."

"You're a real son of a bitch, Dunn."

But they followed his direction. After detectives and officers struggled together to secure the third child to the bars, the wild screaming rose to a new pitch.

Noah looked over at the entrance to Assault, where all the children had turned to look, too.

Tara pressed her hands on both sides of her head, crouching on the linoleum and screaming at a higher frequency than the children. Her eyes were closed, but tears poured from between the clenched lids again, as though she couldn't hold all of whatever she was feeling inside her skull.

And with her, the children's screaming grew higher and louder, higher and louder, until Tara collapsed on the tile, her screaming abruptly cut short. She pounded the floor with her fists, sobbing. This was different than how she'd wept in front of the library. Instead of sorrow, she cried as though she'd been in the worst pain she'd ever experienced in her life that suddenly stopped. The waters behind the dam of that pain flooded out in utter relief.

Noah rushed around the desks and clamoring children, even vaulted over one of the desks that had already been disturbed of its contents. He slid to his knees before grabbing her by the shoulders and helping her upright again. "I told you to stay in the office."

"They were so loud, and they hurt so *much*. Calling." Tara reached out toward the children, which was when Noah finally noticed that they'd stopped screaming, too.

Now their scratched, punched, bitten faces showed an expression he was far more familiar with on children than animal fury — terror. Most of them had fallen to the floor like Tara, holding their knees and elbows and abdomens, wailing for their mothers and fathers. But some of them noticed Tara there on the floor and stretched their hands out toward her the way she did to them.

Noah's first impulse was to hold her back. They were violent. They were dangerous. She was dangerous.

But he let her go, because as much as it hurt in his chest when a woman cried like that, it was even worse with kids. He didn't have any himself, but his sister did. He hadn't been able to stand them crying ever since they were infants, when that was what they were supposed to do. Every time he thought he didn't have a heart, they'd break it all over again because they wanted milk or couldn't have the cookie or needed the green plate instead of the blue plate.

Now here were fifteen kids crying for their mothers, and the closest thing on hand was a nephil who wept as much as they did. When she gathered them into her arms, they didn't hesitate for a moment. They clung to her and she clung to them, just held them while they wept together. Gradually, those who weren't zip-tied to iron bars crawled over to her as well until they were a weepy mass of children, a stick-figure Mary Poppins in the center. The bound children strained against their bonds to join the rest, including a ten-year-old who looked like he wanted to be too old for this nonsense but still needed maternal reassurance.

Andrea sprawled on the linoleum next to Noah, panting. "What was that? Did she stop it? Did she cause it? Was it on purpose?"

Noah rested back on his hands with her. "Whatever happened to the kids started before they got to the station. But I do think she stopped it."

Chapter Five

Other officers crowded into the room in front of paramedics, shouting, waving their guns now that their own weren't in the line of fire, and scaring the children even more. Tara clutched them closer and glared at the officers, although they couldn't have known that the situation had been so abruptly neutralized.

Noah held up his badge. "Lower your weapons! There are children here. Paramedics *in*, officers and children injured."

The police finally holstered their weapons, lethal and non-lethal, because the kids were clearly being kid-like, feral fear and loathing shifted to understandable confusion.

While the officers tried to figure out if they were supposed to call the kids' parents, lock the kids up, or let them go back to school after the paramedics were done, Mattea pediatric ward doctors and nurses arrived, more harried than one might expect from professionals who handled troubled children all the time.

When the doctor in front saw that the kids had calmed down—relatively, considering their hysterical state—he showed such relief that Noah was immediately suspicious. There was no reason why the doctor would be relieved unless he'd expected worse, and the only way he would have expected worse was if he'd seen it before.

"Who's in charge here?" the doctor asked.

Noah stepped out from behind the desk. "Not me, but you're going to talk with me anyway."

Andrea took his place next to Tara to begin the gentler version of what they'd done with the children when they were violent, peeling them away one by one and reassuring them that everything was going to be okay. Other officers more familiar with how to handle crying children stepped in to help. When Noah looked at his colleagues, he recognized them again, the panic that had turned them just as much into frightened animals receding.

Violence was contagious, even without drugs involved, but he wondered...

Sergeant Hale, of Assault Division, pushed through the onlookers. "Dunn, what the hell did you do?"

"Cleaned up your mess," Andrea snapped, holding a little girl on her hip. "Your guys brought a bunch of kids to the station? What did they think they were, miniature criminals? They were clearly juiced on something."

"Oh, did they play with the wrong Ouija board? This isn't your department." Hale put his fists on his hips, puffing up his chest like a goddamn rooster.

"Considering our Jane Doe was the only one able to calm them down, I'd say this is definitely our department."

"Someone was able to calm them down?" the doctor interrupted. "Who? God, tell us who."

"This isn't the first time it's happened, is it?" Noah said.

"It's the third confirmed large-scale incident in the last few days, but for the last week or so, we've received similar calls that suggest there've been some smaller incidents as well."

"And why has no one informed us of this?" Hale snapped. "Why hasn't this been on the news or in our memos? How are we supposed to help people if we don't know what to look out for?

"We hoped the first incident was isolated," the doctor said. "At the second location, your people looked for some kind of substance the kids might have ingested but found nothing. I think we'll have to contact the CDC after this. They'll want to test for a foreign substance or gas, do some blood tests, I'm sure. We simply don't have the resources to take care of this many violent kids at once. I've never seen anything like it—absolute rage from such young children. The kids from the other incidents, they're still in our pediatric ward. When they're not violent, they're just too worn out from their outburst but still so *angry*. Yet they're unable to articulate why or what triggered the initial attack. These kids, though... They're upset, but they're not angry anymore. They're lucid, talking... If fury is a sickness, they're cured." The doctor bypassed the sergeant and Noah to approach Tara. "If you don't mind, ma'am, could you tell me what you did? How did you calm them down?"

Tara had stopped crying, but her face was all wet. Noah handed her some tissues from someone else's desk. Five children still clung to her—a little more manageable than twelve. She blew her nose and wiped her cheeks. With the leftover tissues, she started tending to other kids' faces. "I'm so tired. Crying is exhausting. Why is crying so exhausting?"

"Now you know why we don't like doing it," Andrea said, passing a child to a nurse. "You're exhausting just to watch, and you've cried twice today."

"I came out from the office because they were so loud, so loud in my head, so very angry, and I was so very angry, so very loud. The headache...more pressure in and pressure out. Then I couldn't stand it anymore, and the headache and anger burst, released. They were so afraid, but we're less afraid together. I didn't do anything. I just...*felt* everything. I don't anymore. Thank goodness. The headache is still there, but it's quiet, though they're still confused and upset, and why not? They don't understand what happened. They don't know why they hurt or why they hurt other people. I'd be afraid, too." She hugged one of the children still holding on to her. "I think they need a cherry limeade."

Noah was startled into a snort. "I think everyone is due a nice cup of ice cream, I agree."

"Would you like that, sweetheart?" Tara kissed the top of a towhead's hair. The towhead boy nodded.

"Best medicine I know," Noah said.

"I'm absolutely flabbergasted," the doctor said. "We'll probably want to bring these kids to the hospital for observation, do some tests to compare them against the other kids."

"They're not going anywhere until we settle what happened here," Hale said.

"And you're not going to settle what happened here until the doctors figure it out," Noah said. "Are you really going to charge these poor kids with assault and battery when they're either sick, poisoned, or drugged?"

"Until I know what happened, no one's going *anywhere*."

"Good luck with that once parents and lawyers get involved." Noah had no patience left for a blustering man desperately trying to pretend he could gain control in a room of fifteen scared children, clueless distressed medical professionals, and cops who were just as damn confused but mostly glad they weren't fighting kids half their size anymore.

"Dunn, get back here!"

But he wasn't Noah's supervisor. Loretta would field the complaint and promptly file it in the round file. Q Division had almost complete discretion, and Hale knew it.

"Do you mind if we speak with you again, Doctor?" Noah handed him a business card, which included his personal number. "This may be relevant to our present case, or it might be one we pursue independently."

"This is Assault's case, Dunn!" Hale called after him.

"Absolutely, Hale. No question." Noah occupied himself with helping Tara off the floor and freeing her from the last clinging children, who were retrieved by other officers.

The department would become a different brand of chaos when parents arrived and freaked out in whole new ways. Let Hale and his people take over the paperwork. For now, Noah's priority was making sure

Tara was okay. He hooked his arm around her and led her out of Assault. Instead of taking her back toward Homicide, he veered them toward the stairs and led her up.

"You think he's a fool, don't you?" Tara said.

"I think a lot of people are fools."

"Where are you taking me?"

"Somewhere you can breathe not-so-fresh air and where we won't be overheard."

"What about Andrea?"

"She's a parent. She knows how to deal with upset kids better than I do." Noah waited until they were out of the stairway and on the flat open roof to add, "And she understands that what happened with you is just as important as what happened to those kids."

MPD boasted one gargoyle per corner, so by Meridian standards, the rooftop decoration was sparse. Gravel lined the flattop, and the sound of traffic was mostly drowned out by all the HVAC units rumbling to keep the interior cool. September was still hot. A jacket was more professional than necessary for him and Andrea, but Tara didn't remove it.

"So what did happen?" he said. "Because if those kids had been poisoned or drugged, they would have followed the same pattern as the last incidents, and your presence wouldn't have meant shit." The same frustration she'd inspired from the very beginning surfaced in Noah once again, hooded and hissing, and this time he was sure she was keeping something from him. "What's going on here is some kind of supernatural phenomenon. And it started about the same time you arrived, Tara."

"I'm not doing it. Let go of me." She wrenched against his grip on her upper arms, although he'd deliberately kept himself from squeezing like he wanted to do. She was still his case, not his suspect, and she didn't have a lot of cushion. "I can't tolerate their pain. I would never hurt those children."

"You clearly influenced them to stop being violent, and it looked like you didn't do it on purpose. Is it so much of a stretch to assume you could also be influencing them to be violent and not aware you're doing it? On the other hand, we didn't drive by any playgrounds on the way here, and right now, I'm not inclined to think you're just sending out bubbles of violence to randomly hit the nearest clutch of children. It doesn't seem likely. But you *did* do something to make them stop. That means there's something supernatural going on with you, and there's probably something supernatural going on with them."

"I don't know what I did." Tara brought her hands to her head, a less ferocious repetition of what she'd done below. "What I said down there to the doctor is just as true here. The headache was too much, and the closer I came to the violence, the worse the headache became. I think this pressure, in and out, everywhere… I think it's everybody else. When I'm just around a few people, it's manageable. But when there are more and when what they're feeling is…louder, I feel it, too."

"And you can change what they're feeling."

"Not on purpose. It burst in my head on its own. I thought my skull had actually exploded until I realized I was still there and in less pain — not no pain, because then they were scared and everybody was still upset. But it was nowhere near the deafening peak that it was when they were so furious. There was no reason, no logic, no meaning. It was just dark and heavy and prickly and so big that it erased everything else in their minds. Whatever burst out of my mind chased that terrible dark thing away, relieving me and them. I'm not entirely sure what I *did* so much as that it *happened* to me, like it happened to them."

"So you're telling me an angel falls from heaven with amnesia, then gains just enough memory that she knows her name and that she fell, but nothing about these strange powers."

Tara released her head and stepped closer to touch his temples instead. "Do you remember what it was like in the womb? Do you remember what it was like to be born? Do you remember what it was like to learn to walk, talk? Do you remember your first tantrum, your first birthday, your first Communion? What do you know about falling, Noah?"

Her hands on his hair derailed him more than he wanted to admit and undid his frustration until he wanted her to lower those hands to his cheek, the rough of his jaw. But that was a ridiculous thought, and he told himself to push it away. She was unnervingly direct with her gaze, too. Made him feel as though he were utterly transparent. And perhaps he was, because although she didn't move her hands, she tilted her head in an unspoken query.

"What we are in heaven is separate from what we become here," she said. "What use are angels on the physical plane? It's why we fall so violently. Imagine ascending to heaven and all that's left of you by the time you reach it is a skeleton. That would drastically change how you accomplish things, don't you think?"

She moved her hands from his temples to his shoulders, but it still seemed intimate, although they were hardly in a private place, out on an open roof. Her thumb found the hollow above his collarbone.

Jesus Christ, do not turn me on right now.

Jesus didn't listen to him. Noah silently prayed to the same indifferent God that she wouldn't think to notice.

"I am not what I was," she said. "I don't know what I'm capable of. I don't know how any of this works. I don't even necessarily know what's strange, because this is all I know. And if you want to know how this is supposed to go, perhaps you should look to those who might be in a better position to answer your questions than the new nephil in your company."

"It wouldn't hurt to try that line of inquiry, I guess," Noah said, making every attempt to sound more normal than he felt. He only had to swallow once in the middle of the sentence. "But what we do know is that you're influenced by other people's emotions, and you influence theirs."

Tara finally let her hands fall away from him and tucked them instead into the jacket pockets. "Do we really know that?"

"You've been sensitive to other people since the beginning, but now I think the influence you have on other people is academic. When you cry, I cry, and I'm not a crier. Your emotions are contagious, but you're also unfortunately susceptible to infection."

She stepped closer to him. "Then could you explain what you're infecting me with right now?"

Noah opened his mouth, then shut it. He stepped back, but Tara followed, that inquisitive expression returning. She withdrew her hands from the pockets to grab the front of his shirt and keep him from retreating.

"Whatever it is, it's not pain, although it travels the same paths. And you're afraid of it. Is it me you're afraid of?"

"No." Oh God, his voice had sunk into the raspy place lower in his chest, and he hadn't meant it to. "Stop reading my mind."

"I'm not. I don't know what you're thinking. I think I just feel…what you're feeling, and it's…" She let her eyelids flutter closed for a moment, and Noah nearly had to bite back a moan. "It's much nicer than pain, although it almost wants to be. Does it?"

"Flirts with it now and then," Noah admitted, but he grabbed her arms — still gently — and guided her back again. She released his shirt and let herself be moved. "We should go back down into the station. I know it won't be pleasant for you, but seems like Andrea and I need to take you somewhere new."

As he headed back to roof access, Tara gave a short laugh. "What are you running from? What is it you're afraid I'm going to feel?"

She came up behind him before he could open the roof access door and touched his forearm, bare below his T-shirt sleeve. He couldn't quite look straight at her like she could to him. God, he was being such a teenager, in the early throes of a silly crush. Funny how it still sometimes hit that hard. He could pick up a woman at a bar or entertain himself with videos and it was nothing — just a fling, a diversion. But then a person would surprise him, make his chest hurt when she hurt, and she didn't have to do anything but exist a little too close to him.

She smiled, still bewildered, but mortifying understanding rose within it. "Noah, are you— I thought you didn't— Is that what this—" She couldn't seem to articulate her own interpretation.

And he couldn't cobble together so much as a single lie, which meant he couldn't convince himself to answer, either.

He was a professional. He'd rescued sacrifices, sacrifices who were sometimes quite appreciative. Naked bodies on their own didn't keep him from being professional, and if he had a physical reaction, he usually had ways to deal with it, from forcing himself to think about things he didn't like to physically adjusting himself so that what he felt wasn't as apparent. The fact that he'd seen her naked in the hospital wasn't what distracted him now.

Instead, he was preoccupied with the memory of seeing her naked in the bed across from his bedroom. Naked in his bed. No more hospital gown or dressing. Then no self-consciousness when she'd needed a shoulder to cry on. She wore his jacket better than anything of hers.

Andrea was prettier than her, but there was something, *something*...and not just because she was vulnerable, not just because she was new.

Noah moved slowly. What he was doing was impulsive, but he didn't want to let himself claim that he didn't realize what he was doing, didn't want to make his own impulse hers. He touched her cheek — not even a stroke or a caress, just testing, letting her know what he was doing and giving her a chance to retreat.

This wasn't a good idea. He was on duty, and she was the subject of an investigation. She could be causing these kids to go feral, accidentally or on purpose. She could be a demon.

What harm is there in a kiss? It wasn't like she'd had one before.

And she wasn't moving away, wasn't protesting. The swollen, bruised, cut face from the hospital was gone, as though never there. Her skin was translucent and clear, and she seemed utterly transparent, too, intrigued as he leaned in, lifting her chin with the curve of his finger. He wanted to dive down to taste her surprise, and as though in response to the power of his wish, she gasped before he even touched her mouth.

That was enough to draw him in to press his lips against hers.

Oh, this isn't good. Her gasp had already been enough to stir his desire, but the way she whimpered — in quite a different way than she did when she was in pain — drew a groan from him as well as he pushed her gently against the roof access door.

She brought her fingers to his chest first to brace herself, then to search over his body with the freedom of the curious, up to his neck as he kissed her again and again, then down the front of his shirt, as though following the path of his arousal. His arousal followed her instead. He slid his hand into her tousled hair, his other over her waist to draw her hips to his, almost against his own will, except he very much wanted her body closer, very much enjoyed how she kissed him back — with the hesitancy of novelty, but as they settled into a rhythm between the caress of their mouths, the soft slide of their tongues, the cant of their hips, she quickly lost that hesitancy.

She became as enthusiastic in her kisses as she was when she ate. That's what it felt like to him — as though she was consuming him slowly, sweetly. He wanted nothing more than that absolute sensory devotion to remain on his lips but also stray everywhere, to where she slid her hand with more boldness against where he was hard in his trousers.

Tara moved her hips as though she had the same need as him, the same pace, the same pulse. "Oh, this is…" She moaned as she stroked over him, gripping him as well as she could through his clothing. Using the door as leverage, she hooked one long leg around his, and for a moment, all he could think about was that long, long leg stepping out of a shower, then those long, long legs, heels up, over tangled sheets.

What's wrong with one little kiss? You know better, you son of a bitch.

He knew better, but this felt too good, even though it was all moving so fast now instead of slow, careful, considered. She was as entangled and engaged in him as she was with food, with the same unbridled enthusiasm and eagerness to sample, taste, feast. She'd been sensitive from the beginning. Sensitive to feelings, sensitive to stimulation. That was what this was as much as a meal.

Noah kissed away from her mouth to bury his nose in her hair. She smelled clean, not floral or fruity or like unsettled earth under broken concrete. Witches trapped incense in their skin like vanillin in old books. Some demons smelled of ash or of the pheromones in their musk. When they were in their truer state, they sometimes smelled of brimstone. Gargoyles and stone angels smelled like, well, stone. She smelled unsettlingly human, and her hair was soft between his fingers.

As he kissed down her neck, Tara let her head fall back, but she doubled her efforts on his cock until he could barely think.

He wasn't supposed to get this hard this fast. He wasn't supposed to want to rut like a teenager in a public space where they could be interrupted at any moment. Yet here they were, with her rubbing up against the natural stiffness of his trouser placket and him jerking into her grip, and she didn't know or didn't care about holding herself back. Moaning near his ear with the same enthusiasm as she'd moaned over food, Tara arched into his touch as he massaged her scalp and slid his other hand under his jacket to trace up her back.

The sensation of a wing stump under his palm almost tore him out of the moment but didn't seem to cause her pain, so he tried to avoid it, didn't let himself think of it any further. That would complicate how good this felt, so easy, so swift, as she felt what he felt, then mirrored that back to him so that he felt what she felt and he felt what she felt he felt, both of them at the same time, climbing, climbing, climbing over each other…

He wasn't a biter, but he took the base of her neck between his teeth to keep from advertising to the world that he'd come in a matter of minutes just from her hand over his pants. She had no such compunction about the cries of her climax, any more than she had about crying in general, but she was at least muffled against his shoulder.

"What the fuck was that?" To soften how angry he sounded, he kissed over the bitemark he'd left—no broken flesh, but given her thin skin, it could end up bruising. He continued to apologize for his impulsivity and the harshness of his exclamation with his mouth over the dents he'd left behind until Tara's tension released again.

"I was going to ask you the same thing."

Tara didn't lean back on the door anymore, and she'd unwrapped her leg from around his, but she still gripped his shirt and held herself against him. Noah wondered if at least part of her clinging was because he ran as hot as she ran cold and he was simply comfortably warm. She rested her head on the same shoulder she'd cried on, eyes closed with trust given too freely.

"Is that what people feel all the time?" she murmured. "You're all so fascinating with your indulgences, but it's a distant kind of fascination. We don't have many of these parts and pieces of bodies, and I don't remember it ever *feeling* this strong. No wonder you're as preoccupied with sex as you are with food."

"Yes, we're quite preoccupied with both, but not like... Tara, I need to clean myself before things...stain. And I think both of us need to get away from each other right now."

She raised her head to breathe him in under the edge of his shaven beard, her lips against his neck not quite in a kiss but as though she were considering it. He shouldn't have been responding so soon, but he stirred in the mess in his underwear. He couldn't remember the last time this had happened, and since he was pretty sure he was responding to *her* arousal right now, he'd probably end up doing it again if he just let her explore at her leisure.

This wasn't the time or the place. It should never have been the time or the place. If Tara was a demon, it had been a terrible decision. If she was an angel, it had been a questionable decision, possibly a corrupting one. Not that sex in itself was corruptive, but there were probably rules about this sort of thing. Not that they'd had *sex* sex, but...

His mind was reeling and his body was waking back up, and he absolutely could not allow this to happen again.

Tara permitted herself to be displaced, although she seemed to see him in a completely new light, the same way she'd looked at popcorn chicken, a substandard burger, and her second cup of cherry limeade. He was pretty sure she had to learn the lesson of moderation at some point anyway, doctor's orders to feed her notwithstanding.

Fuck. Now he was imagining her in tangled sheets with food all around her, watching him as she ate and ate and ate…

"Go back down and wait for me in the office," Noah finally said. "Try not to jump anyone's bones along the way. It's generally frowned upon. I'll join you soon."

He gestured for her go downstairs ahead of him. Although she looked back at him on her way down in a way both amusing and appealing in turns, she managed to keep her hands to herself, and he didn't need to worry that she'd come up from behind to tempt him again.

It was ridiculous that he was tempted at all, especially at work, especially after everything that had happened. But he was still struggling not to imagine her in all manner of provocative positions, with her characteristic straight-forwardness.

She hadn't yet learned playfulness, nuance, subtlety, or even much in the way of foreplay, didn't swing her hips at she descended the stairs, didn't bat her eyelashes or lick her lips, at least not to make him want her. But just the sight of her was enough to make him profoundly uncomfortable even more than he'd already been from finishing in his pants.

And from knowing that she knew how he was feeling, given how every new fantasy and twitch in his briefs was followed by her backward glance.

Even more disconcerting than his feelings was knowing that at least some of his feelings were hers.

It was like a switch had been flicked, and he had to ask himself how much worse this distraction was going to become, as well as the way this was going to change how she interacted with the world, and how the world interacted with her.

Chapter Six

Tara hid herself in Q Division's office while Andrea continued working in the Assault Department and Noah did whatever he needed to do to run away from her for a short while.

The wooden panels, windows, and blinds didn't protect her entirely from what pressed in on her from all sides. And now she knew that at least some of that pressure and pain wasn't just the normal tribulations of a physical body. It came from other people. All that anger, fury, fear, grief, sorrow, hatred, contempt... Like dull fork tines needling through her muscles and joints.

She had also discovered pleasure.

Tara had known before she'd fallen that there was pain on Earth, but she couldn't have anticipated how awful it was, her metaphysical angelic body ill-equipped to experience the same stimulation. Nor could she have anticipated how pleasure ran through a human body as completely as a crashing wave. No reproductive organ or complicated gastrointestinal tract meant that she'd been completely incapable of understanding food or sex.

The human body was such a messy, complicated thing, filled with mush and grumbles and fiber and fat—and so much mucus and other salty fluids. But good heavens, the things that sometimes produced those fluids... Terrible, wonderful, exhausting, exhilarating, and she'd only been out of the hospital for a day.

Now that she knew some of the things she felt were what other people were feeling, she was better able to differentiate what was coming in and what she was sending out, but that didn't mean she had any idea how to close that door, if there was even a way to close it. The office was a shield, but not an impenetrable one. Solitude was also a shield, but although it might be a possibility—perhaps her temperament wasn't suited for the city—it wasn't necessarily helpful to her right now, while Q Division was still investigating her and she might be relevant—or at least helpful—to a new epidemic of prepubescent viciousness.

She wondered if she would be of greater use to Andrea than Noah in helping the children. Maybe she could help the parents calm down when they saw their children so distraught and treated like criminals in a police station. Or maybe she could help that sergeant lower his blood pressure and ensure the matter was handled more responsibly.

But the bursting of violent feeling in her head, while a relief, had left her surprised that gray matter hadn't leaked out with burst blood vessels through her nose. And the continuously rising panic that had led to it had wrapped piano wire around and around and around her neck, tighter and tighter each second.

No, she was as useless outside the hospital as she had been inside it. She didn't understand why she felt like this if she couldn't use it for anyone's good.

When Noah returned, he looked the same, so if he'd changed, it wasn't something she could see. He looked as composed as ever, as he had been even when the feelings had become too much for her and he'd shuddered under her touch in response. There had only been one break in that composure, when he'd gone rigid and what emanated from him hadn't been controlled or considered but a blissfully empty yet chaotic darkness—which didn't make it bad. There could be peace and pleasure in darkness, especially during a headache.

And she'd met and matched his chaotic darkness with her own. As it had been building and building inside her, she'd thought, *Surely it can't keep going. Oh, this has to be as far as it goes. Oh, dear heavens, how far does it go?*

It had been a much less alarming burst when she'd finally reached that apex, and she'd been comforted in the end, that there had been an end at all, that it didn't just keep intensifying indefinitely, like the opposite of a fall—although she supposed that ended, too, but not without transformation.

He looked composed, but she knew he wasn't, even though he was on the other side of wood and glass and she couldn't easily parse him out from the barrage of everyone else in Homicide, Assault, and the holding cells. But for a man who hadn't been an angel in another life, he stood as squarely as his jaw, as though his insides weren't as mushy as her own. She'd felt that solid body, felt how he tended to himself to meet the demands of his job, would like to feel his body again.

Low in her abdomen, something tightened in a much nicer way than when she needed to use the bathroom. Messy, messy things, these bodies. But perhaps some of the messy things made up for other messy things.

She sat back in the uncomfortable chair and waited for him to gather his pride enough to come to her. Once he did, Tara shifted in her seat. Her body and mind seemed to light up like the globe pendants that hung from the department ceilings as he approached. He was familiar, there from the moment she'd awakened in the strange place, both gentle and insistent in his interrogation of her. Which hadn't yet ended, she reminded herself, despite his lapse on the roof. He'd been careful there, too, albeit conflicted. Less conflicted about giving her food than giving her sex. She knew why, but it amused her nonetheless. She made no such distinction.

Although it is distracting, isn't it? When she started thinking about either of those, she was hard-pressed to think of something else. Noah hesitated at the door, which meant he probably had a good idea where her thoughts strayed when she looked at him.

"You need to get a handle on that," he said. "Or else we're going to need to find a eunuch to put between us."

"Can't you just foist me onto Andrea?" She bit her lip against the desire that hit her at her suggestion, although she wasn't sure why.

"Sadly, no. I may need to warn her, though, if you can't establish some kind of control."

"I didn't even know I was doing it until thirty minutes ago, Noah, although I suspect I'm adapting as quickly as I heal. You need to adjust your expectations."

He braced both his hands on the door frame and lowered his head with a sigh. "You're right. It's just really difficult to focus now that you've figured out attraction and desire and all those other things that we usually save for other areas of our lives, if at all. If I'd been distracted by you like this, or if you'd been distracted by me, that incident in Assault might not have ended as well as it did."

"*Has* it ended?" Tara asked.

"I caught Andrea outside the bathrooms. She said there's going to be a lot more drama coming our way. She'd rather stay here to provide answers and an understanding ear to incoming concerned parents. If she gets the opportunity, she'll start the process of gathering your IDs. We'll reconvene at end of shift. I apologize again for us being night shift. You'll have to readjust when you actually join the rest of the society, which your circadian rhythm will probably prefer."

"Does yours?" The good thing about her genuine curiosity was that it drew her thoughts away from his body and her pain. She followed him out of Homicide via another hall than the one connecting with Assault, which was still full, although most onlookers had returned to work. Yelling, screaming, and crying from that vicinity poked and prickled under her skin like claws, but moving away meant it wasn't nearly as bad as before. Besides, these were all more reasonable reactions and emotions. Quite different from the mindless screams and sharpened blades of the children's feral energy.

As she turned her mind to other things, Noah relaxed as well, his stride surer through the halls as he led her back to the building's entrance, with its maze of stairs.

"If demons started doing more evil deeds during the day, we would be day-shifters in a hot second," Noah said. "Some of them *do* their evil deeds during the day, of course, but it's less likely to be illegal, which means we don't have much of a leg to stand on to stop them. Less pustulant pestilence demons, avarice demons — that sort of thing — can function almost invisibly in our world. If they're caught out by law enforcement, it's generally through fraud or other white-collar crimes. Andrea and I don't have the technological resources or skills to beat demons and cults at that kind of game.

"No, the kind of demons and monsters we deal with on a regular basis are most active at night. Some people live in the dark just fine, but neither Andrea nor I tolerate it very well. We do what we can with sun lamps and trying to be up for more sunlight hours during our days off, especially Andrea when she has the kids. But every shift feels like two days, and we never get enough sleep, even if it's the right number of hours. Repairs, maintenance, construction, and medical appointments all happen during the hours we're supposed to be asleep. Summers are a little easier, because the light lasts longer. Winters are the worst. Really, the only upside is that Meridian does have a thriving nightlife, so while some things close at regular hours, there are more twenty-four-hour joints and places are open a lot later than average, even for a city. Did you know there's a twenty-four-hour bowling alley just twenty minutes from here? You wouldn't think they'd be all that successful, but as it turns out, demons love bowling. It's nuts."

"You talk about demons as though you want to eradicate them, like hunters. Then you mention they like bowling. Do you eradicate them while they're bowling? Because it sounds like you don't."

"We're not hunters. We sometimes help hunters and they sometimes help us, but they're vigilantes. With a few exceptions, such as those who adhere to the Alliance treaty, they'll kill a demon just because it's a demon. In order to operate at all, Andrea and I must do so under strict guidelines, because most of what we do isn't something we can put in a police report, but at the same time, we must be above reproach in case a report is necessary. One of the fundamental tenets is that it isn't open season on monsters or demons just because of what they are. Andrea and I are more concerned about the victims in most of these cases, which means we've occasionally had to free a monster or demon before, if a cult of humans got their hands on someone who hadn't caused any direct harm."

With the sun already going down, Tara understood how nightshift could be disorienting. The rest of the world was winding down while they were just getting started. Their eyes, designed for the light of day, had to suffer the insult of so many shadows, despite occasionally blinding attempts to illuminate that darkness.

Tara slid into the passenger's seat. "Noah?"

"Yes."

"Andrea's getting me a driver's license, isn't she?"

"Yes."

"I can't drive."

"Between rideshare, taxis, and a decent public transit in the heart of the city, you might not need to. One thing at a time."

* * * *

When the graveyard gate was locked, Noah tried the front door of the chapel. No one answered, so he shifted over to the offices, where someone opened the door.

Tara stayed by the cemetery fence, gazing upon the gravestones in the dimming light.

She was a few days old as a human but ageless as an angel. Mortality was something that she'd known from a distance. It was something else to look upon the broad swath of fertilized field and know that every single stone disturbance marked a person's death. Child, mother, brother, together, alone... Everyone died on the physical plane. The humans had it coded into their design. Demons could be killed. Even the stone angels would eventually be nothing but dust.

The physical plane had never been built to last. For all that people pursued immortality — metaphorically or literally — it was the ephemeral nature of that architecture that made it as urgent and beautiful and frightening as a bee sting.

This was just one field. There were more cemeteries in Meridian than churches, all of them held the dead, and there were more dead left to bury, such that there would be other cemeteries in the future when these were finally all full.

Falling hadn't improved Tara's concept of death. To live was to be inimical to death, utterly unable to fathom. She understood food and sex now, things that depended on the transcendence of the temporary, the inevitability and desperation of decay. Death, even when right in front of her, planted in fertile soil, was harder.

"We're in luck. Reverend Ballesteros will let us in the cemetery for a few minutes while he finishes up in his office," Noah said, approaching with the reverend.

"Here you are, ma'am." The reverend unlocked the padlock, then shook out the chain. "Good luck with your assignment. I hope the dead can speak to you like they do for me. God be with you."

"And also with you," Noah responded automatically.

When she glanced back at him after the reverend headed back to his office, Noah's expression was slightly self-deprecating.

"Lapsed Methodist," he whispered.

"Why lapsed, if you don't mind my asking?" Tara asked.

"Oh, I don't know. More like a lapsed churchgoer, I guess. It was one thing to attend Sunday school as a kid, but I don't have to go to church to witness the supernatural, and I don't need some dusty minister telling me the truth that Andrea and I live. Also, about the time church is gearing up, I just want to go to sleep." He shrugged. "I talk to plenty of spiritual leaders through work anyway. And I visit plenty of churches, as you might imagine. Get my fill of crosses in the cemeteries."

He took out a flashlight to help make sure she didn't trip on the smaller stones and markers. His company was companionable, even though they weren't talking about anything substantive, even though it was nighttime and cemeteries weren't traditional places to while away the hours.

Tara couldn't remember entirely, but she thought she preferred limited company rather than being alone. Someone didn't fall to Earth to be alone.

Yet she appreciated being alone with Noah. Despite the buildings crowded around the cemetery and cars trundling past, things were quiet again, without and within. So maybe she didn't need to run away to the country to function. She just needed space — in admittedly short supply in a city, but not impossible to find.

"Do you know where you're going?" Tara asked, as they strolled down the tenth row.

Noah pointed the flashlight at her, making her squint. "These are your people, Tara, not mine. I thought you were trying to find one to talk to."

"I thought you were taking me to an angel you knew."

Noah rolled his eyes, but he laughed and she sensed no frustration. "No. They'll whisper with me around, but I told you that most of them don't talk to me."

"I assumed you were taking me to one that does."

"I'm sorry. I should have been clearer." He pointed the flashlight back out to the gravestones and passed the beam over the many angel toppers, large and small, sitting, standing, or lying on the gravestones. "They don't talk to me because I'm not one of them. But you are. So it shouldn't matter which one you try to talk to, if they acknowledge you as one of their own. I think."

"You think?"

"They don't talk to me. How would I know?"

Their mini comedy of errors gave her a fit of giggles — like the fizzy bubbles of a cherry limeade but in a different part of her throat. Then Noah joined her, the flashlight beam jiggling when he couldn't keep it steady. Before they knew it, they were both laughing in a cemetery and probably getting nasty looks in the dark.

When she could finally stop giggling so madly, she held out her hand. "May I use the flashlight?"

He handed it to her, then stepped back and let her explore on her own. He followed a few steps behind.

Tara finally found a cluster of angels—different sizes, different stones, different poses, some feminine, others masculine, and one uncertain, but all of them with beautiful, magnificent wings that made where hers had been itch from the absence. She automatically tried to move them, stretch them out, but although the wing hinges shifted under her skin, there was nothing to stretch.

She abruptly sobered from the fit of humor with the reminder of what she'd lost.

She shrugged off Noah's jacket and handed it to him without a word. She still didn't like cold, but she wanted her arms to feel free as she spread them in the midst of the copse of angels. When she closed her eyes, she could almost remember all four wings at their full wingspan, flying rather than falling. Then she pulled her arms back in to hold her shoulders, pulling them in to the point of discomfort, as though if she split her shoulder skin, wings would unfurl out again, tearing through the T-shirt.

"I am Tara, nephil of only a few days." She didn't need her voice to carry. She spoke only to the small group of angels while Noah looked on from a crypt about twenty feet away. Close enough to hear. She didn't mind if he did and hoped the other angels didn't, either. She didn't know why they would exclude him when he was a protector of Meridian as much as they were. Falling had a way of humbling the proud.

"I fell in the middle of the city and was taken to one of their hospitals. I don't think it was supposed to happen like that, but I have no recollection of falling beyond the pain, and I don't remember who I was before the fall or why I fell. If I had a plan for when I came down here, it escapes me now."

She heard no whispering to acknowledge that these angels were more than stone.

"Noah and Andrea are human and don't have any reason to trust me, but they're doing their best to help. I don't make it easy. I have an inadvertent influence upon the world, and the world presses its oppressive influence upon me. I could benefit from some guidance. I don't think I fell to become a demon, but how would I know when I almost forgot my own name?"

"We all had an adjustment period."

Tara swept the flashlight beam toward the voice, which came from a three-foot-tall angel with a delicate curve to her hips and a soft, covered swell of chest. She'd been draped over the back of the gravestone, but now she perched on its ledge.

"The rest of us emerged from our daze alone," the angel continued. "If you fell in such a populous area, you must have had a reason."

"I don't know what it is."

"Most people—angel, human, demon—do not know their purpose. You're hardly unique in losing yours." The stone angel beckoned her closer and for her to lower her flashlight. "You probably feel like you've been put in a gyroscope and expected to land on your feet."

"I landed on what was left of my wings."

"It's not meant to be gentle," the angel said. "We have to choose the amputation, the diminishment, the humiliation. It's not so often that we let humans witness that degradation, but you must have had a reason to be caught when we have so many other places to fall and recover in our own time, disoriented in the wilderness — sometimes tempted. A city center can be its own wilderness, though, with its own temptations."

"How am I supposed to traverse this wilderness alone?" Tara asked. "How do we arrive without a name or papers or any sense of who we are and still live in this world? The demons have a network, but we must depend upon the kindness of strangers?"

The angel smiled with the infinite patience one could expect of stone. "If you are to become demon, you will have your network. If you are to remain an angel, you have already been found by those who were meant to find you."

"Are you saying I fell where Noah and Andrea would help me?"

"You fall where you mean to fall. It is a helpless feeling, to need them, but that's the price and pleasure of making ourselves small."

"Then how do I know if I fell to serve on earth or in hell, if I can't remember why I fell?"

"If you need to ask the question, you probably already have your answer, my love."

The angel rested her forehead against Tara's, and Tara closed her eyes. She felt nothing coming from the angel, nothing exiting her into the stone. It was such sweet comfort not to be pulled, pushed, crushed, and broken by raw emotion. There was almost no pain, except that the angel's head was exceptionally hard and cold, but such exquisite silence was worth a little discomfort.

"Ultimately, Tara, the choice is yours," the angel whispered. She stroked Tara's hair and cheeks. There was terrible loneliness in her expression, and Tara was glad not to know it more than what she saw. To have the cosmos within reach of their wings and many eyes, then to be confined to stone for an untold number of years…another price, another humiliation, but all for a reason. Mortification in return for understanding.

She remembers staring down. It isn't really down, any more than heaven is up or hell is deep. Angels fall from outside Earth to help them burn through, but they are in and out and in-between, not from a distance or from on high but merely separate. As the dimension allows, they look down because they are never among.

And she — though 'she' is too simple for how she started — stares down so often and yearns so to feel, to embrace, to see with two eyes, to taste with tongue that only knows song, to smell everything from a steaming plate to a steaming grate, to hear the crude inventiveness and endless variation of their plunking, whining, declarative music as it is meant to be heard, to feel gravel and sackcloth and wool and skin and hunger and grief, every texture within and without flesh.

It is all so beautifully, elaborately simple from where she observes every attempt to reach beyond their plodding bodies, to describe and speak to things unseen and unknowable, yet how far and close they come, and how far and close they seem. She does not sleep, but she dreams of their world, their loud, towering world stretching for more and higher, ugliness and beauty, paradise and inferno. She wants to know their suffering, to become a part of their transcendence.

"Sometimes angels fall for benign or benevolent reasons but never find their footing," the angel said. "They seek instead another pair of wings rather than wait ten years to receive theirs back in return for servitude in stone."

"I think I fell to feel," Tara murmured, lingering in her distant yet distinct memory. "But now I feel *everything*. I feel them, and then I make them feel."

"Not every angel is given such a blessing when they come down to live as human, but every blessing has its corresponding curse. As an angel, you were fortunate enough to have the free will to fall. Now that you are human, you have the free will to choose whether to serve heaven or hell. What you choose is what is meant, my love."

"But how do I control it, either way I choose?" Tara asked. "What they feel overwhelms me, and I can't control how I make them feel."

"Angels were created full-fledged, knowing and known. We never had to learn. As a human, you have to learn. You have to be patient."

"I don't want to hurt them."

"I know. But you will fail, Tara, as they fail. You will fail and you will succeed, you will exult and you will despair, you will exalt and you will condemn, you will climb and you will stumble. This is the life you chose."

"Is the time given enough?"

"Never. Ten years, ten thousand, it is never enough. But ten is what we are given. It's your choice what to do with it. Whatever you choose, my love, may it bring you joy."

"I want to say this wasn't helpful, but that would only be my frustration, and it would be a lie," Tara said. "I do thank you, though, for clarifying that there's little clarity."

The angel laughed. "You've only been here a few days. Grant yourself grace. But you are not alone, neither here nor out there. I hope that gives you some peace."

Tara rested her forehead on the angel's again and wrapped her long arms around the smaller angel, as though cradling a child. "May I return for more wisdom?"

"We would love for someone to talk to. At the very least, it's nice to know what's going on outside the fence," the angel said. "We don't need to speak of heavenly things. Earthly things entertain as well. It does get dull to have all the accoutrements of an angel but no cause except the peace they seek to rest in. All dressed up and nowhere to go."

Tara smiled. "Peace be upon you, too. You know, you might talk to Noah and Andrea now and then when they try to talk to you."

"They're not the kind we usually speak to. I'll spread the word, but I can't make them do more than whisper to those forged without divine light."

"Surely, if you can speak to demons in spiritual battle, you can speak to humans who are only trying to help."

"Just because demons forswore heaven doesn't change what they were created to be. Their divinity is twisted, corrupted, but there's not a one who can't come home."

Chapter Seven

Tara was quiet as they left the cemetery, not brooding but contemplative.

"How much of that did you hear?" she finally asked between calls on the police scanner.

He glanced over at her for a second, but he couldn't search her face for the answer she wanted while he was driving, much less at night. "Some. I wasn't trying to overhear, but you didn't seem to be trying to keep it secret. Was I not supposed to be listening?"

"I have nothing to hide yet."

"It was interesting to finally get confirmation the stone angels are alive, though. The rest of the world thinks the moving Meridian statues are just a trick."

"If they're alive, they move, not just in Meridian," Tara said. "There are just so many here that they're more likely to be caught in a different position. They probably think it's a great joke."

"I hadn't thought about the angels having a sense of humor about the whole thing. I just assumed they were deadly serious."

"We're as varied as you. Did you think only the demons have fun? Granted, it usually takes free will to have proper fun, but that doesn't mean any of us are without our joys as well as sorrows. That's why I fell. I wanted to experience...all of this." Tara gestured vaguely to the skyline lights, indicating the world at large.

"Being an angel wasn't enough for you?"

"I wanted to know what you felt when you composed poetry or listened to music, when you danced, when you ate with family and friends, what made you laugh, what made you cry. Angels can accomplish feats of greater complication, but we don't have the same creativity, inventiveness, wonder, awe, and we have no need for the same intensity of sensation. But that doesn't mean it isn't attractive to us or that we aren't curious. Haven't you ever wanted to be something else? Did you always want to be a cop? Or did you want to be a fighter pilot or a zookeeper when you were a kid?"

He laughed. "I wanted to be an astronaut. And a dinosaur. But it's different when you're a kid — obviously, because you think 'dinosaur' is a viable occupation. As I approached adulthood...I wanted to be a cop. I wanted to be a *good* cop. Turns out that where I am now, on the fringes of the force, is closer to what I thought I wanted to be than if I had a more conventional position."

Tara finally turned back toward him in her seat. "You never thought about what it would be like to be something else? An opera singer, a trash collector, a casino mogul?"

"My mother didn't want me going into law enforcement, so I considered becoming a firefighter. Mom preceded to inform me that wasn't acceptable, either, so I became a cop anyway."

"And after you're done being a cop?"

He hadn't contemplated retirement in a while, not since his last serious relationship that had ended with relative amity after a discussion about precisely this. "I wasn't planning on quitting."

"You may not end up having a choice," Tara replied. "At least in the way you want to be a cop."

"I guess part of me figured I'd die young," Noah said.

"And if you live until you're ninety?"

"I'm tempted to say 'shoot me'."

"Noah."

"I know." He was already over forty and worked out as much to keep himself from falling apart as to keep up with the naturally powerful demons and monsters with which he interacted. Those interactions weren't always violent. On the contrary, they usually wanted nothing to do with him and scattered. But sometimes he also needed to deadlift people out of warehouses. Not everyone was as light as Tara. "I just don't want to think that far ahead because it might not happen. If I'm going to do something, it might as well be now. If I can't do it now, I probably won't be able to do it later, either."

"You could have a career-ending injury tomorrow. Would you still want to be a cop if all you could do was ride a desk?"

"I've been recruited a few times for Internal Affairs, mostly because Andrea and I already have a tense relationship with the other departments, so they figure I'd be used to the antagonism. But I've seen too much. I can't just pretend I don't know what's going on in this city. I can't do nothing. I'd probably end up mentoring the new cops they'd have to bring into Q Division. Make them do the heavy lifting."

"Some angels can't imagine being anything else, either. Plenty with free will still choose to stay as they are. They bow and praise and serve, and if they question their existence, it's not strong enough curiosity to leave for a short time. It's not a bad thing, Noah, being nephilim. Just because we fall doesn't mean we were cast out. It's an opportunity to experience for a short time what it's like to be human — that is, if we want to stay an angel when our time is up. If we fall to become a demon, the rules change."

"But even demons have a path back to heaven, don't they? As gargoyles."

"Exactly. Different rules. They can be demons for thousands of years but still can change at any time."

"What about the hybrids? I never quite understood that part."

"There are many ways for angels to fall and for demons to incarnate, and different levels of power when they do. Hybrids are probably the closest people come to that image of a devil on one shoulder and an angel on another. Humans don't need angels and demons for them to do good or bad things, but with hybrids, there's the added element of the divine and demonic. They intertwine with a human soul, inextricably bound to it until it expires. It's really quite fascinating from an angelic perspective, but hard to explain down here."

"So you didn't fall to cause murder and mayhem or any other shenanigans?" Noah asked. "Because I could drop you off right here, just say you ran. I don't need to get in the way of your agenda, unless you get in my way."

"I wasn't planning on it," she said lightly.

"But you have a choice, don't you? I heard that much. You *could*."

"You could decide to shoot someone in cold blood tonight. Does that mean you want to?"

"You've only been here a few days, and we had clothed sex on the station roof."

"I know you've probably heard otherwise all your life, but there's nothing wrong with what we did."

"Sounds like something a demon would say." Noah wasn't being entirely serious, but neither was he teasing.

"There are all kinds of sexual immorality, but sex before marriage is not one of them. Of course, by Old Testament standards, we married each other up there on that roof. But you and I both know that, by modern standards, that's ridiculous. Some rules change, some don't. The rules of marriage have changed. The rules of sexual immorality have not, but as you're aware, they've been misinterpreted, and where there's room for misinterpretation, there's grace."

"Can I quote you to a priest?"

"You believe what you want, Noah. If you don't want to touch me again, that's your choice."

"You don't make it feel like a choice. I don't think you meant to, but it kind of seemed like you dragged me along for that ride."

"I know." She turned away from him again, and this time, discomfort tightened her voice. "Please forgive me while I learn. The angel didn't exactly give me any tips on how to control myself, just that I would need to practice."

"Why did she call you 'my love'? Did you already know her from heaven or something?"

"It's just a term of endearment, like 'good friend'. As you've probably guessed, we don't have men and women quite like you imagine them. We don't have genitals or mammary glands, although if we have chests, sometimes the breasts are more prominent. 'Love' is just the love we show or give. It's not romantic, if that's what you're wondering."

"I was. Thank you."

What he didn't ask about and what lingered in his mind like the aftertaste of her kiss was overhearing that, if she was an angel, she was exactly where she needed to be because she'd put herself in his path.

It was the closest Noah had ever experienced to some cosmic being having a plan for him. Unsettling confirmation that everything his Mom and Grandma had scolded him with was true— Someone was always watching. She'd fallen in the middle of Meridian to get his attention.

He knew what he'd like to think. He'd like to believe that he'd been chosen by an angel to be her guide on Earth. He'd like to believe that extramarital sex as sin was silly and impractical so that he could release some of the guilt his family had given him. He'd like to believe that her breaking the hold of feral violence on the children was because she had a special empathic gift designed to help them. He'd like to believe that her taking hold of his arousal and giving him hers in an inevitably explosive cycle was an anomaly, that she really hadn't meant to do it.

He'd like to believe every word that came out of her mouth.

But while she wasn't necessarily too good to be true, she seemed too good to be likely.

Noah periodically checked in with Andrea on how the Assault snafu was going. From her profanity-laden descriptions, there'd be some extra-fun lawsuits to look forward to, but she'd checked and copied the security footage before the department tech got hold of it so that no one could accuse Q Division of the same questionable decision-making as Assault.

He perked up when dispatch said through the scanner that someone had called in a couple of kids acting weird in Cemetery Grove.

Tara shared a look with him.

"We don't have to go," Noah said, "if you don't feel comfortable encountering more feral children so soon. This might not even be the same thing."

"Don't let me keep you from doing your job."

* * * *

Cemetery Grove felt older than all the places she'd seen so far—at the very least less cared for, the buildings not so tall, the upper windows dirty, the signs outdated. The cemeteries there were somehow more raggedy but also more elaborate and bigger, older. There weren't enough lights and not all the ones they had worked. The nightlife here wasn't as lively as in the main thoroughfare, which didn't mean there wasn't any. There were still crowds, but everyone felt more alone. Careful. Wary.

She wished these things meant that she felt less intensely, that all the walls people hid behind and dark rooms people did things in—for business or pleasure—

provided some protection for her. But the streets were narrower, the population denser, so the pressure only increased. She almost didn't want to get out of the car when they arrived at the alley cited in the call.

And she didn't have to get out. This was Noah's job, not hers.

But if it was the same strange thing that had infected those other kids, then it was her job, too, wasn't it? If she could defuse one melee, she could conceivably defuse another.

Noah didn't tell her to get back in the car, but he instructed her to stay behind him. He kept his hand on his gun and entered the quiet alley first.

After just a few steps, Tara squinted her eyes against pinpricks of pain, white-hot in her eyeballs from wordless, reasonless anger.

"They're here," she murmured. "It's the same thing."

"Do you know what it is?"

"I only know what they're feeling, not why they're feeling it."

"Can you break it up without us even going in there?"

"I only know what they're feeling, not *where* they're feeling it."

Noah gave her a semi-annoyed look over his shoulder.

"You're not going to use the gun, are you?"

Noah didn't take his hand off the grip. "Just because they haven't shown fully homicidal intent doesn't mean they won't. If they come after me, it won't matter that they're kids. They're demonstrably violent and dangerous, like people with rabies. Oh God, it isn't rabies, is it?"

"You think I can cure rabies? No, your first instinct that this is mystical is correct. I just couldn't tell you where it comes from or even how many kids are in the alley. I can't tell you if they're attacking each other or if they'll attack you. I just know they're there because I can feel how angry they are. It's..." Tara pressed her hand to her head. She didn't know why she kept doing that when it didn't help. "We must be getting closer. The pain is getting worse."

"I'm sorry. You really don't have to stay."

"You came here with no backup because you wanted to test if I could control these kids. I'd say you should stop pretending that you care what happens to me, but I know you do. I also know that a room full of scared cops wasn't the ideal environment for these kids, and neither is an alley of them. I can do this."

Noah reached back to touch her arm in apology and reassurance. "Are you sure?"

"Not in the slightest."

The deeper they went into the alley, the louder the other noises became, snarls that were unsettlingly animal for something coming from human throats, especially those of children.

Tara fought not to whimper, but she also tried pushing back against what was pushing in. It was like pressing her palm against a board with nails hammered into it. She thought she was making some headway when the first child stepped around the blind corner. He was covered with blood from his mouth down to his waist.

"I've seen werewolf children who breached the treaty by losing control of their wolf side." Noah's entire body under his fitted shirt and pants practically quivered with tension. "That is not a werewolf child.

Damn. Could you imagine whatever this is reaching the wolf packs, though?"

"Do you think it's contagious?"

"Fear and violence are always contagious," Noah said.

Another three children came out from around the corner. One of them held an adult hand. Just the hand.

"Oh, fuck me." Noah pulled out his gun.

"Are you really going to kill them?"

"If they try to kill me, do I have much of a choice?" he shot back.

"What about 'fear and violence are always contagious'?"

"Looks like I caught it, then. More importantly, my fear and the violence it might cause is justified. Theirs isn't. If you're going to fix them, now is the time. *Fuck.*"

Another five kids joined the others.

If it's some kind of metaphysical curse passed around like disease, how would kids from different playgrounds and completely different parts of town catch the same thing? This felt less like a contagion than...

"Chemical warfare," she muttered.

"What?"

"This isn't a disease, being passed from child to child. Someone is *doing* this. They're going to different places in Meridian and setting off mindless violence like a chemical bomb."

"Been in a lot of battles?"

"More than you." She put her hand on his back to indicate that she was stepping forward.

He cursed a blue streak of whispers and kept his gun up, but he didn't stop her, even as the kids were joined by seven others. Some had scratch marks, but most of them appeared covered in blood that wasn't theirs.

The children tilted their head at her as she took point. Strangely, she could have sworn that, amid the barely repressed fury, she sensed recognition, although she'd never met these children and couldn't possibly have been the one to set the emotional bomb off. She'd been with Noah when the call had come in. Unless she'd sent it out unconsciously, and the infection of each group of kids was random.

But her instincts told her that none of this was random. The whole setup — including getting Noah and her into a blind alley in a rougher part of town — seemed deliberate. To hurt them? Kill them?

She staggered to her knees ten feet from the boy in front. She couldn't get any closer, not without the rage behind her eyes burning so hot that she feared her brain and vitreous humor would boil. Where she was still conscious, she thought of the children, how their brains felt the same way, but they couldn't shake it off, couldn't do anything about it but change to fit their new neurological environment. They bared their teeth but didn't snarl or growl until Noah tried to help her. She bared her teeth in response, as much grimace as aggression, and Noah quickly backed away.

The children crept forward, tentative, dropping ripped-off body parts with wet slaps onto the slick alley concrete.

This wasn't hunting behavior. Why weren't they stalking her? Why didn't they run at her, attack her, tear her head off her shoulders so she wouldn't have to feel this way anymore?

She pressed against the pressure pushing out of her skull with the same reflexive futility, then screamed at the city-lit night sky. The closer they came, the more the pressure and sense of being impaled through her limbs and abdomen intensified. But although they slowly swarmed her, they still didn't sting. They reached for her, like the last group of kids.

But not quite like the last. Instead of collapsing into tears, these children clustered around her, rubbing against her sides and her back, sniffing her like pups to their mother. They snarled not at her, but at what was behind her.

She turned around to see what unsettled their minds and hers.

Noah. She recognized him as Noah, as a man she knew, but anger and the pain that accompanied it spiked just by looking at him. Rage refined and bubbled into something unbearable that compelled her back to her feet to join the pack of feral children as they continued down the alley. *Now* they were stalking.

"Tara... Tara, are you okay?"

She heard the words, but they meant nothing to her, not even her name. She had no words of her own. She just wanted the pain to stop. The children were causing the boiling, deep-brain fever but weren't the source of it. Even though everything hurt to move, she staggered toward the man in the alley, shrieking through clenched teeth. He wasn't the origin, either, but he'd brought her here, hadn't he? He'd known it would hurt, but he'd brought her anyway.

How dare he. How fucking *dare* he hurt her like this.

She ran at him, fingers curved to claw at his bare arms, her cry ear-splitting against the head-splitting rage.

"Oh, shit." He backpedaled but didn't run, caught between wide-eyed panic and clench-jawed resolve. "Tara, it's me. It's Noah. Tara, snap out of it. *Shit*, shit, shit..."

He grabbed her arms through his jacket to keep her from clawing him. Then he kicked out to catch one of the children in the stomach, which just made the rest of them angrier.

"Tara!"

When she couldn't claw at him, she ran her feet up his body and the brick wall of the building behind him, changing the angle of his arms so that he couldn't hold her as easily. While she went high, the children went low, attacking his jeans and boots. When their nails didn't tear through, they tried teeth. He had to let go of her arms, and she descended upon him from above, using her legs, hands, and teeth to try to rip him to pieces.

He fell back against the wall, muttering to himself under his breath with his eyes closed.

Something abruptly shoved into her stomach, stealing her air and sending her falling back on top of children who'd been struck by the same invisible sucker punch that plastered them to the ground in every direction.

"Tara, for God's sake, wake up. It's me."

She couldn't get up — not while her vision went gray from not being able to breathe, despite her gasping efforts — but that didn't stop her or the others from trying.

"Fuck it."

He crouched among the struggling, gaping, gasping children and hauled her up. Her attempts to scratch his face weren't half-hearted, but her body was too busy trying to get oxygen to her brain, not her limbs. She had neither power nor coordination.

He hooked his arm around her waist to pull her against him and made a fist in her hair to hold her head back so she wouldn't bite his neck, where he was especially vulnerable to exsanguination by someone without any inhibitions to shallow her bite.

Then he pressed his lips under her jaw, groaning a little as he tasted her, all tongue and no teeth — as though teaching her through action what he would prefer from her mouth than violence.

But it wasn't just teaching. It was *feeling*. Texture of tongue, of lips, of affection. The early stirrings of lust slithered in among the needles and rusty nails of abject fearful fury that had chased away words. This chased away words, too, but in another way.

Noah bled himself into her, like watercolor onto already wet paper. Just as the first children managed to sit up from what had stunned them, Tara stopped scratching at his chest or struggling against the fist in her hair and instead arched her head back to encourage the drag of his lips against her skin, bringing in the first tease of his teeth now that he wasn't afraid she would bite to kill.

Some of the children climbed to their feet.

Tara shook as though in seizure against him and *pushed*, like before. This time, her mind had more grip on the anger rather than simply flailing out at it without finesse or control.

She thought she might be able to find that grip again.

But she didn't need to now because the violence dissipated as quickly as it had taken her, leaving behind only the children's horror, upset, and confusion and the low, languid pleasure of Noah's mouth over her neck and along her jaw.

He pulled her back, though, panting, with the contortion of regret. There were too many crying children around them, and like the last group, they clustered around Tara, as though they knew she was the source of their freedom.

But they'd clustered to her before they'd been freed from their rage, too. They'd surrounded her but hadn't attacked. They'd somehow *recognized* her, even within their violence, enough to gather her into their maelstrom minds and carry her with them instead of doing to her what they'd done to others or what they'd tried to do to Noah.

Either she was a uniquely comforting and nurturing presence to the vicious, or…

She was missing something. Something she was supposed to know but didn't. Something that, if she knew it, would make sense of all this chaos.

Noah stepped to the side, making sure that the children were all children again and reacting in the normal way a child would once they realized what was happening.

"I need to call this in. Can you keep them here?" he asked.

She nodded. As the beautiful simplicity of desire receded, she wanted nothing more than for her more complicated fear, spiked with confusion and sorrow, to subside. She let the children embrace her and embraced them back, although her stomach was turning with their knots, because these children were covered with too much blood and had left behind too many pieces.

She hoped to God they didn't remember.

"We're going to need that doctor who handled the kids from Assault to take these in, and I think we have at least one 10-54. I need backup, homicide detectives to take over the case, a crime scene unit, and a bus. Remaining on scene until detectives arrive." Without saying anything to disturb the children, Noah pointed to the blind corner and indicated that he was going to take a look. She nodded.

She felt his disgust from fifty feet away.

Chapter Eight

Tara stamped her foot against the weatherproof mat on the passenger side of Noah's vehicle.

Noah only jumped a little. "I'm not going to tell you not to be so upset that my insides turn into a pit of vipers. You feel what you feel. But it's probably not a good idea to startle the driver."

"Sorry. I'm going to hit the floor a few more times."

"Go nuts."

She stamped both feet over and over again until her aching body protested.

"Are you okay? Silly question, but I'm asking it anyway."

"Whoever's doing this isn't playing games anymore," Tara said. "And someone *is* doing this. I know you think it might be me, because it's clearly not a coincidence that this is happening around the same time I arrived. You may even think I'm accidentally sending violent suggestion out into the world like weather balloons to burst and fall upon unsuspecting children. But this is a coordinated campaign, and it started before I was even conscious. Someone is trying to make it look like it's me, but — "

"I don't think it was you," Noah said. "And I agree that this seems somehow coordinated. If it were accidental, there's no reason for you to be accidentally targeting kids. You're very good with them and apparently radiate maternal energy, but as far as I can tell, you've shown more unbridled enthusiasm for tater tots."

That made her smile a little.

"But I'm afraid that leaves us no closer to what's causing this than before. What makes you think someone is targeting you specifically? You've only encountered two of these groups, and this last one we sought out."

"The children... The children *knew* me. They were perfectly comfortable with me, before and after the anger possessed me. I'm missing something so important, and if I can't think of it, some other child is going to wake up with someone else's blood in their mouth. I can't let that happen..."

"It's Meridian, Tara. It's bound to happen," Noah said. "I know that sounds callous, but if there's one thing you learn while trying to protect the people here, it's that you can't save everyone. You can't carry the weight of the whole city on your shoulders. You'll win, you'll lose, you'll never be a hero every time. The cemeteries are a testament to that. You're just one person. You've got some power, and I've got a few magic tricks. We're two beleaguered superheroes in a population-dense city. So you take the wins. And there were wins today. You were sucked into their violence, but you came out of it well, all things considered, and you pulled them out of it more quickly and with fewer waterworks. These kids you've saved aren't like the first few from before you were involved. You've released them entirely from whatever's affecting them. And that's a win. We take what we can get, yeah? And we'll figure this out."

"What if we don't?"

"We will. You want to know how I know?"

She nodded.

"Because whoever's doing this wants us to figure it out. They're escalating, which means they're planning an eventual confrontation. They want you to be part of it. They want you to know who they are."

"But I don't."

"You will. You'll figure it out or they'll unmask themselves."

"Not every criminal wants to be caught."

"They don't want to be caught by me," Noah corrected her. "Even if I did catch them, though, what could I do? That's my despair. So much of what Andrea and I do exists in the gray areas cops or courts aren't designed to handle, even if they worked the way they were supposed to. So, whatever happens, I think it'll come down to you, Tara. Don't beat yourself up and do their job for them. You want something to eat?"

Tara sighed as she leaned back against her seat again. "Always."

* * * *

Gas-station Hostess Zingers were probably not going to be a sustainable treat. They didn't even taste like real food, so much as flavored wax desserts.

Yet she still had to lick the filling and the last bits of cake from the waxy cardboard. She kept telling herself that she could literally have another package another day, that this was probably not the one and only time she'd have the opportunity. They didn't *need* to stop by another gas station to buy another four packages for her to eat as fast as possible. But it was hard to convince herself to throw away the wrapper in front of the police station and let go of the fact that there weren't any more for now.

"You will eat again before the next time you sleep. I promise." Watching her eat had lifted Noah's mood, too. Her attachment to food amused him so much that it briefly distracted him from what he had seen, what he hadn't let her see, which allowed her stomach to untwist as well.

"I know. But I predict that moderation is going to be a problem for a while."

"To be fair, it's harder to do healthy during the graveyard shift. You won't be nocturnal forever."

"Maybe I'll stop being hungry?" But she didn't have any confidence while she said it.

"The entire food industry suggests otherwise. I stress-eat as much as the next person, and the amount of emotions you go through... How did you not fall asleep in the car?"

"I woke up tired. It's not pleasant, but I just assumed it's supposed to be like this. Like the hunger. Is it not?"

Noah put an arm around her shoulder in a moment of unexpected intimacy. "You'll have a better sense of what normal is when your life approximates it."

When they entered the police station, it was quieter than before, in sound and in emotion, but there were still plenty of third-shift workers. First responder was a twenty-four-hour job.

The specialized departments were largely empty, although there were a few people in holding and a guard on duty over them. Homicide was empty, too, except for Andrea working at her desk. She noticed their movement before they reached the door, and she clambered up from her seat to step outside the office.

"You just let her walk around like that?" Andrea pointed at him. "You, stay out there." Then she pointed at Tara. "You, come in here."

Tara looked down, expecting Zinger chocolate smeared on her shirt. Instead, Noah had literally walked her into the gas station with her shirt and some of her jeans smeared with blood. Probably from the kids' victim or victims.

"We're both fine. Thanks for asking. Go on." Noah nodded her in with Andrea, who was closing the blinds. He helped her out of his jacket. "She's got spare clothes in her desk. I should probably deal with some of these stains on my jeans while I'm here."

His jeans were a dark wash on which blood was less apparent, especially out at night, but her T-shirt was gray, and the character on it was dressed in a mix of pink and red that only emphasized the stains.

As soon as Tara closed the door behind her in the office, Andrea's hand was there.

"Shirt."

Tara pulled off her shirt and draped it over Andrea's hand. Andrea dropped it into her trash can.

"I bought you a bra."

"It didn't fit."

"Okay. Pants."

Tara removed her pants and did the same. Andrea threw them in with the shirt.

"At least the underwear fits and doesn't appear to be stained. Wipes. Good for all occasions." She handed Tara wipe after wipe for her to get rid of where blood had seeped through her shirt. Andrea cleaned the dried blood on Tara's back.

"Pants." She handed Tara a pair of sweatpants. They were short and too big in the waist, but Andrea indicated the drawstring, which at least kept them from falling down. "Shirt." Again, just a T-shirt, this time of a thicker fabric and different structure, and it was too big, but it served its purpose.

"In this business, clothes are like poker," Andrea said while she checked Tara's hair like the doctor had done in the hospital. "You've got to know when to hold 'em or fold 'em. Some of them just aren't good enough quality to justify getting the bloodstains out, but Noah's cleaned blood out of that jacket I don't know how many times. I'm pretty sure he uses magic. Or maybe he just has a whole closet full of those jackets and replenishes them when the number gets too low. Which is kind of genius, when you think about it."

"I didn't know he could use magic until he pushed the kids and me away," Tara said.

"Oh, we learn our little tricks along the way. Neither of us are witches or anything, but a spell's a spell, and we have a few augmentation tattoos that let us do magic now and then with some degree of success. There are ways to get more power, but there's a cost to that, which neither of us are willing to pay. I apparently have a pinch of intuitive magic that helps us sometimes, but I think magic makes people complacent, sloppy. Like depending too much on smart technology, and then your phone dies. I'd rather have contingency plans than expect magic to save my skin. We mostly keep the spells in our back pockets as a last resort."

Andrea framed Tara's face with her hands, staring up at her as though to confirm that she was all right. Then her hold softened. She stroked her thumbs along the finer hairs at Tara's temples.

Tara was surprised to find herself becoming aroused and that the feeling didn't arise from her—no less powerful than what she'd felt from Noah, but subtler somehow. She curled her thin, cold fingers around Andrea's wrists but neither pushed her away nor drew her in. Noah's waitress comment made more sense to Tara now, but she didn't know what to do with it, didn't know what else to do but lower her head to meet Andrea's lips as the woman stood on tiptoes to kiss her. Lightly at first, but the moment her tongue touched Tara's, electricity shot from Tara's head to between her legs, from Andrea to her, and back and forth like a closed but intensifying loop. Andrea slipped her fingers into Tara's hair and moaned, canting her hips forward against Tara's.

There was a knock on the office door. "Everyone decent in there?"

"God, that feels good. And you taste like chocolate," Andrea whispered before kissing her softly one more time. Tara chased the kiss, the electricity fighting to close its circuit, but Andrea laughed a little and shook her head as she stepped back. "I was worried when Noah told me what happened. I'm glad you're still with us. I would hate to lose you so soon after you arrived."

"What—" Tara stepped toward her.

Andrea held up a hand to silence her. She took a seat, putting her desk between them, although she licked her lower lip as though she wanted to taste something else. She glanced at the door, then slowly brought her hand between her legs where Tara couldn't see and did something that made Tara stumble back against the blinds.

"Decent as can be," Andrea called to Noah as she brought both hands back up to her desk.

Tara tried to recover as fast as Andrea had, running her hand through her tousled hair, caught in an eddy of desire and confusion that threatened to become frustration, because she didn't understand what had just happened and what it meant. As Noah entered the room, Andrea acted like it hadn't happened at all, but arousal hovered between them like low floating fog and was slow to dissipate, especially as Noah stepped between them and responded to Tara's desire again. He met her eyes before letting his gaze fall to her lips, which yearned to be kissed, and at that moment, she wasn't sure by whom.

She'd been put in both of their paths, and although she hadn't considered Andrea as a source of this kind of pleasure, now she couldn't unconsider it.

However, Andrea was a lot better at hiding what she was feeling than Noah, and when Noah sat behind his desk and adjusted himself, he would think the desire he was responding to all came from Tara.

She struggled to determine what *she* wanted when most of her desire cues were triggered by them rather than herself, and although Tara very much wanted to explore the feelings they each inspired, she wasn't sure she wanted to be shared.

When she'd fallen from grace to land where Noah and Andrea would find her, she didn't think she'd had this kind of conflict in mind.

Noah gave Andrea a more detailed rundown of what had happened in the alley and showed her photographs he'd taken at the scene. Then Andrea ran them through the havoc that cops versus kids had wreaked upon the Assault Department after the parents had arrived. On her computer, she showed some of the video she'd given to IA to prove that she and Noah had been helping and that Tara had been instrumental in defusing the situation entirely.

"So, we know something is happening to these kids," Noah said. "But there's no trail to follow to figure out what. Tara thinks she *should* know what was going on, but we can't speed up her getting her memory back, if she gets that part of the memory back at all."

"If I had to give us a plan of action," Andrea chimed in, all business now, "we go to the hospital in the morning before end of shift and talk to Dr. Kim. We need to interview him about the other incidents, and I'm pretty sure he wants Tara there to try something with the kids who are still recovering. Tara, after everything that's happened tonight, are you okay with that? The kids at Mattea aren't supposed to be nearly as bad. You won't be going in there to fully feral children."

"It'll be easier to learn how to control this if I'm not fighting something so powerful to begin with," Tara said. "And I don't want to leave the remaining children in whatever state they're in. Anything I can do to help."

"Okay. I'll contact the night nurses to give us an early morning meeting. If we can't get morning, we'll ask for late afternoon or evening after we wake up. You'll have to stay with Noah one more day, but I'm off until Sunday night at that point. Noah will be working or on call the rest of the weekend, so you can join me and Hannah at the Wheel for some shopping and stay over with me. Isaac's staying with their dad, but I've already cleared it with him for Hannah to spend some extra days with me."

Tara looked between Noah and Andrea. Andrea was still being eminently professional, but when Tara met her eyes, there was heat there, even without Tara feeling it in her chest, in her abdomen, lower. It all seemed so very abrupt, but so had Noah's desire — sudden, sweeping, overwhelming, exacerbated by the magic within that gave her what she'd wished as an angel, to understand how people felt. But there was as yet no animosity, no jealousy of time spent elsewhere, no notice of attraction. Each thought that the arousal she felt was for them alone.

Should I say something?

Everything she'd experienced since her arrival was the very definition of 'be careful what you wish for', but at the same time, she *wanted* to know more. She *wanted* to explore. She *wanted* to try everything. But this wasn't just her life. It was Noah's life and Andrea's life, and she didn't want to play with them in such a way that it left bloodstains on something she'd have to throw away. As far as she knew, she hadn't fallen to hurt them. *Would* she hurt them? Was she overthinking? Maybe she'd misinterpreted something. Maybe she'd misinterpreted everything.

It would be so much more useful to read their thoughts rather than feelings.

"That sounds like a good plan," Tara finally said. "And I'd love to meet your daughter. She seems like a formidable child."

"Oh, she is. She's a pain in our asses, of course, but I'm hoping she doesn't lose how opinionated or intimidating she is."

"She learns it from her mother. I think she'll be fine," Noah said. "And I'm fine taking her for the day. Are you okay with patrolling with us the rest of the night after Andrea makes her phone call to Mattea, or should one of us stay here?"

"I can join you," Tara replied. "There could be other children in need, and it might be better if both of you are there to protect each other if I cannot calm them or myself down."

"Or perhaps you'll take us down with you," Noah said. "I'm used to keeping a lid on my temper. How about you, Andrea?"

Andrea threw her stapler at him. Noah grinned and caught it before it could hit him.

Chapter Nine

The Mattea front desk couldn't arrange a meeting until late afternoon the next day, so Noah and Andrea took Tara on a patrol tour of nighttime Meridian. Tara sat in the back seat of Andrea's car while Noah drove.

Where there were clusters of unhoused in a few notable alleyways, one or both of them left the car to account for who they found and speak with some of the people. They kept a bin of bottled water, snack packs, and toiletry bags in the trunk that they passed out. Then they stopped at the forest splitting the city to warn werewolf packs about a potential curse that might hit their young ones, threatening the tenuous peace between most hunters and wolves.

Although they invited her to join them, Tara was happy watching from a distance. She sensed tension, antagonism, fear — roiling with sophisticated motivations, and a little madness here and there. She wanted to leave them to their feelings without feeling them too strongly or making them worse. She might eventually be useful, but her head was full enough for the night.

Without Tara between them, Andrea and Noah moved like an established team, communication more nonverbal than verbal. In an instant, they made themselves non-threatening, authoritative, sympathetic, professional, whatever someone needed them to be for them to keep population counts, maintain diplomacy, make sure someone walking past a dark alley wasn't pulled into that darkness. They recognized other night-shifters, raised their hands to those who walked or waited for a bus, suggesting the familiarity of routine — their nightly beat.

"Well, that's what we do," Andrea said as they pulled back into the station parking lot after sunrise. "And what I need to do right now is head home so I can relieve my babysitter — she's over eighteen from UTM and sleeps over so I'm not the negligent parent my ex said I was. Easy pay for her. That way I catch my kids at breakfast before they go to school and their dad picks up their things." She reached back to touch Tara's knee. "I'll see you tomorrow. Try not to turn feral."

"I'll do my best." Tara was still disoriented by dawn after the world had seemed like it would stay dark forever. As an angel, dark and light didn't matter like they did on a revolving globe. But her eyes and somehow her body craved light, and now she was expected to close her eyes to sink into darkness again while the light climbed higher in the sky and offered much-needed warmth as well. She didn't think she was going to be able to maintain Noah's and Andrea's schedule, nor did she want to. There was so much more to the city when most of it was awake.

She blinked in bewilderment when Noah got out of the car and Andrea took over the driver's seat.

"Oh!" Tara joined Noah once she remembered they were in Andrea's car.

"I mean, if you want to come with me..." Andrea joked. She waved goodbye and pulled out of the lot. Most people were pulling in for the day shift.

"Want me to make you some potato and egg breakfast tacos back at the house?"

"Do you have to ask?"

* * * *

Noah warmed up flour tortillas, then showed her how to put her taco together with freshly fried potatoes and eggs, then some onions, cheese, hot sauce, and sour cream to taste. She tried a little of everything before settling on hot sauce and cheese as her toppings of choice. Noah stopped after three tacos, but she finished off the potatoes and eggs with a fourth, because everything stayed good the whole way through.

Her first homecooked meal. Now she knew why Noah and Andrea looked at her funny for exclaiming over a hospital cheeseburger, although she wouldn't say no to another.

"I wonder if you're kind of like a kid that way," Noah said. "They're so new to the world that they can do something over and over and over and ask for the same food over and over and over without getting bored like their frustrated parents. It takes a while for diminishing returns to hit. You're experiencing things you've never experienced before in your life. Your happy hormone maker isn't tired yet. At least I hope that's the case. Otherwise, you might want to be careful about things that tend to be addictive."

"Like what?" Tara asked.

"Oh, you know. Drugs, nicotine, alcohol, caffeine, cheese, sugar, exercise, gambling, television, videogames, sex... A lot of the things that make life a little more fun. No happy hormone for you." Although he sounded like he was joking on that last part.

"Noah..." She wasn't sure if she wanted to bring it up now, but he was the one who'd opened the door.

He seemed to realize he had, too, because he barreled forward past the implication. "I need to head to bed. More specifically, I need to head to the bathroom for a shower. You'll probably want one of your own. You don't have to go to sleep, but..."

"But you'd prefer if I went to bed in the spare room while you go to bed in yours," she finished for him. "And I'll need sleep if I'm going to meet those kids later today. I'm exhausted. Can I bring this up to drink?" She picked a can of soda out of his fridge.

"Not that one. It has caffeine. Have this." He handed her a ginger ale instead of the Dr Pepper she'd chosen. "Caffeine is a stimulant, so it can keep you up. With our twelve-to-fifteen-hour shifts, Andrea and I are a bit dependent on it in soda or coffee form. If you can avoid getting hooked, you're a step ahead of the rest."

He walked her up the stairs to the hall that separated the rooms.

"Good sleep, then." Noah cupped her shoulder, then slid his hand down to her elbow. He looked like he wanted to say something else—and she felt what else he wanted—but he pulled away and she let him.

He didn't lock her in this time.

She took his advice to shower using what Andrea had bought her and Poppy had shown her how to use, although she was still a little baffled by the razor and would have to ask Andrea about it when she stayed over at her house.

It was so nice under the hot spray, the little room turning into a sauna, but she really was tired and, as much as she wanted to stay under the hot water forever, she also wanted to crawl between the sheets under the soft, soft comforter and let weariness wash over her like the water over her head. It was also nice to be somewhere that she barely felt anyone, and although she still ached in muscle and bone, she was getting used to it — that legendary human adaptiveness.

Tara crawled into bed without clothes, as she had the night before, and watched some more nature documentaries while she drank her ginger ale. Within an hour she was nodding off and happy to turn off the television and cover her head to give herself the darkness that the heavy curtains couldn't quite manage.

But when she woke up, she jerked as though she'd fallen from the tallest Meridian skyscraper, or perhaps from higher, higher, with the flutter and scorch of wings, then the resounding *snap*, as profound as a crack in the largest bell in its tower, then falling all the faster and without sense of direction, screaming, her features melting and melding, new ones ripping through her like she was being gored, sinking from light into darkness.

Then striking ground, every bone in her body breaking and her squishy insides sloshing and spilling within. Yet she wasn't alone. She stared over herself, her wings spread wide to block out what light was left of the evening. Smiling over pain that didn't seem worthy of such a small word and which she shouldn't have survived. Yet they all did, didn't they?

She was in bed, fallen, yet falling, yet felled, the breaking of her wings bringing phantom pain not just to her shoulders but her whole back. As consciousness took hold of her, she thought she might have just wrenched her back from moving so quickly, lost on which way was up and how to move her limited limbs.

Tara finally found the top of her sheets and comforter so she could reach the light of day penetrating the darkness of the room. She gasped and panted through the aftermath of panic and the settling pain in her back as she relaxed.

"Noah?" She didn't know if he could hear her, but he'd told her to holler if she needed him.

Tara climbed out of bed onto her hands and knees, then pulled herself to her feet with the nightstand. The more she moved, the more the muscle tension released. She pulled herself over to the door and opened it, not sure if she still needed his help but thinking about going downstairs for another soda, since she wasn't locked in.

She couldn't step across the threshold – as though there was a plastic shower curtain at the door frame. No matter how she tried to cross over, she pressed against the barrier, soft but otherwise implacable.

Tara pushed at the air, shoved her shoulder against it, leaned her entire weight against it, but she couldn't enter the hall. She switched on the bedroom light and stepped back to try to make sense of why she'd been able to enter the room but not exit it.

Symbols and runes, carved up in the corners of the door frame. If she hadn't known better, she would have assumed they were scuff marks or cracks from an unsettled foundation. She'd already noticed the ones around the windows and the corners, but she hadn't seen these.

Symbols and spells of protection. Of captivity. He'd put her in a room magically designed to keep something of mystical origin from entering if not invited, but also from exiting if not invited.

He hadn't slide-locked her in this time because he hadn't had to. The slide lock had been misdirection. She'd assumed she couldn't leave because of the lock, so she hadn't even looked for what else could be keeping her there.

"I can't believe I lost my wings for you." She turned to the bed and struck the mattress with her fists. It wasn't satisfying in the slightest. "Noah!" This time her yell was no longer mild from semi-consciousness. "Noah!"

He stumbled out of his room in pajama pants and no shirt, hair sticking out in every direction. He rubbed at his eyes, but when he reached the open door, he let his hands drop and squinted in against the light, after waking up in a bedroom with blackout shades. At the sight of her, his heavy lids opened all the way.

"You locked me in a damn cage!"

He blinked several times. Then he looked up at the symbols on the door frame. "Oh. Yeah. It's not personal, Tara. Andrea and I both keep a room in our homes where we can house supernatural beings while we figure out what to do with them. We put these runes all over our house so that certain demons and hybrids can't come in unless we invite them, but they ensure that the invitation is rescinded as soon as we let them back out. In being a bit more diplomatic with the supernatural side of Meridian, we sometimes shelter dangerous beings whom we can't necessarily trust. I didn't put these things up for *you*."

"But you didn't tell me you did more than just use a physical lock. I had to figure it out trying to walk out of the room for a drink or a snack."

"That's why you have snacks on the side table," Noah said.

"That's not the point!"

"No, I know. I'm sorry. When I physically locked you in, you didn't know what you were at all, and more importantly, *I* didn't know what you were, demon or angel or something else entirely. I would have told you when you went to bed this morning, but it really didn't cross my mind. A lot of things happened yesterday. I'm sorry I didn't tell you."

"But you still put me in *here*. Not the other bedroom, but here."

"This is your room. It doesn't hurt you to be in it. It just means I have to let you out."

"What were you worried I'd do?" she snapped.

"I wasn't worried you'd do anything, but maybe I should have been," he shot back. "What if whoever was responsible for you losing your fucking mind back in that alley found you, and you stabbed me thirty-seven times in my sleep? The magic protects you, but it also protects me. I don't want being a Good Samaritan to be the reason why bagpipes start playing this weekend."

"You think I'm dangerous?"

"You've already proven that you have a little difficulty wrangling your feelings, and you have the free will to be evil as much as good. What if you tried to use that shit on me in the other room?"

"If I'm so dangerous, what if I'm using it right now?"

Noah opened his mouth, closed it, clenched his fist, clenched his jaw. "Are you?"

"Not on purpose, if I am."

"Tara... Why are you naked again?"

She looked down at herself. She hadn't thought about it, but now she was far more aware that she was, and that he wasn't wearing a shirt.

Dim, stubborn sunlight etched a lovely cast of his form, emphasizing how he had disciplined himself. He wasn't perfectly chiseled, and he was hairier than she remembered most angels being, but the sight wasn't unpleasant, defining his body as much as the light.

Tara touched the swell of her belly from all she'd eaten before bed, brought her hand up to cup her breast. Looked back up, breathed in what emanated from him as he responded to the sight of her amid his receding anger. She slowly brought both her other hand to her other breast. Not much there, just enough for a little weight upon the natural curve of her palm. His breathing grew shallower as the outline of his cock pressed against his loose pajama pants.

She felt his desire inside her, yes, but her own intrigue unfurled and swayed not just low in her pelvis but in her mind. This felt different than before. Just as pleasant, but also nuanced, seasoned, layered. Darker, as her bed was dark and warm, as her dreams were dark and strange. Was this attraction? Hers?

Tara let her hands fall away from her breasts, let herself be naked. Then, without a word, she stepped toward him and gripped his shoulders, then his hair, as she brought her mouth to his, lips parted, and he opened for her without an attempt at protest.

It was different, bare body to bare chest. Her fingers were more sensitive than most of the rest of her, but everywhere her skin met his practically tingled from how intimate it felt, as intimate as feeling his feelings — that swirl of wariness, even suspicion, with arousal that overwhelmed it all and ultimately pushed it down.

All the ways she didn't like to be cold, he heated through. Her breasts seemed heavy just by being against him, her nipples almost as sensitive as her fingers, if not with as much detail. It drove her crazy, the sensation of the little peaks of dark flesh rubbing against the hotter skin and silky fur of his chest.

She moaned and pressed herself closer, wrapping her arms around his neck as they stumbled until he was against the wall. This time, he slid his hands down her back to grab Tara's legs and lift her up to rub her pussy over his cock through his pants instead of her trying to tear him to pieces.

But it felt like she was doing that anyway, and it felt like he was doing it to her in her head, spinning up and down her body in waves of lust as she rocked down on him and he gripped her back and ass to thrust with greater and greater urgency to meet hers, which met his. They were moaning so loudly that the neighbors on the other side of the townhouse wall might have heard them, but she couldn't care about that now.

She pushed at his waistband with her heels, but she didn't get to him in time before her head and her pussy seemed to explode with the same force as anger and pain, but so much nicer. She could live in that pleasure forever, because it chased away the pain for as long as it surged through her to the rhythm of orgasm.

He broke the kiss, the back of his head striking the drywall so hard that it crunched. His grip could have been pushing bruises into her bony flesh, but he groaned loudly enough to wake the quick and the dead as he came.

She unhooked her legs from around his hips and slid down his abdomen, over his erection where his cum made a damp spot in the front of his pajamas. He hissed as she pushed at his sensitive cock, but when she threaded her fingers through his hair once more to bring him in for another kiss, his hiss turned into another groan. Her desire hadn't abated, and she sent it into him, like blowing smoke into his mouth.

Noah broke the kiss again, pressing his forehead against hers in a way that reminded her of the stone angel. He smoothed his hands up her back, pausing at her shoulders where her wings had once been. Then he slid them back down again to hook her thighs and lift her up.

"Fuck it."

She met his kiss moment for moment as he carried her from her room—effectively giving her permission to leave—and into his. He kicked the door closed behind them, then switched on a lamp. It felt like nighttime again, as though she needed any more disorientation. The blackout shades were much more effective than her curtains.

"I had a bed," she murmured between kisses.

"Your nightstand doesn't have condoms," he said. "I'm not fucking getting you pregnant within a few days of you falling."

As if to punctuate his reply, he fell with her onto the tangled sheets of his bed. At some point, his comforter had been kicked to the foot of the bed, and it looked like he barely even sleep with his sheets, based on how they'd been twisted.

He pushed himself up on his hands and knees over her as she stroked his chest, exploring his fleshly physicality — crude and a little damp to the touch, but so was she, sweating over her scalp and the back of her neck, the small of her back. Their slicker skin made touch easier. He hesitated halfway to reaching for the nightstand drawer and stared down at her as she let her fingertips drift lower to the waistband of his pants.

As she pushed them down the jut of his hips, they caught on his reawakening erection. Hair that clustered around his navel led down to the thatch of wirier hair at the base of his cock.

Even more than the hair, this was what she wasn't used to with angels. She'd been familiar with human genitalia prior to falling, and as though compensating for the absence in their angelic counterparts, they tended to be exaggerated in demons. It was different now, confronting the carnality of a penis when she was just as carnal between her legs, but in a different way. Both were points of vulnerability, but she was too aware from things she'd witnessed that her vulnerability was different from his.

She couldn't begin to imagine what it was like to have what her body yearned for when she'd never had these parts before. She loved the way an orgasm made her feel, but touching, stroking, over, inside, penetrating, thrusting? Her imagination reeled with the images of what she wanted without context for what it would feel like.

Noah withdrew from the drawer and touched her cheek, caressed the curl of hair in front of her ear. "I assumed… But it's only been a few days, even if… If you don't want to do this, Tara, we don't have to. I don't want you to think you have to. I don't want what I want to make you…"

Tara brought the hooks of her fingers to the front of his pajama pants and carefully pulled them down, then pushed them the rest of the way down his thighs. He had to settle to the side of her to take them off completely. He used them to clean cum off his cock, then kicked them away with his comforter.

"Are you sure?" he asked.

"Does it hurt?" she asked.

"Wow. I didn't think about that, either. Then again, there's not a lot of thinking when you're.., No, it shouldn't hurt. But it's been a long time since I've done this with someone who hadn't before. It would be really helpful if you held back how you feel from me. It's probably difficult for you to think right now, too, and maybe my short-circuiting brain isn't helping, but could you try?"

"I can't make any promises. It's easier to send something out than to hold it back."

"Well, it'll be less likely to hurt if you're completely aroused, which doesn't seem to be a problem when we're sharing. It helps to be…wet." He stroked up between her legs to her pussy, where he raked his fingers between and outside the folds.

He drew juices from her pussy up to her clit, which made her spread her legs wide for him in encouragement as she lay back on his pillow. It smelled of his soap and shampoo, and deeper, the particular fragrance of his skin itself.

"No," he said a little breathlessly as he pressed and rubbed around her clit in slow rhythm, sending sparks through her that made her purr, arch, rock her hips up to meet his touch, then cover his hands to learn what she liked best and encourage him to do that. "*That* shouldn't be a problem. Fuck. I don't know if I can do this."

"We don't have to. We can just...this. Oh, please don't stop doing that, though. Please don't stop touching me."

"I don't want to. I just don't know if I can...have sex with you in a way that does sex justice if I keep coming too soon."

"I don't care about that." Tara pressed his fingers and hers more firmly just above her clit in deep rubbing circles that made her pussy clench around what felt increasingly hollow. "I don't care as long as it keeps feeling this good, Noah. Don't stop. *Fuck*, no, *don't* stop. What did I just say?"

Noah laughed as he withdrew his hand from under hers. "I don't know how I feel about being the one to make an angel curse." He crawled over her again, massaging the length of her legs as though fascinated by how long they stretched on either side of him. "You're used to sex going fast, and I've got to say, it's kind of refreshing, even though I know it's because of our little feedback loop. But we climb the ladder way too quickly, which is why I keep having to do the kind of laundry I haven't done since I was a teenager. But as nice as it is to come, when we do things that way, you don't get to enjoy foreplay. I've had girlfriends, I've had one-night stands, and I have an ex-wife. I'm perfectly content being selfish now and then, but among all my faults, finishing too early and leaving my partner unsatisfied isn't one of them."

"Do I seem unsatisfied to you?" Tara reached down to touch herself the way she'd been urging Noah to touch her, but her arousal had pulled back and didn't start where she'd stopped. She huffed in frustration.

Noah left his fascination with her legs to settle himself on the sheets between her thighs. "You seem hungry. I think you can just keep going and going and going, and that'll help with my staying power, but I do have limits. Sex for you in general is probably going to be different than it is for other women because of your super-empathy thing. But I do want you to know what pleasure is like when it's just yours. So you can know that it's *yours*."

As though he knew what had been weighing on her mind since the rooftop and since Andrea had kissed her just as unexpectedly. When he nudged her hand away from her clit with his nose, she rested back on the pillows, propped up so she could see him better as he acquainted his mouth with her thighs in tickling kisses and licks. It seemed strange to her that he was more familiar with a pussy than she was, since she'd only had one for less than a week. But for all of his experience, that didn't mean he really understood what the things he did made a woman feel.

"Can I... Oh." At the first flick of the tip of his tongue over her folds, she twitched. "Oh, how do you stand having bodies?"

"We don't know any different. They're a pain in the ass sometimes, but we just have to find the ways to make them feel good."

"Can I share? Can I share — oh, *that*?"

He lifted his head again from where he'd slithered his tongue through the furrow of her folds to follow the path he'd made with his fingers, but this sensation was entirely different — the difference between clothes and skin.

"Can you share what?" His voice had lowered into something scratchy and husky, like his stubble brushing her thighs when she tightened them over his face, but as a tonal quality.

"You think you know how to give a woman pleasure. You take pride in it. I don't doubt you, but would you like to *know*? Can I share that? Make me come again. It'll make you come again, too."

He stared at her with blankness in his expression, other than the slight wrinkle of his forehead. His eyes were pupil-deep in the dim light. "Fuck."

"Is that a yes?"

"Fuck. Yes. I'll eat you out and eat myself out in the process. That isn't selfish in the slightest or turning me the fuck on like I'm a fucking teenager again."

"You said you could be selfish."

"Oh, I'll be selfish. I'll be so selfish that I'll make you scream if I can." He kissed her belly just above her mound. "I'm kidding — about the selfish part. I'm doing this for you, but fuck yeah, I want to know what you feel. Give it to me, then, if you can. So the fuck what if I get cum on my sheets. We've already negated our showers."

He mouthed his way back from her other thigh to the crux, to the thin lips below the dark black patch of hair. Then he dipped down to flick his tongue over her entrance again, but this time he delved in, pushed against what seemed to tighten around him, almost uncomfortably, but he was more interested in the wetness there than in entering in. He hummed with approval.

Noah looked back up at her and drew the flat of his tongue slowly back up to her clit, where he pushed her hair away and stretched the flesh more taut, drawing the hood back. He rubbed his tongue over the clit directly, but he'd already withdrawn when she wrenched to the side, tightening her legs on either side of his head again, and not with pleasure.

"Should have expected that," he said, righting her again and holding her open with his arms hooked underneath her thighs. "You're so damn sensitive, you'd be especially sensitive there. It was kind of like sticking my cock in the vacuum attachment from the theory that mouth suction was good so more suction would be better. Do not recommend."

Tara giggled, falling back on the pillows. She grabbed his sleep-tousled hair to push him down again. He both obliged and frustrated by licking along her folds, over the thinner lips, between them and the thicker flesh outside, then sucking over both, using tongue and teeth—not biting, but like how he used his blunt nails over her thighs as he continued to hold her open. The more he played with her lower lips, the heavier she felt between her legs and in her cunt, as though desire itself had weight.

She kept a hand in his hair, but with her other, she stroked circles around her nipple, fascinated by how the flesh tightened, wrinkled, had its own weight, too, but also seemed to connect on a fleshly string to her clit, which he was emphatically not stimulating, even though it twitched and pulsed with the same swollen need as the rest of her, inside and out.

He slowly drew back from a luxurious suck upon her lower lips. "I can't believe I'm saying this to a woman when my first few girlfriends had their work cut out to get it through my thick skull. An orgasm is amazing, Tara, but it's not all there is. I'm feeling your pleasure but also your tension. You're trying to get there fast, like the way you shovel food into your mouth, two-fisted. But we're not in a public place. We don't need to hurry. Just lie back and enjoy the sensations. If I'm doing this right, the climb will take care of itself."

Tara forced herself to let go of Noah's hair, which she'd been using to try to direct him and control his speed. She convinced her upper half to relax on the mattress and pillows, gathered fistfuls of the sheets as he released one of her thighs to bring his fingers to her folds and rub on either side of them. He brought his tongue not to her clit but instead to the hood, almost cradling it.

She cried out, but this time the sensation wasn't so powerful that her body considered it pain. She hadn't expected that where one cluster of nerves was too much, the cluster protecting it was just right.

With his fingers, then his thumb, he massaged deep into all her other nerves until he found the ones that made her jerk her hips up to meet his mouth or made her moan. She clenched her fists in the sheets with a much more pleasant tension. He relinquished her other thigh to mirror the deep-tissue massages that left her moaning with every exhale.

She brought her freer thighs to his head when he stopped, just as the build he'd promised began. "Damn it, Noah."

"I know. Damn it, me. God, I'm good."

She laughed so hard that she was even more breathless when he sucked two fingers into his mouth, then pushed them against the entrance that had, like her clit, treated contact as too much.

Her chest hitched, and Noah winced with her, but he continued to push his fingers in, slow and gentle but not stopping until his knuckles nudged the entrance. It didn't hurt. Not really. She didn't have a word for the discomfort. But he left his fingers inside for her to adjust to them as he kissed over her abdomen, licking her navel as though it were her clit. Like her nipples, her navel seemed to have an unexpected connection. Her clit twitched as he delved into the dip and laved the thin taut circle around it.

She let go of the sheets to hold her hair at her temples, once again as though she could hold her feelings in by pressure alone. She canted her hips up to encourage him, and in doing so, his fingers moved inside, rocking him deeper, bringing the slight curve of his fingers to press against the wall of her pussy. It felt less unpleasant when she was the one moving him within her, and he moaned as he kissed up to the breast she hadn't played with. When she lay on her back, her chest was almost completely flat, but that didn't seem to bother Noah as he sucked, licked, and circled her nipple like he had her navel and clit.

She gripped the headboard as she arched over and over, to urge her nipple deeper into the wet, velvet heat of his mouth, to urge his fingers inside her swelling softness to move, and because he felt what she yearned for, he did both. She couldn't see his cock from the way he rested on the bed, but he moved his hips to her rhythm, rubbing himself against the sheets, which were probably just as damp under him as they were under her.

He pumped his fingers in and out, with the tips still curved inward, and he sucked at her nipple hard, nearly painful, but somehow her mind and her cunt didn't treat it that way. Every nerve of her throbbed to the beat of her desire, and as though to punish him for it, Tara sent along every bit that she could manage. It slipped away from her sometimes, but that didn't seem to matter to him. He still groaned through their shared lust.

Then he squeezed in another finger, opening the knuckles just enough to stretch her — a little uncomfortable again, pulling her back from her galloping pleasure and staving off the build. But he also continued to keep his fingers curved, and while he thrust them into her, his fingertips rubbed a place inside that straightened her spine and sent her jolting up with a small scream. She slammed her feet down on either side of him and bore down on his fingers.

"Found it. Oh, that's fucking dangerous," he groaned into her chest before kissing his way back down.

He flicked his tongue over her clitoral hood as he rubbed against that spot inside her, which pushed his knuckles against her entrance more. She found she didn't mind anymore. She ground down against his hand.

Her pleasure climbed too fast again, and Noah groaned as he sank his mouth over her clit and hood, flattening his tongue and sucking with soft pressure over the hypersensitive clit.

She cried out in a screaming sob. Her pussy clenched around his frantic fingers, all that heavy heat and wetness released around him, and her clit contracted in beautiful, intense twitches in his mouth. He doubled down as he grunted his own climax into the sheets without even touching himself, occupied as he was with her body that made his body feel so good. She rode his face and fingers as long as she could until her climax fell over the other side.

He softened his mouth over her into a gentle kiss, easing his fingers from her pussy. In the dim lamplight, they glistened from her arousal. He climbed to his knees, licking his fingers as though he'd had a particularly good meal. She didn't hesitate to pull him down over her to kiss him and taste herself. The muskiness was almost too strong of a scent, but the taste was pleasant, especially on his tongue as he settled over her.

They kissed, tasting lazily, sweat and cum cooling on their skin, until his erection returned to probe at her thigh and abdomen. They moved their bodies over each other, a glorious celebration of carnal texture. He tortured her nipples with his fingers, his palms, his teeth, his chest, stroked between her legs, but mostly lingered on her limbs, mesmerized once again by their length over and around him.

Then she reached between them to explore where he was long as well, and hotter than anywhere else. His skin moved over the rigid organ with delightful elasticity. He buried his mouth at the base of her neck and groaned, hips making involuntarily jerks as she stroked over him, then reached farther down to test the texture and weight of desire in his scrotum. It was strange enough having her genitalia largely internal, but even stranger for his to be so much on the outside all the time. They were both such funny things, and yet such funny things were the source of such pleasure. She massaged over the wrinkly flesh behind his scrotum, and he thrust hard against her, bumping between her legs, with a barely restrained moan that sounded like her name.

They both reached for the nightstand, but Noah had the benefit of routine and being on top. He clambered away from her to draw the condom down the thick length of his erection to the flushed, thicker base. Something about clothing his erection in something so tight and flesh-colored, something meant to protect him, when the rest of him was completely naked... Her mouth watered as though four tacos hadn't been enough.

As soon as he was finished, she pushed herself up on her knees to kiss him down again, exploring his neck, his chest, the way he had with her, except he'd already had an idea how certain things would feel good for her. She just wondered if they would feel good for him in turn.

Given how quickly he capitulated to her guidance down onto his back as she straddled him — and given the buzz inside her from all the places she stimulated on him — they felt quite good indeed. There were differences between men and women, but they were still not all different, which was comforting for her.

From her experience with his fingers, she arranged her knees on either side of his hips and positioned his cock at her entrance, and with his help holding the base, she slid down him. They tandem-groaned as she felt how she felt to him and he felt how he felt to her.

The penetration was still a little uncomfortable, because he was thicker than three fingers and the angle didn't lend itself to the spot inside that he'd found. It wasn't so much the physical sensation of stretch and vulnerability that reeled her mind and spurred the urge to ride him, taking him in over and over until he was pumping his cock up to meet her. What drove her was the utter intimacy of the practice. Prophylactics notwithstanding, he was *inside* her, pushing her open like an escape route. She was part of him, and he was part of her — cleaved together. He was inside her and she surrounded him, and when she rocked over him, used his chest to lift her hips so that she moved him inside her, then leaned backward to encourage the same angle that he'd given her with his fingers, for a moment she was him and he was her and they were moaning together, groaning together, singing together, the exact same note in different registers, the exact same gasps, the exact same rising cry as they strove for the inevitable conclusion.

Noah grasped for her hips as she found the perfect angle for his cock pushing against the place that felt so good — not as effective as his fingers, but she used hers to stroke relentlessly against the bone beneath her clit, urging the both of them to join together in their orgasm. She just had to keep doing that, right there, right there, she had no words anymore, just their moans, but they were almost there, almost there, right *there*.

He was beautiful as he fell back and tensed from toes to neck in his own orgasm, shouting and thrusting deep inside her with each pulse of his cum to match the clench of her pussy around him. His orgasm extended hers and hers extended his until he had to use his grip on her hips to lift her off.

Noah curled to the side, squeezing the base of his cock to both finish himself off and stop himself from getting hard again. He pulled the condom off and discarded it in the trash can on his other side, then slumped back, panting.

"Jesus, I thought I was going to have a heart attack. Wouldn't have been the worst way to go, I guess. That was…" He ran his hand through his hair, tugging at his scalp. "That was amazing from my end. I hope it was just as good from yours."

Tara crawled over him to settle beside him. "You don't have to fish for compliments. You know you did good."

He laughed. "So you've figured out how to share more deliberately. Have you figured out how to hold it back?"

"Easier to share. It hurts holding it in. Like there's not enough room in me."

"Of course there's not enough room in you. You're fucking tiny." But she didn't think he was being serious.

"But I'll work on it." She stroked over his chest, enjoying the texture of him. "This didn't exactly give me much incentive, though."

He laughed again, still a little out of breath. "No kidding. But better to learn on something with lower stakes rather than on something you really don't want to share."

"True. Perhaps we should keep practicing."

"I don't know if I can... Jesus H. Christ, woman. Was that not enough for you?"

She tucked herself closer, licking the salt on his skin from his flatter nipple up to the stubble on his neck and then to his mouth, where she could still taste herself. She insinuated her leg between his, sliding the length along his thigh until her knee nudged his scrotum. His erection twitched awake.

"Noah," she murmured against his lips as he leaned into her kiss, "how many tacos did I have?"

"Fuck. I do have to sleep again eventually."

"I'll be happy to exhaust you."

"*Fuck*." He rolled over her, pressing her into the mattress with his beautiful weight and heat, and reached again for his nightstand drawer.

Chapter Ten

As Noah had expected, waking up with his alarm made him angry that the world hadn't been destroyed during his last hour of sleep. He switched off the beeping a little too aggressively.

Tara groaned at being awakened as well.

Settling back against his pillow with her in his arms wasn't the worst thing in the world to wake up to, though.

She wasn't the typical kind of woman he had sex with, especially the ones who stayed overnight instead of just meeting him at some hotel. The definition of gorgeous differed from person to person, of course. But Tara was... Even without her own ambiguity of identity, she was also ambiguous at first and sometimes second glance. He'd always liked a woman's curves, and she barely had any. There was little soft on her other than her mop of hair.

She was intensely emotional, stiff in movement and gait from what he assumed was both adapting to a new body and the aches she suffered, straightforward and sometimes tactless because she didn't know better, young yet old, dangerous yet guileless. And she had a sexual appetite that had left him so replete that his penis was nearly numb.

Yet he couldn't stop looking at her as she tried to fall back to sleep on his chest, couldn't stop enjoying just lying there with her and thinking she was the most interesting thing he'd ever had in his bed. The more he stared, the more beautiful her strangeness became, wing stumps and all.

And he didn't know what to do with that.

He wanted to tell himself that he only felt how she felt while she tucked against him like he was her personal heater, unselfconscious in her nudity and the general mess of sex, affectionate and comfortable and comforted, and that was why he didn't want to let her go to get ready for work.

He wanted to tell himself he wasn't getting attached to a nephil who was unstable at best. That wasn't her fault. Someone was sabotaging her stability, and it couldn't have been easy feeling everyone's feelings when it was sometimes hard enough to deal with one's own. But the fact was that she'd tried to kill him. He could also swear in court that he'd nearly died from the sex they'd had. The only reason they hadn't fucked all the way through the day was because *she'd* finally tired herself out.

He didn't think she would always be like this. Like the novelty of food, he really did think her sexual appetite would settle. When she was finally satiated, she wouldn't require as *much* of everything.

But he had a premonition of his own, although he had none of Andrea's natural intuition. Tara would always be hungry, just like she would always be in some pain. She'd fallen sensitive, and that wasn't going to change. It scared him, not least because he realized that the only reason he was scared was because he just *assumed* she would still be part of his life by the time she'd fully acclimated to being human.

He stroked her hair, heart racing again for a different reason.

She looked up at him, dark feather eyebrows furrowed. He should have known better than to have strong feelings with her right there.

"It's okay. Just some anxiety. It's not you." He wasn't lying. The fear was his own.

Tara buried her face against his chest. "Do we have to get up?"

He found the app that controlled his blackout shades and raised them to force the issue.

"Ow." She shielded her eyes against the sunlight that was still well high in the sky at three in the afternoon. "I hate you."

"So do I. I told you we'd be tired. I guess you had to learn about consequences eventually." He worked out one of the tangles in her hair. "You may be less than a week old down here, but your body's adult. You need sleep as much as you need food and water."

"That sounds like some bullshit."

She surprised him into a harsh laugh.

"Wait until your first hangover. But we do need to get up. And we desperately need to shower. I think my bed's a biohazard."

He'd worn condoms when he'd been able to get one on in time, and he'd made every effort if he was going to be inside her, but she'd come so easily that it had sometimes been a hopeless case. That would probably settle with time, too, but when her orgasms were so tied to her partner's, perhaps it wasn't so surprising. She could weaponize herself with an electric bullet.

Noah slapped her ass. There wasn't much flesh there, more flank than cushion, but it was still a satisfying sound. "Time to get up. You can sleep on the way to the station, if you want. Shower. Then breakfast. I don't know about you, but I expended some serious calories last night."

She let him pull her out of the bed, then stood on her own power, although she winced and her legs shook like a newborn foal. Using his nightstand, she bent and stretched in a way that called attention to how much he loved the long length of her legs. And when she exposed her pussy like that, it made him think about taking her from behind, although his cock couldn't so much as twitch.

"Aching?" he asked.

She nodded. "That would be more consequences, yes? On top of how I already hurt."

"Shower and more movement will help." He led her out of his bedroom but stopped her before she could veer into his bathroom. "Oh no. We are not showering together. I may not be able to feel anything below my waist, but that still seems like a bad idea."

"You're putting me back in the bedroom box?"

"It's the only other shower. It's also where your clothes are. I'll let you out again."

"Oh, will you?" So she'd learned sarcasm as well as swear words.

"Get yourself in that shower and I'll make you Belgian waffles. Like pancakes, but with little compartments for your syrup."

The rumble in her stomach decided her. She headed back into her room without another complaint.

Noah's phone went off as he was brushing his teeth. He spit out the toothpaste foam and put his phone on speaker. "Couldn't wait until we got to the station, Black?"

"Just wanted to let you know we were going to be a little late getting in. We lost the, um, hot water, and I need to wait for a plumber to get here to fix the damn heater."

Someone said something too far from the receiver for him to tell who. It sounded like a woman, though, not Hannah, who would have still been at school.

"Uh-huh." He infused every bit of his skepticism and amusement into the grunt. He wasn't mad. If anything, it would give him and Tara more time to recover.

"And exactly what does 'uh-huh' mean?" Andrea said, annoyed. The woman in the background laughed.

"It means I'll see you at the station a little later than usual. Enjoy your plumber."

"Fuck you."

He ended the call without responding, but he shook his head with a smile. She was probably with that hunter she saw off and on. He didn't know why she thought she had to stay in the closet. Sure, this was Texas, but Meridian buildings turned rainbow during Pride. And if she thought she successfully hid how she felt when they were interacting with succubi, she had another think coming.

He couldn't throw stones about divorce. He was mostly just happy that she was enjoying herself after her marriage had fallen apart in a far uglier way than his. Andrea and her ex put on happy faces for their children. Those kids would never know how nasty it had gotten during mediation, the splitting of their assets, and especially the custody battle when he worked a standard, safe nine-to-five and she was a nightshift detective who'd been in the hospital five times in one year. If she was shacking up with a nice woman and coming in late for herself now rather than bowing out because of her kids, more power to her. They needed something to relieve the stress of their work. Kids were wonderful, and she loved hers more than life itself, but kids were not stress-relieving.

Noah turned on some music and stepped under the shower spray. There was stress relief, and then there was whatever he'd done before his alarm had gone off. Muscles he didn't normally use that way felt much better under the warm spray, and the rest of him was blissfully relaxed from an excess of those happy hormones he'd warned Tara about.

Careful, Dunn.

Demons were sly, and angels never stayed. He didn't need to go getting attached to someone who didn't know yet which she wanted to be.

* * * *

Noah thought he'd be okay until she started in on the Belgian waffles, which he'd topped with strawberries and whipped cream as a little treat in addition to the syrup. Of all his splurges on pointless kitchen appliances, the Belgian waffle maker was one that actually did get some good use.

She'd come down in jeans that were a little too loose, but the long-sleeved black shirt wasn't, and she wasn't wearing a bra. He wanted to say something, and maybe she would have listened, but unless there was an unintentional hole or stain, he'd learned a long time ago that he was *not* supposed to tell a woman how to dress. The shirt wasn't really tight, and her breasts weren't prominent, but the shirt was thin enough and fit her a little better than some of the others, so the fact she was braless was more apparent, and it was hard not to notice while he watched her eat.

Whipped cream. And sticky syrup. She wasn't even trying to be sexy. She was just eating with her usual enthusiasm and expressing appreciation for how good it was, sucking syrup off her fork like a normal person.

He was the one who wasn't normal because the cock he'd hoped had settled in for a long autumn nap woke up again. Knowing how she looked and moved and sounded when she was having sex made all the difference in the world. She just ate syrup and whipped cream and he remembered her kissing under his jaw and her uninhibited moans, breathy or loud as she felt them, felt him. He remembered his goddamn wastebasket looking like a frat house bin.

She glanced up at him halfway through her waffle and slowly smiled. He didn't know whether she was trying to look wicked, but the expression was emphatically Not Helping.

"Really?" she asked as she continued eating.

"You're going to get used to it," he grumbled, picking at his strawberries. "I'm going to get used to it. You're amazing. I'm a creep. Can you help with this?"

"Nope. Not yet."

"Are you trying?"

"Yep. Not yet."

"Andrea had a good 'night' and is having a good 'morning', too. I guess it's going around."

* * * *

On the way to the station, he kept getting distracted by her at traffic lights. He'd forget that he was supposed to be driving until the car behind him honked.

This is ridiculous. It apparently wasn't just his penis that thought he was fourteen again.

As beautiful as she was in dim light, she was all the more real in sunlight. She wasn't radiant unless she smiled, but he kept getting caught in the slight green of her hazel eyes and the wild way her hair had dried. And he thought about how her lips probably still tasted like maple syrup.

He'd done gone and got attached. Complicated as his life was, he'd had to go and make it more complicated, and he was having a devil of a time trying to hide that fact when she kept looking over at him, too. She had to know what he was thinking, in emotion if not in words.

They made it to the station without him rearending some poor Hyundai or some Chevy rearending him in their end-of-day impatience. He went up the stairs and entered the building first so that he wouldn't get the opportunity to stare at her legs. Her baggy jeans did nothing to flatter her, but her legs didn't need extra flattering.

What he didn't expect was that he'd end up feeling secondhand intrigue and heat of arousal settling in his already stirred cock to push it against his trousers. Fool that he was, he hadn't worn denim, which was usually sturdy enough to keep him bound down until he could surreptitiously adjust himself. He looked back to catch *her* staring at *his* body, and she seemed so soft and enticing in one of his leather jackets…

This is getting out of hand.

In the lobby, he stopped her. "I need to take care of something. Do you know how to get to Homicide?"

She nodded, seeming captivated by his mouth. When he started to leave, she pulled him toward her by his shirt and pressed her lips to his.

They were in the middle of the lobby, people coming and going, closing out or starting their shift, guests coming in to make a statement or report a crime. Officers and detectives who recognized him exclaimed, hooted, howled, or whistled. Even if they didn't like him much, this was juicy office gossip—not least because Tara's case wasn't closed. She knew they weren't supposed to be having sex on the roof, but she couldn't have known that they weren't supposed to be kissing where other people could see. And that was his fault.

Yet he couldn't convince himself to pull back, not immediately. It wasn't like it was anything more than a kiss, although it wasn't exactly the most chaste.

But the hoots and hollers were intensifying rather than dying away, and he realized that the pulsing hum of her arousal inside of him was probably creeping out beyond just them. Other people wouldn't know what was happening. They'd think the desire was their own. If it settled in and they responded the way he did, getting more turned on, then she was going to get more turned on, too, ad infinitum. Except it wouldn't go on forever, just until...

With every last fiber of his self-control, he broke the kiss, then brought his mouth her ear. "It's contagious to more than just me. Try to get a hold of yourself."

"I'm sorry." She shook her head and held her hands up between them, clenching them into fists. "I don't know if I—"

"I'm not mad, Tara. Just... It might not be as bad as everyone catching anger, panic, or fear, but lust has its problems, too. Try some—I don't know—meditation techniques to empty your mind. Count to ninety-nine or read a pamphlet. You've been watching those nature documentaries, right? Try to remember a scene from that and hone in on the details. Now, I'm going to try to control *myself*. I'll meet you in the office, okay?"

"I'll do what I can."

He cradled the back of her head, kissed her hair, then patted her shoulder to direct her toward Homicide. He gave a wry grin to the people who'd been watching and cheering but offered no more, hoping they'd just forget about what they saw. He might get a reprimand from Loretta, but it wasn't like Tara was a person of interest in a criminal case so much as the subject of an investigation into a weird occurrence. He should close that up as soon as possible, though, for propriety's sake, mark the cause of the incident as *Origin unknown*. He couldn't very well put *Angel fallen from heaven*. Just one more mystery to be filed among all of Meridian's other unsolved cases.

He ducked into a bathroom stall to arrange his erection so it would be less noticeable and he could go about his day until it subsided or he passed Tara on to Andrea, whichever came first. Precedent suggested that having Tara join Andrea on weekend leave would be the only way he'd get any work done without Tara sending him desire like heat shimmering off the DFW tarmac in dead summer.

Away from her, he did his own meditation—breathing exercises he'd learned in anger management courses way back when he was a young buck in college who'd thought that because his head was hard as a hammer and he could throw a football that he could get whatever he wanted in life. He'd made bad decisions. He'd burned bridges. He'd hurt people and sought a million ways to make himself seem bigger when he felt half his own size.

It had taken him a few years and those anger management classes — mentor-suggested, not court-appointed — before he'd finally realized how much he wanted to help people and he'd stopped seeing everyone else as having a victim mentality while considering himself the only real victim. Being shown that feeling victimized wasn't the same as being a victim had gone a long way to changing how he saw the world.

That, and controlled breathing. Who knew that something you had to do to survive could be so useful in making you remember you were glad to be alive and that not everyone was so fortunate?

Finally, his erection somewhat subsided on its own. He washed his hands and splashed some water on his face, then headed out toward Homicide, trying to maintain the same even breathing as he went.

Between Homicide and Assault, he recognized Tara's silhouette at the end of the hallway, and he sensed something was wrong. He'd told her to go to his office. That she wasn't in his office set off the first silent alarm. He slowly approached.

It hit him like a wall of succubus magic, although the quality of arousal was different — more layered, multi-faceted. Because he was feeling Tara feeling everyone else in the whole goddamn Homicide Department. She braced herself against the wall, breathing shallowly, her shoulders near her ears, her eyes clenched shut as she shook her head. Trying to control it. But it was still coming into her, going out to them, and coming into her stronger.

Noah hesitated to look in Homicide because gossip was one thing, but he didn't really want or need to know about his colleagues' sexuality. He peered in from behind her anyway.

It almost seemed normal. People were talking to their partners, clattering on their keyboards, interviewing witnesses, and someone in holding clanged on their bars. Business as usual.

Except Mercer, at the desk he shared with his partner Cardenas, kept adjusting himself. He tried to make it understated, but he kept doing it. A woman handcuffed to a chair while Hunsacker did some paperwork on her looked at him with slightly glazed eyes, as though she felt the arousal and just assigned it to the closest person, even though Hunsacker wasn't anything special. Jefferson, who had a corner desk that allowed him to put his back to the wall and see everything else in the room, was pressed into that corner, eyes closed with a slightly pained expression. He wore a coat and kept his hands in the pockets, covering himself.

Conners was one of the few homicide detectives with whom Noah and Andrea got along because she'd faced a demon cult and burned her hand on a demon's brimstone—hard to deny they existed when scars reminded you every day. She shifted uncomfortably in her seat while she worked, her cheeks flushed.

Noah closed his fingers around Tara's upper arms.

"There's so many of them," Tara said, her voice a little higher, breathy, and no, that wasn't helping at all. "How do you all live with this every day?"

"Well, we don't feel when other people are turned on, for starters."

"I can't stop it."

"Okay, here's what I want you to try to do. Imagine puppies and kittens. Do you know what puppies and kittens are, or do I need to pull up a video?"

"I remember what puppies and kittens are, although I would love to meet some in real life."

"Okay, just think about how much you want to see puppies and kittens in person. Maybe Andrea can take you by a shelter this weekend. I'm sure Hannah wouldn't mind. Maybe you can get a kitten for yourself when you get an apartment or something. See, that's nice, isn't it?"

She wouldn't be able to do anything about the ambient arousal left from what she'd inspired, but what came from her was much milder as delight replaced lust. Jefferson finally let go of the breath he'd been holding, and Conners stopped shifting. The woman with Hunsacker didn't appear to have changed her mind about him, which was odd, but hey, whatever iced her cookies.

And he still desired Tara, but he imagined puppies and kittens, too, and it was hard to associate little balls of adorable fluff with what they'd done in and out of bed. "Better?" he asked.

"Yes. Oh, that's a wonderful distraction."

"I use it to dispel any strong emotions when I need to be in control of a situation and not let that situation control me. It's not foolproof, but it's a start. Now, think you can make it to the office?"

"Hold my hand?"

Noah slipped his hand into hers. "Here we go. Puppies and kittens."

"Puppies and kittens," she whispered. "Puppies and kittens."

He led her into the large and still quite active room, imagining the last time he'd been at his sister's house and played with their brown lab.

However, as Tara walked past Hunsacker's desk, she clenched her hand tighter over Noah's. Both Hunsacker and the woman he'd either arrested or detained were staring at each other, the woman biting her lip and Hunsacker's posture suggesting that he, like Jefferson, was trying to hide an erection.

Tara's breathing deepened, then caught into something shallower. Both Hunsacker and the woman groaned under their breath.

"Noah," Tara gasped.

"Shit." He could feel it too, growing, growing, climbing. He hooked his arm around her shoulder and led her faster to his office. "To me. To me. If you can focus it anywhere, send it to me alone. I can take it. *Oh. Oh, fuck.*"

Tara might not have been a succubus, but she was just as powerful in her own way, and she was pulling arousal from other people in the room on top of her own and his. He was fortunate he'd already done his little tuck trick, or else he wasn't sure he'd be able to hide his erection at all, given that Tara was wearing his jacket.

"You want me to stop?" Tara said breathily, because he'd paused in the middle of the room, not quite hunched like Hunsacker but still leaning slightly forward as what felt like all his blood directed itself to the heavier and heavier place straining against the front of his pants.

Why did his office need to be all the way on the other side of the room anyway?

"No. No, God, don't stop." He didn't mean it to sound like that, but he couldn't unsay or unhear it.

"Not helping, Noah." Her legs shook.

"Puppies and kittens. Hurry. Hurry."

He rushed her like they were coming in from the rain. People they passed along the way usually ignored Noah and Andrea as they worked, but they perked up like they were goosed, and what Tara felt from them she sent to him. So she couldn't stop the intensity, but perhaps in her panic, she could direct it.

Finally, they reached the office. He fumbled with his keys to unlock the door, then closed and locked the door behind them. Then he went window by window and snapped the blinds shut before grabbing Tara's arm and pulling her back to his desk, where he kissed her furiously, then twisted her around to shove against his desk.

"God, you're impossible," he groaned as he ground against her ass. She pushed back to meet him, mashing her mound and her clit against the front of the desk when she canted her hips forward.

"I'm trying. Oh, fuck, I'm trying. Noah, I'm going to…"

"I ain't complaining too hard. In a matter of speaking." He pulled her back so that she couldn't get herself off on the desk, but he didn't think he was going to make it, either.

Tara reached behind her to hold him by his hair, massaging his scalp as she met his kiss. It was awkward and sloppy and rough and should have been awful. Instead, it was all too delicious, and he could feel the climax happening.

He didn't want to come in his pants again, didn't want to come anywhere but inside her.

"You know walls don't block the feelings much, in or out, right?" she gasped.

"I did not. That's okay, as long as they can't see in. Fuck, Tara, I can't...

She pushed her jeans down and her underwear with them.

Noah nearly lost it right there. He jostled his right drawer and found the box of condoms at the back.

"Really?" she said, briefly more amused than aroused, which at least spared him some control to open the foil.

"I leave for dates from work, and it gets too damn hot in Texas to keep them in the car."

He almost couldn't open his trousers fast enough because she kept pushing her pussy back against his pants, and he could tell she was wet. He jerked her up by her shoulder and whispered in her ear, "Take off the jacket."

That gave her something to do while he wrapped himself with a groan. Then he positioned himself. She cried out at the first breach, but he covered her mouth.

"Not a sound," he whispered. "Oh, fuck, fuck, fuck, not a sound." He pressed his mouth against the back of her head in a quiet groan as he thrust into her again, again, reached his other hand in front to stroke on either side of her clit, pinching the hood between his fingers.

She braced herself on the blotter and bucked into his fingers. "Noah..." Not a cry, but a gasp. "Harder."

Someone knocked on the door.

"Dunn?" Loretta. His boss. While he was screwing a subject of investigation on his desk.

Not that anyone could see in, but Noah pulled Tara down with him to hide in the small, awkward space under his desk. He was wedged against the desktop and a corner and still buried inside her while she rocked in his lap. She covered her own mouth now as she rested her head back on his shoulder.

He covered her hand covering her mouth and held her still when a key inserted into the lock and opened the door.

Tara's eyelids fluttered and her eyes rolled back underneath as she clenched around him, her gasps the only indication that she was coming, but he had to shove his arm into his mouth to bite down as he came inside her. He jostled the desk, but he didn't think it was loud enough for Loretta to hear. Hoped to God it wasn't.

"Dunn?" Loretta called again.

Tara was doing well focusing pleasure to just him if Loretta couldn't feel their simultaneous orgasm, but she was also doing so well focusing that pleasure that the orgasm lasted forever again. He didn't think he could hold his breath to hold back his groan much longer.

"I swear he was in there," someone said—probably Hunsacker. "Must have sneaked out."

"Well, let him know I'm looking for him. And to turn his damn phone on."

The office door closed.

Tara couldn't stop the moan that wasn't completely muffled by either of their hands. She bore down on him for the last throes of her climax, so tight at that angle that he shouted into his arm and bucked up to bury himself inside her pussy while it throttled him so damn sweetly. His head struck the desktop. He groaned in pain rather than pleasure as he released his arm from his teeth.

"Son of a bitch," he swore as Tara giggled madly behind their hands. She pushed his away, still laughing.

"Me first." She raised herself up off him with a broken moan, then grunted as she climbed out from under the desk. She was still naked from her waist to her knees. She hadn't come down from her desire fast enough for him to be unaffected by the sight.

He removed his condom, tied it off, then crawled out after her as she started to pull her jeans back up. She looked over her shoulder at him. Her nipples were pressing against her shirt, because she was still fucking turned on and sending it straight to him. Like he'd told her to. He couldn't get mad. He wasn't mad. God, he wasn't mad. But he was losing control of his...well, control.

He grabbed another condom, then crawled behind her and shoved her against the office wall. Her fingers disturbed the blinds as she grabbed the windowsill. Tara sighed into a moan as his erection pressed between her cheeks. He brought his own fingers back around to stroke a little more softly over her, but she wriggled her ass against him in a wordless plea, sending wave after wave of how much she wanted him until he thrust back inside her and fucked her harder against the wall—disturbing the blinds more, but he didn't care.

"It might fall off if we keep going like this," he said through clenched teeth. "I'm just one man."

"I can't keep doing this," she sobbed, hiding her face in her arm. "I don't remember seeing humans do this this much. I don't think I can... Yes, yes, there, there, oh, yes..."

He brought her off with his fingers and embraced her from behind to sit her on his lap where he knelt as she came around him and he came inside her.

"Why is it not enough?" Even though she wept harder, she still moved over his cock.

Noah heard something out in the bullpen that suggested she hadn't managed to hold it all back, but at least they wouldn't associate it with her anymore.

"Focus on me. On me. Good God, you're insatiable."

Her laughter shifted into tears and back, and she lifted off him to try once more to crawl away but hit him with her need anyway. He kissed over her hip, up her spine through the shirt, then bent between her legs to gently lick over her wet entrance, cleaning her and making a mess of himself. He just wanted Tara to stop crying.

Her arousal didn't dissipate, but it did calm. He removed his second condom as he continued to lick over her. His tenderness forced her to slow down, even as she made him hard again and he scrambled to get another condom on. It was one thing to come on his sheets, another to come on his office carpet.

Noah massaged over her thighs, more reassuring than sensual. He'd had sex before with someone who cried after orgasm because the flood of emotions overwhelmed her, but this was on a completely different level. He hated Tara's sadness, felt it in his bones as much as her desire. Instead of hard and rough, which they'd enjoyed multiple times over, he wanted to show her that climax didn't have to be violent, that it wasn't always tension but sometimes the product of a complete lack of that tension.

Tara's tears dampened the carpet beneath his desk, but her sobs subsided. She slowly relaxed under his patient tongue and the deep digging of his fingers into her muscles, which also released a dull throbbing pain in his legs that were probably echoes of what Tara had been dealing with since she'd woken up. He'd just assumed it was his own, leftover from overdoing sex in his home. He made a note to follow up on massage treatment for her in the future.

"Noah, that's... Oh, that's..."

She lowered herself bit by bit down to her arms on the floor, her hips up for him to feast upon her but the rigidity in her shoulders and spine slowly unraveling. His erection ached to be touched, but the part of his conscious brain still connected to his penis told him to end this nonsense as soon as possible for rest and replenishment of fluids and proteins. And a long period of abstinence. The weekend would do nicely.

He almost sobbed himself as she came with softer sighs.

She finally let her bottom half settle down until she was huddled under his desk. He helped her hitch her underwear and pants back over her hips. Sweat dampened her hair and the back of her shirt.

"Puppies and kittens, sweetheart." Noah stroked up her spine under her shirt, then backed away to remove his third and hopefully last condom.

He hid them under some tissues in his trashcan. Then he hauled himself up by the desktop to do up his trousers and fetch wipes from Andrea's desk. He tucked his hand into his pants to do a quick final clean, then finished off with his hands and his mouth. He brought the wipes to Tara. She sat up, leaning against the drawer side under his desktop with her eyes closed, but she accepted the wipes and tended the tears and her hands.

"I'm so sorry. I didn't mean to be this much trouble." She handed him the wad of wipes, which he tossed as added cover for the condoms.

"You're not exceptional trouble, Tara, and like the rest of my job, it's trouble I choose."

He returned the wipes to Andrea's desk, then sprayed some air freshener. The strength of the scent of sex was greatly exaggerated, but that exaggeration dwindled with each session, and the room was a small and enclosed.

"You must have much better things to do than save an overenthusiastic fallen angel from herself."

"Right now, saving an overenthusiastic fallen angel from herself and doing my job align perfectly. You're still being investigated, don't forget, and we'll need you at Mattea, if you still want to try your hand at helping those kids."

"Yes. Yes. Although, since walls alone don't diminish the effect of my empathy, what if the people in there infect me as well? The kids, yes, but also the others suffering."

"Then you can leave the hospital and spend some quiet time in the car. A parking garage might even be a good spot for you. There are places, Tara, where there are fewer people. You don't have to drive for miles to find them. Hell, a church on any day but Sunday might give you a nice, quiet place to think. You can spend some time in open chapels when you visit your cemeteries. Is talking about solutions helping?"

"Another distraction." She rested her head back again and sighed. "Yes."

"Would chips help? There's a vending machine by the bathrooms. Do you know where those are?" He handed her a few dollars from his wallet when she nodded. "You're going to have to come out from there eventually. Remember, puppies and kittens, solutions, count in fours, feel whatever you're feeling and don't try to make more of it than what it is. Feelings pass, and the more you try to resist them, the more they take you over. Let yourself feel it without making it yours. That's distraction—deliberately thinking about something other than the pink elephant—and mindfulness—reminding yourself that the pink elephant is only a pink elephant and nothing more."

She looked at him funny.

"Try not to think of the pink elephant," he said, by way of explanation.

Her eyes lit up with understanding. "Oh, I get it. That's good."

"It's an old example. I'm not that clever. Need help getting out from under the desk?"

She held out her hand.

Chapter Eleven

While Tara was out getting something to eat, Noah made sure everything looked like he hadn't just had way too much impromptu sex in his office.

And not a moment too soon because Andrea peeked her head in through the half-open door.

"Loretta's on a rampage about yesterday's melee. She's mad we didn't inform her of it immediately. Jesus, I just figured she heard us from her office. Tara's at the vending machines. You want something?"

He shook his head. "How'd the plumbing go?"

"I brought something for you from home, Dunn, and I put it in my pocket so I wouldn't forget. Here." She pulled her fist from her pocket and turned her hand to present her middle finger. "It's your very own 'fuck you.' Isn't it adorable?"

Noah tilted his head. "And so professional."

Andrea backed up as Tara returned to the office. She seemed distracted, but given that he wasn't contemplating adding a waterbed as a permanent fixture to the

Q Division office, he figured that intentional distraction was working.

"Hey." Andrea tousled Tara's already wild hair. "Did you get cold?"

Tara looked a little confused, but she nodded. "I'm always cold. Noah, can I use your jacket again?"

Noah grabbed it from the back of the guest chair and tossed it to her. She had to juggle her Sun Chips while she put her arms back in the sleeves, but when she re-settled in the chair, facing Andrea and next to Noah, she seemed more or less normal again, with the exception of that faraway look.

Andrea blinked and cocked her head slightly, but she raised her eyebrows as though to say 'fuck it' to herself and turned her attention to Noah. "We ready to go?"

Tara chose to go with Noah on the way to Mattea rather than Andrea. Andrea seemed bewildered again by Tara's choice, which Noah didn't understand, because Tara would spend all weekend with Andrea, but she'd been spending most of her time so far with Noah. It made sense she'd choose what was most familiar to her, even without all the sex that they'd had in the last six hours.

Tara ate her chips in Noah's car while she made every effort to put into practice what he'd suggested. He felt twinges of arousal here and there, but the world occupied more of her attention when they were on the road, especially while the sun was still up. He also had to remind himself that he wasn't the center of the universe. He sensed anxiety from her that probably had nothing to do with him and everything to do with meeting the kids and putting herself in the path of other people's suffering.

Mattea Psychiatric Hospital was an intimidating building during the day, even more so at night. If there was ever a place that didn't need the added grotesque elements of the Cabrera New Gothic mode, it was a psychiatric hospital. The windows were barred with wrought iron, almost like ivy over the overly elaborate façade of mild brick and concrete flourishes. It loomed as much as it hulked.

The hospital was beautiful from a distance and protected by the ubiquitous gargoyles, but Noah had never liked it up close. It was as though they were *trying* to create a haunted facility that would become even more notorious twenty years after the insides had been gutted but the stories of tortured souls remained.

However, as clueless as Meridian doctors were about the mystical side of the city, they meant well, and Meridian's mental health numbers — particularly its suicides and incidences of self-harm hospitalizations — were abysmal enough that they probably needed a psychiatric hospital more than the average city.

* * * *

Tara and Noah pulled in just a few spaces away from Andrea's in the parking garage.

"You still okay heading in there?" Andrea asked as they walked toward the hospital. "We're not going to make you. We can always talk to the doctor ourselves and fill you in."

"You don't have to risk yourself to help these kids," Noah added. "They're being taken care of now and improving. You can come back when you have more control."

"I absolutely *should* risk myself to help these kids," Tara replied. "You didn't feel how scared they were. I don't want them to be that kind of afraid anymore. But maybe we just stick with one child at a time instead of a cadre?"

She shook on the inside but squared her shoulders outside the hospital, unintimidated by its size when there were so many gargoyles lining the rooftop above. Whether she remained angel or became demon, the roof was protected by those who had been both, which was oddly comforting.

Upon entering the hospital, Tara realized that walls of the right thickness did, in fact, provide some barrier from other people's emotions. Or perhaps there were supernatural shields etched into the brick or concrete that prevented breach either outside in or inside out. As soon as she passed through the hospital open doors, despair, sadness, anger, and — more than anything — fear hit her like a buffeting wind in a breezeway.

Tara staggered against the wall, her eyelids fluttering as she tried to fight the oppression coming at her from all sides. The only reason she wasn't losing her ever-loving mind was because there was some distance between her and the people suffering. The hall Noah and Andrea walked through was empty until the reception desk at the end.

Andrea was the first to realize Tara wasn't still following them. "Tara?"

Tara held up her hand to ward the two detectives away. "Just give me a minute. Don't come near me."

She had to learn how to deal with this. Fear and panic had been all too quick to get away from her in Assault and the alley, and no one seemed to be a match for the lust. She was as dangerous to other people as she was to herself if she couldn't control it.

Tara focused everything she felt not on Noah—because she didn't want to do that to him—but on the hospital's pistachio-colored linoleum tile that had done nothing to offend anyone but also felt nothing and couldn't be made to feel anything.

That helped get the terrible feelings out of her head, but only temporarily. More came in at every moment, but the feelings she expelled also just bounced off the tile and returned like echoes.

But she wasn't merely a vessel for other people's feelings. She also made people feel her emotions.

She'd known peace in the car, especially at night. She knew what peace should feel like. She tried to remember it, even as the weight of the hospital threatened to crush her—and she didn't even think she was getting the *whole* hospital. The thick barriers between floors seemed sufficient to diffuse some of the impact, like they had in the hospital she'd awakened in.

Holding those memories of peace, she sent them out to meet the terrible feelings coming out at her.

It wasn't perfect—a single umbrella against a whole wall cloud of impending storms.

So she thought of the way she'd felt when she'd made Noah laugh, when all the tension in the Assault room had broken, when she'd been held. The more she dwelled on feelings that directly contradicted those that tried to take her over, the more those other emotions had no hold on her, like oil to water.

Cultivating the emotions that made her feel calm and safe didn't make the other ones go away, but they became more bearable to withstand.

She took a breath, then another, testing her resolve and how much it required her to focus, because she needed to be able to walk through this world doing more than thinking about how to keep it from overtaking her. Most of the time, she could. Most of the time, other people's emotions weren't that strong. She had to remember what her brain was like in those times.

She stood on her own strength instead of depending on the wall to hold her up. She did have to focus, but it didn't take all her energy. Perhaps it would become easier the more she did it.

"Okay, let's keep going. I think I have this managed."

"We can take as long as you need," Noah said.

"If I need to leave, are you sure they're going to let me?" Tara said.

Andrea smiled, but worry still furrowed her forehead.

"We won't let them take you away," Noah said. "If anything happens, we'll blame it on your recent concussion. Okay?"

After the man at the reception desk buzzed the three of them in, another wave of bad feelings hit her — a solid fist of numbness and nothing, both medicated and natural — on the other side of the tempered glass between the entryway and the interior. The only saving grace was that despair, anger, sadness, fear, and numbness weren't the only feelings that hit her. There was peace here, too, and she grabbed on to it like stair railings wherever she found it. There was peace, happiness, playfulness, cheerfulness, excitement, curiosity, and it didn't come from the staff with any greater prevalence than patients.

The pediatric psychiatric department on the third floor consisted primarily of a large open area bathed in sunlight. The kids could get some fresh air amid hanging ferns and bamboo growths that surrounded a cushioned playground, where two orderlies watched and interceded with any conflict.

The overwhelming attempt with the color palette here was Happy. The overwhelming attempt with the color palette in adult spaces was Calm. Neither quite hit the mark. The children's room was too aggressive, like a toybox from a nightmare. The adults' rooms were as bland as melted ice cream. All of it put Tara's teeth on edge. Or maybe that was the citrusy scent of a thousand days of antibacterial cleansers. Nevertheless, there was more cheerfulness up here despite the poor efforts of the atmosphere. Tara heard it as much as felt it.

The orderly led them out of the common area into a series of hallways and rooms — offices, dormitories, some smaller rooms with only one or two beds, windowless as cells except in the doors, with minimal adornment to distinguish one bed from another. Around the corner were more rooms. The windows in the closed doors showed padded walls and no beds. Each had someone's name slipped into the placard.

Dr. Kim's more spacious office was one of two for co-heads of the department. Dr. Kim anxiously studied a series of monitors on his desk as he sorted through folders of paperwork. He stood when the orderly gestured them into the office.

"Detectives. I've been gathering files on the kids still in the facility. Parents took some of them out, of course, since they were here only because the parents permitted it. Some were even ready to go home. In the case of last evening's incident, however, they're being held pending a more thorough evaluation, due to the... due to the deaths, of course. Terrible business. With whatever's spreading among these kids, I feared it was only a matter of time."

"Have you noticed it passing on to adults, too?" Andrea asked. "Kids and the elderly tend to be vulnerable to the same viruses."

"No rash of entrants into the geriatric wing, nor have I received any memos about attacks at senior centers or bingo games."

"I know you've spoken with other officers and detectives, but just to confirm... There's been no account of someone possibly inciting these incidents?" Noah said. "The kids haven't said that they saw anyone there beforehand?"

"You think someone is doing this?" Dr. Kim asked — but not as though curious. More as though it was confirmation of something he'd been afraid to say out loud.

"Tara suggested that this was behaving not like a contagion but a chemical weapon," Noah answered. "Like a bomb went off in the middle of a bunch of kids. But there weren't any weapons at the scenes, and someone surely would have mentioned a smoke bomb or a grenade."

"This is Tara?" Dr. Kim pointed to her.

She nodded.

"The kids are overwhelmingly confused about timelines," the doctor said. "Everything bleeds together, and they can't entirely remember the moment it happened or when it ended, but they also seem to confuse when they met Tara. Some say before the episode, some say after, at least from what little they remember. What's your last name, miss?"

Noah and Andrea glanced at each other. They hadn't gotten her papers yet.

When the detectives didn't provide the information, Tara spoke up herself. "I don't know. I'm afraid I experienced a traumatic brain injury a few days ago upon my arrival in Meridian. I was in Mercy Hospital for…four days, was it? I've only been out in the world for a few days since."

"Curious. Curious." Dr. Kim shuffled through his papers again, troubled and a little flustered. "Detective Dunn asked me a question yesterday at the station about how far back these incidents go. It's hard to confirm whether the smaller incidents with only one or two children are related, but they began two weeks ago. The first larger incident occurred four days ago. Yet the kids describe a similar woman as being there, giving them comfort before or after the incident, like when you were there these last two incidents."

"Tara was definitely in the hospital four days ago," Noah said. "We were there with her in shifts. She was never alone. And ever since she was released from the hospital, she's been with one or both of us as we continue to pursue the investigation into her injury."

"Curious," Dr. Kim muttered again. "Well, there are lots of women who would fit the description they gave — tall, pale skin, dark hair, gold or green eyes. It sounds like some kind of mild mass hysteria."

Tara was too stunned to reply.

"If they do have the image of a woman in their minds, before or after the incident, perhaps we *are* looking for a woman, though," Andrea said. "Do they have any other specifics?"

"Sadly, no. So you really think a woman is engaging in terroristic weaponization of children?"

"But you said the woman gave them comfort," Tara said.

"Perhaps to gain their trust. As a woman, she would already be seen as a safe person for them. Additional comfort might get her close enough to release whatever causes them to become violent," Dr. Kim said. "Women can absolutely be terrorists, but as far as a psychological profile goes, this woman is acting completely contrary to any expectation."

"Women usually do, with violence at this scale," Andrea said. "If they're even caught."

"Given her focus on children, the only explanation I can come up with is thwarted maternal desire of some kind," Dr. Kim said. "If she can't have children, no one can."

Tara finally found her words. "She's not killing children. She's making children try to kill each other and everyone else. And maternal would be gentle or quick. Women *can* be sadistic, cruel, cold, although I seem to feel too strongly, rather than not enough."

Dr. Kim regarded her with some suspicion. Tara didn't blame him. She was suspicious of herself. But Noah and Andrea were adamant that she'd been in their company ever since she'd arrived, so there was no way she could have been there for the children to *see* her. Certainly not over a week ago. There had to be another player here.

But *why*? Why turn children feral? What was the *point*? Tara certainly had no interest or reason to hurt anyone, much less children.

"She's not lying," Noah said, surreptitiously easing himself between Tara and the doctor. "She's intensely empathetic, with a demonstrably contagious affect, which you witnessed yourself. Because of it, you said at the station that you'd like for her to interact with children from previous incidents who still have episodes of violence."

"Not episodes of violence," Tara said. "Violence is only a side effect. They're episodes of fearful anger."

"Interesting," Dr. Kim said, still suspicious, yet fascinated. "We've found no foreign substance in their blood tests, at least the kinds that we test for. What we did find was a frightening amount of cortisol and high levels of adrenaline. If what these children were experiencing was solely fear, we should see variety in their responses — fight, flight, or freeze. There must be another chemical response that this woman is inciting other than fear alone. They're creating designer drugs faster than we can test for them, faster than we can make them illegal. However, there's no *reason* to create a drug that makes people fearful and violent, except…"

"Except terrorism," Andrea finished for him, sitting in the chair across from the desk. "Shit. You don't sell bath salts to children because then you don't get repeat customers. There's no profit in it. And given the randomness of application, we can disregard accidental impurity."

"Precisely," Dr. Kim said.

"It would be helpful if we had some idea of an endgame," Noah said, sitting with Andrea. Tara remained standing next to the door. She didn't like how Dr. Kim kept glancing over at her as though wanting to get her on a surgical table.

"I'm more interested in a solution," Dr. Kim said. "Neither the kids from the station nor those from the alley have demonstrated any relapse — although they suffer their own distress, of course. The children from the other incidences who are still with us, however, continue to have episodes of explosive violence during which they can be neither consoled nor calmed. All we can do through these episodes is sedate and contain them so they won't hurt themselves or others."

"May I see one of them, perhaps somewhere quiet?" Tara asked. "You can observe, of course, but it's quieter when there aren't so many heads in the room."

Dr. Kim hesitated. Then, perhaps in professional despair, he softened his gaze. "There *was* something different about these last two groups. Maybe you can reach whatever wasn't fixed in the previous ones. Do you have any medical training?"

"I don't think I do."

"You just like children, then?"

"I don't like when people suffer," Tara said. "I want to help."

Dr. Kim rounded the desk. "But how? How do you help them?"

She instinctively understood that she couldn't explain her powers in any more detail than Noah had. This man would never consider a supernatural cause, nor a supernatural cure. He would rather stay confused than consider a world in which therapy and carefully applied psychopharmacology couldn't solve all problems within these walls.

"I don't know," she replied. "If I can, does it matter how?"

"Well, I'd like to be able to repeat the process when you're not here," Dr. Kim said. "I can't just keep you hostage in the building until the terrorist is finished with her plan. Well, I could, but it would be highly frowned upon."

"Let's start with one." Tara held out her hands to Dr. Kim, who allowed her to grasp his. As she sent him a fraction of her peace memories, he warmed to her further, with not enough room left for suspicion—at least for now.

"I'd like to look at the records of all the children, if possible," Noah interjected. "We might find a pattern you couldn't."

"HIPAA forbids me, and you know that," Dr. Kim said. "At least when I introduce Tara to them, it will be within the realm of therapy. Their names are in the police reports. If you want to speak to any of them, you'll have to ask the parents or get a warrant for their files. But no one's filing criminal charges. It's abundantly clear to everyone involved that children don't just become feral by choice."

"Could it be some milder form of rabies?" Andrea asked.

"There is no milder form of rabies."

"That you're aware of," Andrea pointed out.

Dr. Kim tilted his head in half-agreement. "The test for rabies requires a biopsy of their brain, which can only occur after they're dead. However, even though they're still having episodes, they're getting better, and there's no cure for rabies. Certainly not anything this young lady could do with a soothing mien. Shall we, Miss Tara?"

* * * *

Noah and Andrea were allowed to stay behind the window glass because they were concerned about Tara's well-being, but they couldn't turn on the speaker out of respect for the boy's medical privacy. Dr. Kim entered into the room with Tara, on behalf of the child.

The child in question was a ten-year-old boy named Caleb, who Dr. Kim felt could be more articulate about what he remembered. Dr. Kim had also chosen him because he was still coming down from his last violent episode. He crouched in a corner, wide-eyed and more suspicious than Dr. Kim as he scratched his arms, twitching with adrenaline.

Dr. Kim stood in the corner by the door, visible to Noah and Andrea. Tara sat on the cushioned floor across from Caleb. She scratched her arms, too, mirroring him. His anxiety left her nervy, but the cushioned walls, floors, and ceilings were actually effective at muffling more than just acoustics. All she could feel and hear were Dr. Kim, Caleb, and herself.

Maybe good insulation was the grand solution. Something to experiment with another day.

"Hello, Caleb. My name is Tara. Do you know who I am?"

Caleb didn't say anything or shake or nod his head. He opened his mouth but eventually chattered his teeth closed.

"Do I look familiar to you? Is that it?"

Caleb shrugged.

"On the day that what happened to you happened, did someone who looked similar to me do something to you?"

Caleb pushed himself harder into the corner to keep himself from shaking apart entirely.

Tara crawled forward like a crab and settled closer to him. "I know you might have a hard time believing it, but I know what you're going through. That's why I'm here. Just the other night, I briefly experienced what you experienced. I know it's scary."

"At the playground," Caleb said, violently shivering again.

"What?"

"Like you, but different."

Tara nodded. "How is she different?"

Caleb chewed on his tongue, his lips, his cheeks. He indicated on his head that the hair was longer, then made the shape of an hourglass in front of her to indicate that the woman in question was curvier. "Eyes bright. Glowing. Like headlights. I liked her. I liked her in a... I liked her."

"How did you like her, Caleb?"

"She was... She was...you know...pretty. And she was warm."

"Like she had a fever?"

"No. She made *me* feel warm. Like I was safe and held."

"Did she touch you?" Tara asked.

"She held my hand."

"Do you remember her name?"

"What she said didn't matter. Only what she made me feel. Weird. I don't want to talk about it anymore."

"It's okay," Tara said quickly. His agitation had calmed as he'd talked with her, because she'd tried sending her peace to him, but when she'd pushed him on how the other woman made him feel, that agitation had spiked right back up again. "We don't have to talk about that. We don't have to talk about anything if you don't want to. Sometimes it feels like the world is a very noisy place. It's nice to just sit and be quiet for a while. Would you like that?"

Caleb closed his eyes, and so did Tara. As she continued to pour her peace into him, the calmer he became, the calmer she became, and the easier it was to calm him down more, to strip away the lingering parasite of anger and fear hanging on him like fabric caught on chain-link fence. She untangled it from him until she couldn't find anything else to untangle. Then she stopped feeding him her peace and let him sit with his own until he fell asleep in the corner. He whistled lightly through his open mouth.

Tara climbed to her feet and turned to Dr. Kim. "Can I meet the other kids? One at a time, please."

Chapter Twelve

As Andrea drove them away from Mattea, Tara could admit to herself that she was glad to see the building in the passenger-side mirror. Even with the angels and gargoyles, she couldn't wait to leave all that pain behind.

"That was pretty amazing, what you did in there," Andrea said.

"I'm exhausted."

"We can save shopping for tomorrow if you like. I'm sure Hannah won't mind another pizza night with a nice movie. I can't guarantee she'll choose one with low stakes. She's as serious about her movies as everything else."

"I'll be fine. Do you mind if I just kind of drift for a bit? I don't think I need to sleep, but I didn't get much sleep, either."

Andrea snorted. "Yeah, go ahead. Mind if I turn on the radio?"

Tara rested her head against the cool window glass while Andrea switched her radio on to a rock station. Tara let it and the sound of traffic wash over her. She was so tired, in mind, in body, in ways she'd never experienced before. She'd maintained the mental shield around herself and poured out her peace instead — hot shower, warm towels, and cool sheets — until she almost couldn't remember what any of these things were, just the feeling of having had them. Human bodies had such limits, which certainly explained why they had to spend a significant percentage of time repairing and renewing.

Tara fell into a dream that was more like memory — of wings and eyes and gazing down and into the world, desiring so to understand pleasures and pains, but also angry, hurt, although angels didn't hurt the same way that humans did. She *was* hurt, though, and angry like the fire some angels were made of, and when she jumped from the edge to fall, she tried to hold on to that anger, but it burned away with her feathers and her other eyes. She fell to Meridian for a reason, and she was so damn close…

Tara jolted awake like she'd fallen again. She wondered how long she would really be falling.

"You okay?" Andrea asked, putting the car in park. "We're at the school. I need to go in to the afterschool program to get her."

"Yeah, I'm…" Tara looked around. "I'm fine. Just dreaming, I think."

Andrea rested her hand on Tara's arm, then left the car with the keys in the ignition and the radio still on.

By the time Andrea returned with Hannah holding her hand, Tara felt more present, although she wished she could have slept a little bit longer so that she could remember what she was supposed to remember. But she couldn't force it. Like the rest of who she was, it would arrive when it was good and ready.

Hannah climbed into the back onto her booster seat. She was wearing a pink jacket that she immediately took off and folded next to her.

"Hannah, this is one of Mommy's friends from work," Andrea said. "Tara's going to be staying with us for a while, and she's agreed to let you make her over."

"Are you ready for this, Tara?" Hannah asked, solemn as anything. "You look nice now, but Mommy told me that she bought your clothes from Target, and that's not acceptable."

"We do have a budget, Hannah," Andrea replied.

Tara immediately loved having Hannah in the car. Her energy was a lot less chaotic than most of the children she'd interacted with so far, as well as some adults. She had strong feelings but carried them like building blocks and stacked them as fastidiously as she'd folded her jacket. She was the kind of reliable young girl who would be an absolute terror when she reached her teenage years, because then she would be able to order her thoughts to run circles around her parents.

* * * *

The outdoor mall boasted many more people, so Tara let Hannah take her hand. The added contact helped ground her, because Hannah knew exactly where she wanted to go and exactly what she wanted Tara to try on when she got there.

It was so nice not to have to figure out what went with what. Hannah explained everything while Andrea stood back, her arms crossed, wearing a smile she rarely showed while on the job.

When the stack of clothes on Tara's arm was too heavy for her to hold without almost falling face-forward, Hannah allowed her to go to the dressing room and told her through the curtains which pieces to try on first.

Before Tara closed the curtains, Andrea stopped her to add a few things to the hooks on the wall — some structured camisoles and bralettes. "At least until we can get you in a proper lingerie store."

Tara gave them a fashion show in front of the multi-planar mirrors outside the dressing rooms. The clothes Hannah had chosen at this particular store were similar to those Andrea wore on the job — plainer blouses and shirts, neutral pants, a leather jacket that was a lot like Noah's, so Tara loved it.

When Tara asked if Hannah was trying to make her look like her mom, Hannah pursed her lips and said, "I'm giving you outfits you can wear for anything. If you prefer statement pieces, we can do that next."

Tara raised her eyebrows at Andrea. Andrea shrugged while trying not to laugh.

Hannah wanted her to keep so many pieces that it would have broken three cops' budgets, but Andrea subtly suggested that Tara didn't need a million independent outfits so much as a capsule wardrobe. Hannah had a eureka moment and instead pointed to each piece of clothing she wanted Tara to have, explaining the myriad ways she could put those pieces together, then what kinds of things she could look for in the future based on the clothes left behind.

Hannah might have been eight years old, but every suggestion and recommendation was invaluable for

Tara, for whom clothes had only been cursory modesty so far, given that angels didn't wear clothing, although she'd admired them on humans.

"Can we stop by the bookstore before we go to the next place?" Hannah asked.

"We're going somewhere *else*?" Tara said.

"You just got everyday wear and business casual. You'll want a nice dress or a skirt or two to look pretty. You're a pretty lady. I think you'd look really good if you try."

"Hannah..." Andrea said, apologizing with her expression behind her daughter.

"No, she's right. I was just throwing shirts and pants together and wearing other people's jackets and calling it a day," Tara said. "You've been so helpful, Hannah, in more ways than one."

"You're welcome."

"Yes, we can stop by the bookstore first," Andrea conceded. "Want a hot chocolate while we're there?"

The three of them walked out into an evening that had gone from bright to dim, although the number of people had only increased. Tara held Hannah's hand more tightly.

Andrea noticed and hooked her arm around Tara's other arm. "Still okay? I should've warned you this place was only going to get more crowded after people got off work on a Friday night."

Tara shook her head. "It's fine. I need to get used to it."

"What's wrong?" Hannah asked.

"I get headaches and body aches around other people," Tara said.

"That sounds uncomfortable."

"It is. But you're helping with that, too, Hannah. You're very calming, and not just because you're competent."

Hannah was more solemn than her mother, her resting face deadly serious, but she beamed at the compliment.

Crossing the threshold into the bookstore, Tara breathed a sigh of relief.

"That's how I feel about it, too," Hannah said, squeezing Tara's hand before releasing it. "Mommy, I'm going to the Young Adult section."

"I'll bring the drink back to you."

"She's a delight," Tara said as Andrea led her to the in-store café. "I don't think I've met anyone like her yet. Her feelings are like things I can store on the shelves. She's so *tranquil*."

"Oh, she's got a little of her mother in her, too. But by and large, yes, she has her father's steadiness. It's a very lovely quality in both a little girl and a husband, and I'm glad that one of the things so prominent in her happens to be something I still like about him. Even though the damn divorce and custody battles were awful, I can at least trust that he's taking care of the kids and that he'll make good decisions on his own while I'm asleep and can't always collaborate."

"Do you mind my asking—"

"Oh, the same reason most cop marriages don't make it," Andrea replied. "Shit hours and risk. He doesn't believe in all that magic and spiritual hokum, which is also exhausting, but as detectives who work with Homicide, Assault, and Special Cases, we have all the risk of those departments plus the risks of beat cops, plus the risks of exorcists. And when your nightshift spouse comes home and crashes while you're balancing two kids… It's not easy being both a full-time employee and a sometimes-single parent. Hannah understands what I do more than Isaac. Isaac gets that I'm stopping the bad guys, and knowing his mom's a superhero is usually enough. But being a superhero makes it hard to be a mom. As much as I miss my kids and wish I'd gotten full custody, their dad can offer a more stable life than I can. I could have changed mine. I was ready to. But then he won, so…"

She shrugged, trying to pretend it didn't matter, but even if Tara weren't able to feel it, she saw it in the slight lift of Andrea's shoulders, self-protective, tense as humming electrical wires.

"He thinks I'm a superstitious bitch who put her job before her kids, and I think he's a condescending mansplainer who wanted a working wife who was also traditional, but once he got a faceful of what a working wife was like, he decided to chase the traditional wife instead. His new wife knows how to cook all this great organic shit, and I'm the one who's had to figure out healthy takeout. He's a good father. He might even be a good husband to the new wife. We're still mad at each other, and we'll never be friends again, but we're at a better place than we were before the divorce, I think. Otherwise, he would refuse to let Hannah be with me this weekend and say it was my fault I didn't make the most of my allotted visitation. I see what some of the other woman cops have to deal with. I could be luckier, but I appreciate that, at least."

"Is Hannah okay back there by herself?" Tara asked.

Andrea nodded. "I can't see her, but I see everyone entering and exiting her section, and they have an employee back there. She's old enough I have to let her have her free moments. At least it's not a playground, right?"

* * * *

At a sit-down restaurant with a menu as long as one of Hannah's new books, they ordered family style so Tara could try a little bit of everything, plus the obligatory cheesecake. Noah wasn't the only one fascinated by how much she ate and how she enjoyed it, although Tara took her cue from the people around her and tried not to moan quite as much. She'd already entertained Andrea once, but after Hannah finished her meal and half a cheesecake, she gazed with fascination that oscillated between horrified and impressed.

There were leftovers, but perhaps not as many as the waitress had expected when she asked if she needed to bring over some takeout containers.

"Can I touch your food baby?" Hannah asked.

"Hannah! That's beyond tactless and arriving at rude. You're old enough to know better." Andrea fought to look shocked while also fighting not to laugh in surprise.

"I just don't know where it all *went*."

Tara brought Hannah's hand to her belly, where Hannah poked and prodded, but not as uncomfortably as the doctor had. "Technically, most of it is still up here." She led Hannah's hand a little farther up her abdomen. Her stomach didn't look nearly as big as it felt.

Despite the energy spent in Noah's bed and at the station and the energy it took to handle all the feelings around her at all time, she thought she might finally be slowing down on how *much* food she needed. She no longer needed to heal. Now she just had the other expenditures to account for.

"Seriously, where did it all *go*?" Hannah said.

"It does get compressed as it's chewed," Andrea said. "Can we let Miss Tara digest in peace?"

"I think she has superpowers. See, even mine shows in my belly when I'm full." Hannah pushed out her stomach against her shirt.

"Some of that is other things. Hannah, stop looking at your belly and stop poking Miss Tara's. Good grief." But Andrea was giggling as she drew Hannah's hand away.

Tara looked down at herself. She wondered how much she would really gain over time. Even her skeleton seemed to be thin. She didn't feel one way or another about it, but other people seemed to. She just wondered whether, once she was expected to be part of this world properly, she would be able to afford her own appetite.

There was something important about that, something connected, but it left her as soon as she had the thought—like a little rabbit into its den, every time.

"You left us there for a moment," Andrea said. "Anything?"

"No. Sorry."

"Are you sick?" Hannah asked. "Mommy didn't explain why you were staying with us except that you got hurt and can't remember things. Do you not remember who your parents are? What town you were born in?"

"I remember those things. Vaguely." It was the whitest of lies, to keep things simpler.

"I'm glad you remember your parents. I don't want to think about if I couldn't remember Mommy and Daddy. Was it scary?"

"It was absolutely scary," Tara answered. "It's less scary now, and your mom and Noah have been helping me. Do you know Noah?"

"Oh, yes, Uncle Noah. He's not my real uncle, but Mommy and Daddy say he's practically family."

"They've been helping me find out more about myself and why I came here to Meridian. But I promise my parents know where I am. No one's missing me. Does that make you feel better?" Tara offered Hannah her hand again to pull her out of the booth while Andrea left cash on the table.

"Yes. I'd hate for you to wander the world and have no one to come home to," Hannah said.

An unexpected pang of homesickness shot through her chest. She tried to keep it to herself, but she might not have succeeded, because Andrea hooked her arm again and gave her an impromptu hug right there by their leftovers.

"She'll always have Uncle Noah and me as long as she's in town," Andrea said. "Ready to get sized for a bra? It's not the most fun thing in the world to do, but at the very least, people will stop noticing how perky you are when you're cold. And you're as cold as you are hungry."

"Is it that bad? Do people really notice such little things?" Tara didn't think it was any different from a man who was cold.

"It's not bad, but yes, people really do notice such little things," Andrea replied. "Shapewear helps nice clothes look even nicer, cleans up the lines, accentuates like makeup. Of course, it's up to you if you want to wear a bra. Either way, you look great, but I assure you, people are noticing."

"People are strange."

"I don't disagree. Come on, let's get you in a thong."

"Mom!" Hannah said.

"I was just kidding." But she turned to Tara and playfully mouthed, *"No, I wasn't."*

* * * *

Tara expected Andrea to be a part of the process in the lingerie store, but instead she sat with Hannah in the front of the store while the sales associates took Tara into the back for a fitting. Andrea did make sure to preface the session with Tara's concussion to explain why she was mostly unfamiliar with the intricacies of bras. Tara liked fashion in general but had lost track of undergarments somewhere in the eighteen-hundreds out of disinterest.

"Now, this one is going to make a dent in my checking account," Andrea had muttered before Tara had gone back with the associate. "Good thing it's payday."

"I'll pay you back when I get the chance."

"You bet your ass."

But Tara had the oddest impression that they weren't talking about the same thing, because before she'd been ushered back by the gentle associate, she'd been hit with another blow of arousal that had taken her a few long minutes to subside. It wasn't helped by the associate responding to her, amplifying the feeling. However, she didn't seem to associate her reaction with Tara, and she remained completely professional as she urged Tara to remove her top so they could measure her upper half.

As soon as they determined her size, they entered with several styles of bras and underwear for her to try.

Spending so much time in front of a mirror like this, her reflection started seeming less and less like her, especially in the kinds of underwear they brought, although she kept emphasizing she didn't prefer the extra thrills and frills. Eventually, though, she managed to choose three bras and a small selection of underwear.

Just after she left the dressing room, Tara paused at a few racks. A red corset adorned in gold made her think of her wings. A few racks over were shaping slips. She didn't need shaping, but she liked the idea of how they *showed* shape. She found herself connecting for the first time to the sense of being *feminine*, of being a woman and choosing to emphasize that.

Andrea slipped behind her and grabbed the smallest size in both, then brought everything to the counter, including something she'd picked up for herself from the pajama section.

As soon as they were out of the store, Hannah pulled Tara along the wheel-shape of the mall until she found a store she liked, which displayed mostly white and black clothes but also accents in jewel tones.

"Okay. But just one or two things from here," Andrea said.

"This is already too much," Tara said. "I have more than I need."

"You *need* to try one of these." Hannah picked up a red silk dress, then a gray lace sheath. "And this. I want to see you in them."

"She's not a Barbie doll, Han," Andrea said. "If she's not comfortable, she doesn't have to. You *don't* have to if you don't want to, Tara."

"It's all right. It's just two dresses." Tara accepted the hangers from Hannah, who beamed again with more than just a smile, but with the happiness of being taken seriously. "And I should try it with one of my newest purchases, the way it was intended."

The dressing rooms here had doors rather than curtains or stalls. She went in with the bag from the lingerie store and removed her clothing in a gently lit room with yet another massive mirror that made her more uncomfortable than when she'd started this whole exercise. But she unzipped the silk gown and, once she figured out which side was the front, she stepped in and pulled the straps over her arms.

When she tried to zip the dress up, it gaped above where she could reach.

"Andrea? Can you come help me?" Tara called over the top of the door.

"Coming."

Tara unlocked the door so she could slip in. "I can't reach the top of the zipper."

Andrea froze in the doorway, lips parted as she stared at Tara in front of her as well as in the mirror.

"Yeah," she said, breaking her reverie with a little shake and stepping forward for the zipper midway up Tara's back. "You usually get someone to do it up for you like this, but there are also tools you can use for when you're alone. Or you could just unravel one of those large paper clips and hook it in. Same principle. I use that for bracelet clasps, too."

She drew the zipper all the way to the top of the dress, then framed Tara's shoulder blades with her fingers. "Does it hurt?"

"Does what hurt?"

"Well, I'd say, 'Did it hurt when you fell from heaven?' But we already know it did. Did you not know that the stumps of your wings are still here? Most humans can't see them, but Noah and I have the All-Seeing Eye tattoo that pierces through masking spells."

Tara turned around toward Andrea so that she could look in the mirror at her back. The long skirt on the dress and the shape of the bodice made her look seven feet tall, but she was more concerned about her shoulders, where the wing stumps jutted, ugly and vicious.

She winced as she tried to touch them, but they were as out of reach as the zipper. The only open wounds left on her, like broken tree branches. She felt nothing, though, and it wasn't easy to stare at her back — small mercies, but a constant reminder of what she'd lost. Her eyes grew red and watery as she tried harder to feel where her wings had been but kept turning, like a cat trying to catch its tail.

"Oh, sweetheart. It's okay. It means you were an angel, and still are. The demons should remember that when they see their own." Andrea slid her hands up to rub Tara's shoulders. "They're waiting for their wings again. Which means there's something to wait for."

"Unless I choose to be a demon. That'll give me new wings," Tara said quietly, matching Andrea's volume. A gap between the top of the door and the ceiling meant no real privacy in their conversation.

"Tara, I just watched you heal two dozen kids of feral infection," Andrea replied. "You ease people's suffering. You don't cause it. And when you do, it distresses you sick. You're not going to become a demon. You care too much."

"What if I choose to become a demon so I won't have to feel like this all the time, this pain?"

Andrea stroked Tara's cheeks and framed her face with her palms. "I know this probably isn't something you want to hear, but living is painful. I have friends with ME, lupus, Sjögren's. I have friends with bullet and knife wounds. They live with pain all the time. And I know I ache more than I did when I was in my twenties. It's hard to remember when things didn't creak whenever I got up. Pain is the other side of what you love. There's not a way to filter out one without the other. Now, do you want to show Hannah the dress? She'll flip. Or do you think it's too…"

Andrea slid her hands from Tara's face down to her neck, to the top part of her chest as she took in the sight. A good bra made all the difference in the lines created, and it certainly made her breasts seem larger. But Tara was distracted instead by what Andrea felt as she slipped her hands down over those breasts, feeling her through the bra, then down to the structured bodice, which created an hourglass shape where she didn't have much of one.

Tara tried to use what she'd learned in the hospital about creating her own calm against the desire. "Yes. Yes, I should let Hannah see. She chose it."

Andrea took a step back, nodding and licking her lips lightly. She opened the door and led Tara out to where Hannah waited for them with one of her new books in her lap. Her eyes lit up like lanterns.

"Mommy, can you find her some shoes? She needs a heel."

Andrea put her foot next to Tara's to do a quick guess at size, then headed out while Hannah joined Tara in front this store's multiplanar mirror.

"You look like you could be on a magazine cover for Christmas or Valentine's," Hannah said. "Will I look like that when I grow up?"

"You'll probably look like your mom or your father's sisters, if he has any. Or you might look like one of your grandmothers." Tara laughed at Hannah's face.

"Not as they are now, but when they were young. That's how it tends to happen, but you never know. Do you think I need a haircut?" She tousled her messy mop of dark hair.

"You don't need one," Hannah said. "But the look would be improved if you did."

Andrea giggled madly again as she handed Tara heeled black sandals. "God, I love you, Hannah. Can you put these on, or do you need help?"

Tara tried, but she kept losing her balance on the heel, so Andrea knelt to help do up the straps.

"See, this is what heels do to your ass. They also weaken certain areas of your legs, but if you wear them in moderation, you can really dress up a nice outfit or gown like this. Should we try the sheath dress, Han?"

Hannah nodded and headed back to her bench.

"Can you help me?" Tara asked, anticipating trouble opening the dress and closing the next one.

Back in the dressing room, Andrea immediately drew the dress's zipper down, then backed away as Tara shrugged out of the gown. She probably needed to remind herself to be more modest by human standards, but Andrea had already seen her in far less, as well as far less flattering coverings, so she didn't think anything of it except in keeping Andrea's reaction from overwhelming her protective shield.

Tara pulled on the sheath dress, which was apparently designed to cling. Andrea swore in a whisper as she helped Tara zip up the back of this dress, too.

"Yeah, you need to get these. The only danger is that damage could be done to them behind closed doors. Because *damn*."

"They look good?"

"Oh, darling... For an angel, you're pretty as hell."

Hannah expressed her own approval out in the dressing room, especially regarding how long Tara's legs looked between the higher hemline of the dress midthigh and her heels. Tara twirled for her, though the skirt of the other dress would have been better for that. Andrea laughed from the dressing room doorframe, because not only was Tara dizzy from spinning but the shoes weren't conducive to balance. Hannah had to prop her back up.

Tara was laughing, too, all the way back to the dressing room, where Andrea shut the door behind them and slowly pulled down the zipper.

Tara didn't think she was just being careful. She cautiously let her shield fall as Andrea unzipped the dress down to the edge of the new underwear.

Andrea gasped at Tara's reaction to Andrea's reaction, and it rocked back and forth from there.

Andrea pressed ardent lips between where Tara's wings had been. With Tara's additional inches, Andrea couldn't reach much higher, but she brought her hands down over Tara's hips and pulled her back, stroking over the lace. Then, with no resistance from Tara, Andrea spun her around and walked her back against the mirror, then stood on her toes and pulled Tara down for a kiss, this one hungrier than in the station. They were in a much more private setting here.

"Mom, I'm going back out to sit in the store. It's hard to read under these lights."

"Okay, sweetie!" Andrea called back, only a little breathless.

She whimpered slightly as she parted her lips to meet Tara's tongue, a different kind of dessert that Andrea wasn't too full to enjoy. On the contrary, she seemed more and more famished as lust built between them.

Kissing Andrea was as pleasant as kissing Noah, but in a completely different way, not least because of height difference, whereas Tara and Noah were almost at eye level with each other. It gave her a level of control, but Andrea was more aggressive, perhaps from experience that Tara lacked even with what sex she'd already had. She didn't resist as Andrea eased the dress down from her arms and over her hips, helped her out of it to toss it onto the bench and pull them back together again. Tara slid her hands under Andrea's shirt, feeling where she was lusher than any of Tara's angles. She envied as much as enjoyed it.

Andrea panted into her mouth as she pushed Tara down onto the bench to straddle her, making them more even. "God, I've been trying so hard not to think about this, but you tested my resolve with these fashion shows. First, business-lesbian Barbie, and now full-on lipstick even without makeup, which I didn't know you could do." Andrea dipped down to kiss her neck, then lick her earlobe, which made Tara shiver and grasp at Andrea's thighs to draw her closer. "I don't think you should get that haircut. If you got an undercut or one of those fauxhawks, I might just melt every time I see you. It'd be too much pretty for one person."

"I've been trying to hold it back, but I don't know if I can... I don't know if I want to." Tara pushed down her bra straps and the cups, too frustrated to undo the clasp in the front, so Andrea kissed down to her breast to do it for her. "Oh, that's different. That's different."

She was intimately acquainted with how a man's arousal made her feel, like electricity straight down between her legs and an urgency that drove her almost to violence, but although Andrea's was just as powerful, it *spread* more, bubbled up her spine to make her drunk with pleasure. Slower, sweeter, like a lingering bite of chocolate cheesecake. She wanted to groan but respected that they had to keep quiet here, as with Noah in their office.

Instead, she pulled Andrea's hair out of its ponytail and muffled her sighs in it, felt how much Andrea liked that, even as she tested Tara's resolve with her teeth on the nipple, then lashing the tip with her tongue. Tara fell back against the wall, panting hard, caught between the pain and the pleasure, and both were *good*.

Hours in Noah's bed, another few frantic times in the office, now here in a dressing room... And she and Andrea were going to be together all weekend, day, night... Was there an end to her body wanting this, anywhere she was, with anyone at all? Oh, she didn't think she would really do this with everyone, but if their pleasure was powerful enough, could she trust herself to refuse, any more than she could say no to a plate of tasty food?

"You're the wickedest angel I've ever had the pleasure to kiss," Andrea said, climbing down from the bench to push Tara's legs apart and kneel between them. She licked little curlicues over Tara's left thigh up to her new underwear, damp in its center. "Some of it is your power, but I can't remember even a succubus turning me on this well. After everything we did while Hannah was in school, if Mattea hadn't been such a sad place, I would have found a way to get you into an empty room there. I didn't know I could want someone this much, even when you aren't there. I've tried to be professional, but I'm sorry. I just can't..."

She mouthed over the damp spot on Tara's underwear, making her wetter and hotter. Then she pulled them down so she could flick her tongue over the hood like she had the nipple, gentle, then burying her mouth against the hair there to suck at the hood and flood her clit with the swirl of saliva that Andrea drank back down in a desperate swallow.

Tara stuffed her hand into her mouth, biting down instead of crying out. She tangled her other fingers in Andrea's hair just as she found a rhythm that made Tara's eyes roll back.

Then her eyes flew open. She pushed back on Andrea's forehead. "What did you just say?"

"I've tried to be professional?" Andrea wiped her mouth with the back of her hand. She had entirely too many clothes on, but she still looked beautiful, with darkened, shadowed eyes.

"No, something about 'everything we did'…"

"You know, everything we did while the blackout shades were down. Like making love under a midnight sun."

Tara pulled her underwear back up and reached for her jeans and long-sleeved shirt—plain in comparison to everything else she'd worn tonight.

"What's going on?" Andrea tentatively pulled herself up, spinning Tara's head in a storm cloud of thwarted arousal, bewilderment, and hurt.

But Tara was too distracted by trying to make sense of what Andrea had said. She tried to find a path for it to be real—as though if she looked at it from another angle, it would make more sense. It didn't.

"Andrea, I didn't spend off-shift with you. I went to Noah's to sleep."

"No. After the kids went to school, you knocked on my door and said you and Noah had been eating when you decided you wanted to stay with me instead. I was confused why he didn't call or text about it, but since you were there, I had you stay on the couch, because I hadn't cleaned Isaac's sheets yet. Then you had a nightmare and… And you don't remember any of this, do you?"

"I spent off-shift with *Noah*. I woke *him* up, mad at him. We had sex for almost the rest of the day. That's why I was so tired this evening. And that's why you were so late today," Tara realized. Things were falling into place, but the places were all askew. "Because I did the same thing with you. But it wasn't me, Andrea. It wasn't *me*."

"Then why did you let me kiss you at the station? Why did you let me… Oh, God. You were just going to have sex with both of us and not say anything?"

"The both of you were just…" Tara gestured at herself, although fully dressed now. "You took me by surprise. The emotions spiraled for the both of you. You both liked watching me eat. I was spreading desire everywhere after he kissed me on the roof. I didn't know whether you were just responding to that or… But you *weren't* with me off-shift. Which means you were with *her*."

Andrea's eyes widened. "Son of a bitch. The woman who looks like you. The one the kids were talking about. But, Tara, she didn't have long hair. She looked exactly like you. Maybe a *little* different, now that I'm thinking about it, but she sounded like you, and she was sweet and straightforward like you and…"

"I think I know why." Tara dragged Andrea out of the dressing room. "Call Noah. Call Noah right now."

Chapter Thirteen

After Andrea and Tara left, Noah stayed in the Mattea parking garage for a while to work on some reports while he was in the shade and everything was still fresh, which meant he could lie better.

He and Andrea had made lying into an art, embellishing reports that they'd send to the respective detectives in such a way that it was unimpeachable from a legal perspective. If anyone came back and asked pointed questions or gave a more detailed and less likely perspective of the miraculous things that had happened, it would still be in line with what they wrote. Even so, the District Attorney's Office had been briefed long ago to bring him and Andrea to court as infrequently as possible.

Sometimes defense attorneys liked to call them as witnesses to use Q Division's reputation to discredit the prosecution and MPD, but the supernatural side of Meridian didn't particularly like attention. Those green attorneys quickly learned that pointing official attention in their direction quickly led to very scary things in their room at night, or popping up in their cars in darkened lots.

Andrea and Noah weren't untouchable, by any means, but they were an understood Meridian variable, like the twenty-four-hour coffee joints and bars.

No one liked to receive report emails from Q Division, but whether they liked it or not, Noah and Andrea were part of this feral children problem. The good thing was that they had a cure—of a kind. Noah couldn't describe it as magic, but he could write that Tara's skill in calming children bordered on miraculous without being dishonest. Dr. Kim would unequivocally swear to the same. He was probably still singing her praises. He hadn't wanted to let her leave.

But Noah and Andrea had been able to tell how draining the effort had been for her. She'd only just figured out how to control it, and that control wasn't perfect. It was amazing she hadn't tapped out after the first dozen, because every child broke down when they lost their fear, as though she'd worked a constricting snake from around their necks. It must have been such a weight lifted from the children, but that was weight Tara then had to carry. And she'd carried it for all twenty-two children in that pediatric ward.

She'd promised to come back in a few days, though, to offer her services to other children who had already been taken home. Dr. Kim hadn't been able to guarantee that they'd all be there, but after seeing what fear had turned their kids into, the promise of a cure would be nearly irresistible for their parents.

A knock on the passenger-side window made him jump.

"Jesus." Noah rolled down the window. "Don't scare a cop like that. I could have pulled my goddamned gun."

"What would be the solution here?" Tara asked, grinning. "How do I let you know I'm here when you're so occupied by your work? Is there anything I could have done that would have had a better outcome?"

"Maybe calling my name from a distance. Or having Andrea text me before bringing you back. What are you doing here?"

"After such an exhausting day, I told Andrea I wanted to spend the rest of your shift and off with you. I'll sleep in the car as needed."

"Wouldn't it be better to sleep in a bed?" Noah said. "And what about that shopping spree with Hannah she had planned?"

"I'd rather wait until I get some rest. I'm just not up for it after…" She nodded in the direction of Mattea's distinctive architecture. "Andrea dropped me off. She said she was going to text you, but Hannah could have distracted her. I guess it slipped her mind."

"I'll bet Hannah's disappointed. She was looking forward to the princess makeover."

"She'll get one. I promised her. When I'm not too tired to appreciate it. Do you mind?"

"Nope. I should even be able to drive you to wherever they wanted to take you tomorrow. I haven't seen Hannah in a while, and we usually try to make a point of having Uncle Noah time so she knows I'm not stealing her mother away out of spite. Come on in. I'm about done here, but you can take a break while I finish up. Then we can grab something to eat before I go on my rounds. Sound good?"

Tara slipped into the seat and did up her belt. "Ready when you are."

* * * *

Noah took her by a sandwich shop and relished watching her chow down on a complicated sandwich while trying not to make a mess in his car. He chose a less complicated sandwich so he could grab bites at red lights while listening to the scanner for anything that sounded more out of the ordinary than usual. He was only a little disappointed that she might finally be settling into more average eating habits, because she didn't attack the sandwich quite like a deranged hyena. She did, however, polish off the whole sandwich, a cup of soup, her cookie, his cookie, and a cup of soda. She still savored, and she still impressed.

"Did you have anywhere else you needed to go while we're out on rounds? We can stop by another cemetery. Surely one angel doesn't have the answer to everything."

"I'd just like to observe tonight," Tara said. "Maybe nap. I'll need plenty of energy for later."

She looked at him shyly and reached across to slide her hand over his leg. She didn't slide it down to his knee nor up to the front of his pants, but despite her shyness, she met his eyes until the car behind him honked because he'd failed to go on green—mostly because another part of his anatomy had decided to go without him. And when her desire rose to meet his, he feared he'd have to pull over, but she withdrew her hand and pulled her feelings back with it. When next he glanced over at her, she was looking out of her window with a contented smile.

Once again, he was afraid of how powerfully he responded to that smile—not in his penis but somewhere in his chest and all the way down to his toes. Such power in another person's hands was dangerous enough anywhere else, but even more so in Meridian, because she was one of the weird things that happened here, and so was he, and that put both of them in a different kind of crosshairs—not marked for death but strife.

His work gave him enough distraction, though, especially when he reached the eastside enclaves where the standard homeless spent their nights. The unhoused were often the first line of fodder for demons and their cults who wanted to snatch someone who wouldn't be missed by a census' reckoning. Like many big cities, Meridian had its share of shelters, some of which were also churches, but there were plenty unhoused who wanted nothing to do with those shelters, and the church ones in particular.

There were unhoused hunters as well, those who had given their lives to the hunt. When it was a calling rather than a mere occupation, it wasn't as though there were grants they could apply for. Collectives allowed hunters to profit-share off their kills, but for true believers, hunting for profit meant ignoring demons who weren't of sufficient monetary value but still had a detrimental effect on the world. They were more likely than most hunters to go after low-value pestilence demons, not least because pestilence demons also were more likely to attack the unhoused when they wanted something low-risk and fresh.

Unhoused hunters were highly distrustful of most people, especially cops. Noah and Andrea were the exceptions. The hunters could always call and get picked up if they needed medical assistance, and if the hunters had a lead for danger beyond their means, Noah and Andrea would help. And like the other people living in these enclaves, these hunters could use the snacks and meals that Q Division handed out without trying to roust them.

Tara watched him through the passenger-side window, a solemn, pale face with keen eyes, more gold under the streetlights than green.

She was already better since Mattea, which suggested she'd be able to build a life beyond this investigation sooner than she might think. Then maybe he wouldn't see her so often. People passed in and out of his life all the time, but the idea of losing her left him maudlin. Oh, dayshift and nightshift people weren't so far apart. They had almost the same downtime overlap, with one working while the other slept. The problem with a cop's shift was that it was longer, giving them less opportunity for overlap.

And Tara needed to see the sun. She needed her chance in the light, with people and laughter and all the food she could eat. He couldn't be selfish because of how she made him feel, how *much* she made him feel. That was what she did, who she was.

He had to just enjoy the time they had, and if that meant enjoying it a particular way, then he would. Simultaneous orgasms had their problems and were mostly pipe dreams outside the supernatural, but he enjoyed them with her, mess notwithstanding. After the first few times, it didn't even damage his ego.

After his eastside rounds, he drove to Cemetery Grove and surrounding neighborhoods, because the warehouses and abandoned buildings ensured that there would never be an end to the demon cults. The job here was to search for people being abducted where there wasn't another hunter on the case. There were plenty in the area, but since there were an endless number of cults, always getting replaced, individuals could only do so much.

Finally, he headed toward Endicott Park, which was one part of the gash of forestland that carved through the middle of the city near UTM.

Perhaps it wasn't appropriate to view nature as the destructive force, considering it had been there before the city had built itself around it, leaving little more than copses of trees and the creek to help with city drainage when it rained — which wasn't often but could be apocalyptic when it did. When viewed from above, however, the three parks certainly looked like claw marks between more ordered buildings and streets — a little bit of wild to remind settlers that Meridian wasn't tame.

Noah turned up the air conditioning twice before realizing that, one, Tara needed it to be less cold and, two, he was getting warm from something other than the car temperature. Sweat rose to the surface over his flushing skin. His cock — which had been awake since the enclaves, if not necessarily upright — now pressed against the front of his pants. The darker the world outside the car, due to greater foliage and fewer lights, the more he wanted her.

He swerved into a parking lot and switched off the car. No lights now except the dim streetlight above them.

"Is it safe?" That was all Tara had to ask.

"The packs that run here don't bother anyone," Noah said. "Thank God the woman responsible for these attacks hasn't gone after the already half-feral children's packs around here, right?"

He and Tara unbuckled their seatbelts. Tara pulled her shirt over her head, then pushed her jeans down to leave them on the floor. She quickly climbed over him, naked except for her underwear.

"Yes," she murmured against his lips, "thank God."

Noah didn't keep condoms in the glove compartment, and he hadn't been planning to use them this weekend at all, with Tara at Andrea's. He did keep a few in his briefcase in the back seat. However, he couldn't reach them, not while Tara was kissing him like this. All he wanted to do was stroke over her long body, which rubbed with sinuous rhythm against his as she unbuttoned his shirt and pants.

Beat cops broke up trysts like this all the time. Noah hoped to God and baby Jesus no MPD shop made its way along the park's edge for a while. It was late for necking, even for horny teenagers, and neither he nor Tara was a teenager, regardless of how horny Tara made him. It would be more embarrassing than usual to be caught, which made it all the sexier, like the fact he wasn't supposed to be having sex with her while her case was still open. Yet he was all too willing to throw away the rules for her. In the back of his mind, he harbored quiet concern about what else he would be willing to do if she asked it of him.

She grabbed the lever that sent his seat pitching backward, then laughed as she nearly mashed her face against his from the speed of the fall. She pushed herself up by his chest, still laughing. Just the toss of her hair and the sight of her breasts in the low light enchanted him. She was still so new here that she hadn't learned self-consciousness. It was refreshing and sexy and his cock was trying to bore through his briefs.

She licked her palm and reached between her parted legs to take hold of him like that lever and draw him out, sending him pitching in a whole new way.

Here, alone, Noah moaned like they were back in his bed and probably disturbing the neighbors. He raised his hips to meet her hand, which did much better on his cock than someone who'd never done this before should have been able to manage, but he wasn't complaining at all.

His phone rang.

He tore away from Tara's needy kiss with a frustrated groan that wasn't helped as she only stroked his cock faster and harder.

"Leave it," Tara moaned into his ear before rubbing her cheek against his hair like a cat.

"I can't. I'm on shift *and* on call all weekend. I shouldn't be here, but I definitely shouldn't let that go to voicemail."

She fumbled with the phone attached to his dash to keep it out of his reach, but when he tried to lunge for it, her ass pushed against the horn, an abrupt declaration in the dark night way too late. Startled, she dropped it on the passenger-side mat. They both laughed, but he bent with some difficulty to reach it before she could.

"Fine," Tara muttered. She clambered onto her seat.

He turned his phone every which way to figure out where to swipe. By the time he had it right-side up, the caller ID read that Andrea had called. He wasn't concerned. If she really needed something, she would text or leave a voicemail.

Tara crawled forward again and took his cock in her mouth as enthusiastically as she ate everything else, and his brain briefly short-circuited. He couldn't tell anyone his name, much less figure out how to call back.

The light from the phone illuminated the beautiful, almost sinuous motion of her slender back as she bobbed over him with relish. Her wing stumps were just as alarming in dim light as bright, and her largish birthmarks — a misnomer for her — on her left side were still prominent against the paleness of the rest of her. She moaned as she took in him, because every bit of pleasure she gave him, she gave herself.

The phone vibrated with the notification that Andrea had left a voicemail. Then she immediately called him again. She wasn't sending emergency texts yet, but there was no reason she'd call him back like that unless whatever she was calling about was time-sensitive or dangerous.

Just as he was about to answer the phone, he glanced again at the beautiful length of Tara's back. Something was wrong. Not the wing stumps. That was a given. Something was different. She looked like she'd gained a little weight, which was fine, but something... something...

The birthmarks.

He'd been there when the pictures had been taken of her whole healing body. He'd kept a mental record of every significant mark to note in her Jane Doe file. He distinctly remembered not just the scars and scabs of her fall, which were no longer there, but that those three birthmarks were on her *right* side.

These were on her left.

Noah nearly came from what panic sent through him. Adrenaline was a strange hormone — it could make him soft or it could make him harder, and with the woman's mouth both around him and the source of his panic, his cock had decided to go in the direction of the latter. She groaned, reaching between her legs to touch herself, which only brought him closer. Then she slowly sucked up the length of his erection to look up at him with the most glorious bedroom eyes that he would have come for if he hadn't known those eyes weren't Tara's.

"What's wrong? Something happened. What are you afraid of?"

She seemed so innocuous, as innocent as Tara, but her capacity for deception indicated how untrustworthy that innocence was.

"Sorry. It's my partner. She's calling back again. That must mean something's really wrong. I'll just..." Noah swiped to answer the phone. "Hey, Andrea. What's going on?"

"Noah, the woman who the kids described as looking like Tara, she looks *just* like her now. She was with me off shift."

The woman responsible for everything took his cock in her wicked mouth again as his stomach sank like a stone. Everything rushed out of his mind because there wasn't room for anything but his climax. The woman moaned her own around him as she swallowed, swallowed.

"Noah, I have Tara here with me," Andrea said. "Is she there with you?"

"Yes. Yes." He tried not to let it sound so much like afterglow while the woman continued to sweetly suck the last pulses of cum from him. "I know. Yes, we'll be careful."

The woman would be able to feel how conflicted he was, how afraid and turned on and angry and heart-sick, but if she was anything like Tara, she wouldn't know *why*. She was a good liar, but so was he. He'd had to be diplomatic before. He'd had to indulge in delusion. He'd had to let people go he didn't want to, because he had no legal standing to arrest someone for a terrible thing that wasn't against the law. And he'd been selling falsehoods in reports and in court—lying for the truth—for so long that it was nothing to make up a true-enough lie for the woman's benefit while her teeth were a little too close to his dick.

"She made me think she was Tara," Andrea continued. "I didn't question it. I don't know what she wants, but Tara says she knows who she is. Where are you? We'll meet you there."

"We'll keep a lookout while we're in the parks," Noah replied. "We're partway through Endicott. We should reach Crestwood soon. I wanted to talk with pack leaders."

"Try to keep her occupied, and don't get killed. We'll be right there."

"No, you were right to worry," Noah said. "But I think we're fine for now. I'll see you in a few."

He ended the call but kept his phone on. Andrea had a tracker app. If he went MIA, she would follow that, if she wasn't already. But if she was at the Wheel, like she'd planned with Tara, that was on the other side of downtown. Even after midnight, it would take her as long as ten minutes to catch up to Endicott, much less the other parks if he and the woman ended up moving from their parking space.

Now that he knew she wasn't Tara, he could tell how much she wasn't. She had more meat on her bones—

although not a lot more, which suggested a certain shared blueprint in both. He remembered noticing that her eyes had a golden cast, although hazel could be unreliably shifty under different lights. She had more defined hips, and in greater contrast, more defined breasts, whereas Tara had nearly nothing. The woman had hidden the difference under her black long-sleeved T-shirt, which wasn't exactly the same as the one Tara had been wearing, although the jeans were. So she'd known where Andrea had bought the clothes but hadn't been able to find the same long-sleeved T-shirt or hadn't been able to tell the difference herself. And she'd had her hair cut to a similar length to Tara's, but it was a little shorter.

Had the woman been a shapeshifter, she would have made herself look *just* like Tara. So she wasn't a shapeshifter.

Not a copy. Mirror images.

Mirror twins.

He hadn't known that angels could be twins, especially considering they weren't born, but the one who'd created them could create them however He pleased.

This woman had been watching them for long enough to know that Tara was there, long enough to copy her mannerisms and ingratiate herself with the people taking care of her. She knew that Tara had fallen.

Tara fell because of her. Because she'd seen what her twin had been doing.

Goddammit, Tara had lost her wings to stop her. Put herself in the path of Andrea and Noah to stop her. And instead, both Andrea and he had been taken in—in some cases, quite literally—because of her.

"What's going on?" The woman wiped her lips and settled back on her heels.

"Someone on nightshift thought they saw the woman responsible for the feral children in Cemetery Grove, headed in the direction of the parks. We so infrequently get help from the beat cops for the APBs we put out, we have to take this one extra seriously. Andrea is on her way."

The woman smiled, utterly relaxed. "I don't have to have heard all the conversation, nor do I have to read your mind. You know I'm not Tara. I was just having so much fun that I didn't want to stop, and I knew you'd want to play along for as long as you could. That's human self-preservation for you. But I don't have the same instinct, darling."

Noah tucked his cock back in his briefs and did up his pants, and she let him. Completely unconcerned for her life, although his hand was just a few inches away from his weapon.

He buttoned his shirt slowly, then turned on his car to switch the dash on, with its bright lights. He pushed on the overhead lights in the front, illuminating the woman in full.

"How did you know, out of curiosity?" she asked. "You panicked *before* the call. You knew. Andrea didn't know, even though she'd seen Tara just as up close and personal as you. Unless…unless my dear twin was even more personally involved with you than I gave her credit for. Oh, I know about the rooftop, but that was mere curiosity, her powerlessness and yours under the influence of her power. I thought you'd be too much of a white hat to have sex with someone so clearly out of control."

"Your birthmarks are on opposite sides." No point in pretending he didn't know what she was talking about.

She snorted, twisting around to try to see. "Seriously? I didn't even know that one. That's good. That's really good. I thought I came on too strong, but I guess she must have come on strong enough herself. I had to play a far more cautious explorer with Andrea. Sweet girl. Almost felt guilty exploiting her loneliness. I don't feel so bad with you now."

"Are you just saying that because you think it humanizes you? That you feel bad for seducing us?"

"Oh, please. 'Seducing you'? It's just sex, Noah."

"It's not, or else you wouldn't 'feel bad'."

The woman clasped her hands on her thighs and thinned her lips as she considered him. "Not all demons are alike, you know? Some angels desire indulgence, and some demons feel bad when they hurt someone. I feel people's feelings, Noah. I feel how bad I can make people feel, so it feels bad for me, too. And I'm sorry for that."

"Not sorry enough to not do it. And not sorry enough not to turn a bunch of fucking kids feral with fear and anger. How do you feel about that?"

"Vindicated. Is Tara coming, too? With your partner?"

"I assume so. They'll need to drop Hannah off with her sitter, though, so you and I still have some time alone."

The woman smiled. "You want to have another go? I'll do things with you she's never even heard of."

"I'm not interested in anything you could do to me. The only reason I did this was because I thought you were Tara."

"But now that you've gone and done it, what would another go hurt?"

"Ma'am, I'm not the sort to say no to the odd one-night stand, but I draw the line at demons when I can help it."

"That last phrase is doing an awful lot of heavy lifting." The woman leaned against her seat, her smile all the way to her eyes, with the kind of casual adoration that Noah had been afraid he'd show Tara.

"I know my limitations," he replied. "But *this* happened because you tricked me, and I don't want to give it another go. You hurt kids."

"I didn't hurt kids," the woman said. "The kids hurt you. There's a difference."

"What was the purpose of it all? Why make kids into your weapons? Was it just to convince her to fall or…"

"You can't imagine the bond, two angels created together, then split in half, one always part of the other. Sometimes, when her heart hurt, so did mine. Sometimes, when I yearned for more, she yearned, too. That I fell first and lost my wings and became strange to her doesn't mean we ever lost that connection."

She reached down for her shirt and jeans, bending in a way that should have been painful or at least uncomfortable. She gathered all her discarded clothes onto her seat and shook them out to don them again. Certainly not out of modesty, but perhaps she was prone to getting cold like Tara.

"Of course I wanted her to come down. God, she felt so far away. We once rested with our wings around each other, all eyes closed. Don't be afraid, Noah. I would never hurt her."

"You know, it's funny. I've never heard a demon talk about the time they were an angel. Their life seems to start with the fall."

"Well, I'm relatively new, I suppose," she said. "And maybe I'm not like any demon you've met before."

"Forgive me, ma'am, but that's not comforting."

"No, I suppose it's not. Oh, look. Either they have her daughter with them or the sitter was on the way."

His rearview window was obscured in part by the interior light, but he still managed to see the flashing portable bubble lights on Andrea's dash.

"That's my cue. Wish me luck." The woman pecked Noah's cheek before opening the door and stepping out.

He'd considered locking her in, but some demons weren't contained by things like that, and being in a closed car with a demon without a cage between them didn't seem like the smartest idea, either — not when he didn't know what kind of demon she was or what she wanted. He'd never met anyone like Tara, and since this woman had the same powers, he could safely say he'd never met a demon like her before, either.

"Hi, Andrea. Is Tara home?" the woman called.

Noah clambered out of his car after grabbing the good flashlight. Working flashlights were essential for a night-shifter, but this was one was good because it could double as a cudgel without the bulb going out. He confirmed that the car was Andrea's and that both she and Tara were in it. He couldn't tell if they'd brought Hannah with them. He didn't think there was a chance in hell Andrea would have put her daughter in danger, but if she thought Noah was going to die any second...

Noah shone his light on the woman.

"You fucking bitch," Andrea replied through her window.

"Yeah, kind of. But I want to talk with Tara right now, and I'm pretty sure she really wants to talk to me." She was so damn calm and relaxed. Tara could be peaceful, even calm, but not relaxed.

The passenger-side door of Andrea's car opened. Whispers passed between her and Tara, something like *don't go* and *I have to*, before Tara stepped out. Noah trained his flashlight on her instead, since Andrea's brights were covering the twin. Clothed, it was harder to tell the difference between them, other than posture. From the caution and rigidity of her neck and shoulders, though, the woman exiting Andrea's car was definitely Tara.

"Noah, are you okay?" Tara asked.

"Is Andrea?" Noah asked.

"I'm fine, fuckface. Why haven't you shot her yet?" Andrea shouted through her window.

"Because it would have been very loud in my car," Noah replied.

"Not because you were fucking her?"

"You're one to talk."

"If it weren't asshole-dark out there, I'd shoot you instead."

"Children, I think we're all grown-up enough to know how to share." The woman held up her hands to placate the two detectives, but she only had eyes for Tara. "Hello, Tara."

"Hello, Sela."

The woman clapped. "Oh, good. It's finally come back to you."

"Not all," Tara said. "Enough."

"If you knew how it hurt to see you fall, then to visit you in the hospital only to discover that you couldn't remember your own sister."

"Is that what we are?"

"Sister, brother, sibling, twin... Take your pick."

Tara stepped closer to her double. Noah wanted to tell her to stay back, stay away, that Sela had brought her here for a reason, but Tara probably knew that already. Andrea and he had done their jobs for both nephilim. The moves were up to them now — the ones with power.

"I'd already wanted to come down for so long," Tara said, "but then I saw what you were doing, and I had to stop you. I've *been* stopping you. I just didn't know it was you I was stopping."

"Are you sure you came to stop me and not to join me?" Sela stepped closer as well.

Andrea climbed out of her car, her backup pistol aimed. "Give me one reason, bitch."

"I wouldn't take the deception personally. Tara and I are so alike, all I had to do was cut my hair, dress down, pretend I didn't know things. The rest was real, sweetheart. And it seems it translated to the real Tara just fine."

Noah's flashlight wavered, but he didn't let it fall from where it needed to be, fixed on Tara. He couldn't get distracted by his own jealousy.

"We're mirror images of each other, Sela, but that doesn't mean we're alike," Tara said. "You fell out of the same curiosity, the same yearning as me, but you also fell because you wanted freedom to spread that yearning more than you wanted the freedom to indulge in it. We were both made to feel, but you twisted our unique empathy into something that destroys instead of saves. You fell to become the demon. I fell to protect them from you."

"You don't know why you fell yet. You think you know what you want, but you'll soon discover that you want *everything*. It's exhilarating, their love, their hate, their delight, their lust, their anger, their fear, and it's all yours, for the giving and taking. It's why we're *here*, Tara. We have a purpose, but not as angels. I can show you." Sela shook her shoulders. Wings as blue-black as ravens swept out to either side of her, a subtle contrast with their grackle-black hair. "I can give you your wings back."

"Those aren't our wings."

"They can't understand why we're here, Tara. All they know are foot soldiers, princes, drones, warriors in a spiritual battle. They know blood sacrifices and chanting cults. If they look to the pestilence demons, they'll *almost* understand us. We're not bad, Tara. We were simply made for this."

"No. We have a choice. We all have a choice. We *always* had a choice. I chose to fall, but I don't have to choose to be the same thing as you."

Tara was within arm's reach of Sela, but neither of them fought, although something invisible seemed to cycle between them, as powerful as a mighty wind. Noah feared what might happen if it spread beyond the sisters. Andrea hadn't witnessed the blood on the alley kids' faces.

"Why don't you explain it to us?" Noah shouted between the magic binding them together and bringing tears to Tara's eyes. "If we don't understand, why don't you tell us what you're supposed to be, if not bad?"

"You know the conquest demons, you've known pestilence, and you always knew death. It's been following you since your own fall," Sela replied, not looking away from Tara. "Tara and I are many emotions, but at strong enough levels, they all become wrath in the end—the seeds of war."

Andrea lowered her pistol. "Wait. Are you telling me that the Four Horsemen of the Apocalypse are already here?"

"Oh, sweetheart." Sela laughed so hard that Noah wanted to laugh with her, and Andrea cracked a bewildered smile. "What you call apocalypse has always been here. The end started at the beginning. Otherwise, why would we be at odds at all?"

"How does being one of the Four Horsemen make you not bad?" Noah said. "True, we're ambivalent about the pestilence demons, as long as they stick to the dead, but most conquest demons are our adversaries, and while death is inevitable and the death demons as much a part of life as birth, declaring yourself an agent of wrath and war might as well mark you as another enemy."

"We're not the enemy," Sela said. "You are. Tara, let me show you. You know how to bring peace, but do you know how to bring a sword?"

"Stop it, Sela." Tara held her head like she did when pain pressed in on her skull. "Stop pushing."

Andrea raised her gun again. "Let her go, you bitch."

"What do you think you're going to do with that?" Sela asked with a smile, spreading her wings as though to present a better target. "I'm not human."

"Your head can explode like anyone else's."

Sela held her hands out to Tara, beckoning her forward. "Come with me. You're weak, sister, too human for your own good. You think it stops with food and sex? I'll show you how to feel it all. I'll show you how to be strong."

"No, no, no, no... Sela, it hurts. It hurts too much. Stop."

"Let her go!" Noah shouted.

"Step away or I'll shoot, I swear to God!" Andrea added.

"I know it hurts, sister. But sometimes you need to break something to put it back together properly. It hurts because you keep holding it inside you when it wants to flow through, burst from you like sweet meat from ripe fruit."

"No, no, no! Ooooooh!" Tara's shouts rose into a howl as she desperately tried to hold her head together. Blood black in the flashlight beam dripped from her eyes, her nose.

Sela braced her hands on Tara's shoulders. "This isn't mine. This is man's. All yours to feel. All yours to use. As it was meant to be. We help start the wars they want anyway. We remind them that they are animals at their core. We remind ourselves and them that they are as pitiful as they are beautiful. Conquest makes them feel big. War shows them that they are small. Are you small, Tara?"

Tara switched from shouting to screaming, ripping through the skin on her scalp and face with her nails. When she opened her eyes, they weren't bloodshot, but Tara was completely absent. There was just anger and fear, the same anger and fear that had taken over the children, that had taken Tara in the alley.

"Shoot her, shoot her! For God's sake, shoot her!" Noah shouted at Andrea.

Andrea shot Sela in the chest three times. Textbook cluster, like they'd been taught. Sela stepped back with each blow as though punched. Her shirt shone with blood, but she barely blinked. Holy water, silver, fucking garlic… Noah didn't know what killed a wrath demon.

"Aim for the head!"

"You want to do it?" Andrea shouted back.

The flashlight was too big to use in conjunction with his service weapon, and he didn't want to take the light off Tara. "Tara, don't let her take you away. Remember us? Remember me? Tara, look at me. Look at me."

"I don't think you want her to do that, darling." Sela swung her wings in front of her in an X shape, hiding the exact location of her head. Andrea lowered her pistol a fraction in frustration.

Sela then flung her wings behind her and leaped while Tara continued scratching herself and screaming like a mountain lion. Sela whirled around in the air, then hooked her arms and legs under Tara's, becoming her wings. Sela's feathers buffeted the entire parking lot so strongly that dust caught in Noah's eyes, forcing him to cover them.

Andrea ducked against the wind to join him next to his car. "Fuck, you're just letting them go!"

"We don't know how to kill Sela, and I don't want to kill Tara trying." Already the wind was dying down. When he lifted his flashlight, he only caught the odd glimpse of wings in the dark sky, like a circling vulture.

"She practically killed her anyway. And now she's kidnapped Tara like a flying monkey to take her God knows where. To what? Bring about the End of Days?"

"I think the whole Four Horsemen thing is a red herring," Noah replied. "She's just a different kind of demon, and she doesn't think she's bad, which doesn't change that she is. But I think I know where she's going. And we're going to need some serious backup, because I think I gave her the idea."

Chapter Fourteen

Andrea waited until she and Noah had ducked into her car, Noah in the driver's seat, before she punched him in the arm.

"What?" Noah snapped, halfway through scrolling through his hunter contacts and wondering who he could trust to follow his instructions — or whether he had the luxury to make demands at all, given the shitstorm that was coming.

"I don't know. I just find myself overwhelmingly angry at you right now, and not in the wrath-demon feral-child way. I'm just..." Andrea hid her face behind her hands and rubbed at her forehead and eyes. "I had to drop my daughter off with a *bartender*, Noah. A bartender we know will protect her with her life, but still... And I had to realize that the woman I was with off shift *wasn't* Tara, while I was kissing the actual Tara... And then she said she'd been with *you* instead... I didn't foresee banging the same chick on my post-divorce bingo card, Dunn."

"Look, these are a lot of emotions, and valid ones — not just because we've been spending time with a contagious empath or two. I'm upset, too. But we can't afford to talk about them right now," Noah said. "I'm pretty sure Sela's taking Tara to the werewolf children's pack. If we end up with feral *werewolf* children on our streets, do you know what that's going to do to the Alliance?"

"Why is she even doing this?" Andrea said. "If it's not to usher in the End Times, why?"

"I think the first reason why she did it was to give Tara a reason to fall. But I really think she's just doing it because she wants to and she can."

"But why children? Who does that? I mean, demon cults do it, but she didn't invoke any princeling's name."

"I'm sure she has a reason, but will it be any better of a reason than a man who murders his wife and children before himself?" Noah said. "*Why* isn't as important at this point as *what* she's doing. Can you call in regarding your gunshots so no one comes sniffing around?"

While Noah ruminated, Andrea glared but called in to dispatch about a group of kids with cherry bombs near Endicott Park. He was pretty sure some dispatchers had figured out they lied half the time they called in, but if they ever reported it, it never got far enough for Loretta to call them out. One of these days, IA was going to get an idealistic newcomer, and Noah and Andrea would probably have to show someone a peek behind the curtain, but that had only happened once so far. That particular IA drone had resigned. Noah was pretty sure he'd ended up in seminary.

"Why matters," Andrea finally said after finishing with dispatch. "Why helps you figure out how to stop her. Why can break her." She pointed at some names on Noah's phone while he scrolled back and forth through. "These four are your best bet for a first call. And these three. They believe in the Alliance. They'll at least try to contain the situation before bringing out the good silver. Goddamn it, that bitch is going to force the kids *and* the adults protecting them to breach the treaty. The last thing we need is a pack of werewolf kids on the streets, and the second last thing we need is a full-out hunter-hybrid war."

"You take these." He sent her a cluster of contacts. "I'll take the rest. Get them to meet us in the Waffle House lot outside Crestwood."

* * * *

The people who worked at Waffle House didn't give an ever-loving shit what went down in their parking lot, as long as it didn't bleed into their restaurant, but Noah thought they were probably straining that apathetic hospitality with the number and eccentricities of the people who had agreed to come.

Some of their vehicles were clunkers from the previous century. Some were worn-down but reliable working trucks. A not-insignificant number were vanity trucks. But there were also a few luxury cars that indicated to Noah that, one, they were very good hunters or, two, they'd been called while off shift, like Andrea.

Even in Texas, it was a little odd to be in a restaurant parking lot with a bunch of rough-and-ready, mostly male hunters, some checking or storing ammunition, some putting their third gun in an ankle holster, some sharpening their knives while they waited for the assignment. And the group was more than a little tense. Hunters rarely congregated outside of hunter-frequented bars or during a meeting for their informal collectives. There were more formal hunter organizations, but hunters themselves tended to be introverts and loners — not mutually inclusive, but the traits often went hand in hand.

"Thank you for taking our calls and agreeing to come," Noah said. "We have a demon problem."

"What else is new?" chimed a hunter who hadn't shaved or trimmed his beard in a while.

"No commentary or interruption. I need everyone to not just hear me but listen. We have twin nephilim. One chose to become a demon. The other is human-ish with powers. She was the one who fell in front of the Archimedes Library."

There was some murmuring but no outright interruption.

"They are almost identical, and I say this because we really don't want the non-demon hurt. That means being especially observant in the dark if the demon isn't wearing her wings," Noah continued. "The more pressing problem is that the demon's the one who's responsible for children around this city going mean."

"Both nephilim have empathic powers," Andrea said. "Translation — they feel what you're feeling and can make you feel things. Tara, the recent fall, is still figuring out how to control hers. Sela, the demon, has complete control. Tara has learned how to cure the children, but she does better one at a time and hasn't had the opportunity to try a bigger group without hurting herself in the process. But Sela also rendered her feral the last we saw her. We don't know how feral, and we don't know what she's capable of when she's like this."

"They both have the skillset of succubi if they choose to share desire," Noah said, "but I don't know if the protections some of you use for sex demons will work against them, since they're not hybrids. Assume they won't. However, worse than that is Sela's use of fear and anger, and we shouldn't assume that because she's mostly done it to children, she can *only* do it to children, since she made Tara slip into that state twice."

"Interrupting." A hunter incongruously dressed in rockabilly costume—Cam Brumley, the one who Noah thought gave Andrea a ring now and then—kicked her pumps over the concrete as she sat in another hunter's trunk bed. "If she's slipped into that state twice, that implies she was able to slip out of it once. Can she slip out again?"

"The first time, she caught it from the kids. This time, she got it directly from the source," Noah said. "Not saying she can't, but with the demon making it happen and maybe keeping it happening, she might not be able to. That brings us to the kids and the reason we had to be selective about who we called. Sela's been going after human kids, bigger groups each time. I think she's heading for the werewolf children's pack next. And the two of us can't stand against a pack of feral werewolf children alone."

"When you say feral, what does that mean?" another hunter asked, this one older, with coarse gray hair and a coarse, lined face, prematurely aged with scars. "A feral cat will still feed from a hand if you're still long enough."

"Think *Cujo*," Andrea replied.

"Although the last big group of them acted more like a pack than a bunch of kids out of their minds," Noah added. "It's possible that they can become more sophisticated after enough time, but no less violent or effective. Which is even worse."

"And you want us to shoot the werewolf kids?" This hunter wore a dark hoodie, dark skin underneath. "Is that what this is?"

"*No*. We wanted people who *could* shoot the werewolf kids, but only as a last resort rather than a first solution," Noah said. "Caging, trapping, tranquilizers would be better."

More murmuring.

Noah held up his hands. "I *know*. I know it's not ideal. I know it's dangerous. I know that fully feral werewolves, without a single inhibited impulse in their brain, is a terrible idea and must be stopped. I also know that these are just kids who don't know what they're doing or why, and it isn't their fault. And we need to start looking for them now, because Sela has a forty-five-minute head start. We haven't heard any reports of big coyotes acting strange, but it could happen at any time. So, to sum up, we want to keep the children's werewolf pack contained, not killed. *They're* not breaking the Alliance. Someone else is breaking it. And if we could refrain from killing the wrong nephil, that would be nice, too. She might be our *only* chance of curing the werewolf children."

Cam waved. "Interrupting again. If the demon isn't a succubus, what is she? I've never heard of a demon who manipulates *all* the emotions like that. It's usually just one or two, isn't it?"

"And you'd know, Buffy?"

Cam daintily presented both middle fingers to the hunter who'd insulted her.

Andrea stepped between them. "Wrath demon, and they're apparently not the conquest demons or hybrids you're used to dealing with. No known weaknesses. Bullet to the head or decapitation is probably a good start."

"Sounds made up," Cam said.

"We've called in hunters for vampires, sex demons, demon cults, and werewolves, and you're skeptical?" Andrea said.

If there was sexual tension between them, Noah didn't see it. Then again, he hadn't seen it between her and Tara, either.

"We already know that pestilence and death demons are vaguer than the big bads y'all usually go after," Andrea said. "Just because we've never met someone who called themselves a wrath demon or demon of war doesn't mean we haven't met one. Neither Noah nor I could even tell that Sela wasn't Tara until Noah noticed a birthmark was on the wrong side."

"And just where was this birthmark?" Cam asked, immediately putting a finger on the detail Andrea had avoided.

"What matters is that she was completely able to fool us by acting like a typical human nephil."

"Demon twins. That's new."

"Tara's *not* a demon," Andrea shot back.

"How do you know?" the older hunter asked. "You said yourself that you didn't realize the demon was with you. The nephil could have already turned, and you'd never know."

"She's been healing kids instead of making them worse. Generally wanting to help," Noah said. "Yes, she still has a chance to become a demon, but hell, *we* have the chance to be terrible people. Yet most of us manage to avoid the worst of it."

"Speak for yourself," the older hunter said.

"If she becomes a demon, she's fair game, just like her twin," Noah said. "We'll address that if we come to it. For now, the objective is keeping werewolf children from leaving the forest and stopping the demon without killing the other nephil in the process."

"Control is the keyword here, not kill," Andrea said. "If you can't do that, then your services are no longer required, and you may go about your previously scheduled activities. Buh-bye."

Cam turned on her heel to go back to her car, a restored Beetle.

"Cam, don't be a dick," Andrea said.

"And if we decide that the safety of the city is more important than your druthers, what are you going to do about it?" the scruffy hunter asked.

"Guys, this isn't a test. You're not going to pass or fail or get thrown in jail. We know it would be easier to just toss a few grenades in their general direction and wait for the pestilence demons to clean up the mess," Noah said. "If you go off and do your own thing, we can't stop you. We just hope you help us instead. Please. At the very least, breaching the treaty is going to make the city much more unsafe, should the wolf elders decide in favor of retribution."

"We shouldn't even have the Alliance," another hunter, hidden in the shadows, grunted. "What do werewolves want to go running around city streets for anyway?"

"The treaty was made to stave off said bloody retribution when hunters went in and killed werewolves for their pelts, or just because they weren't fully human," Andrea said. "But we're not here for a history lesson. Are you in or out? Frankly, y'all owe us. We're on call for you twenty-four-seven, fetching, carrying, giving out information we technically shouldn't. We put ourselves on the line for you and rarely ask for anything in return. Well, now we're calling in *one* favor."

Chapter Fifteen

Tara didn't wake up so much as emerge. Everything hurt as much as when she'd first awakened in the hospital.

She was splayed on grass outside a playground. The playground was lit with golden public lights, but it seemed like all colors underneath them had been stripped away in favor of sepia tones. The world on the other side was nothing more than an inky blackness.

She groaned as she pushed herself up onto her hands and knees. Her joints and muscles ached like hell, but her fingers and knees stung from raw skin. She held her hands up to the playground light. Blood was black in the dimness. She'd ripped through fingernail and fingerprint as though she'd been scrabbling at shingles or rough concrete. Her shirt was black, too, but shining and wet, the smell as coppery as what was in her mouth. Her jeans were stained with dirt, grass, and the same blood. Some of it was hers, based on the scratches on her arms and legs. But she didn't think she'd shed enough to account for what was on her.

"Good morning, Snow White." Sela jumped down from the roof of the tallest playground tower. "I was wondering how far you'd get on your own power without me holding you under."

"What did you—" Tara stopped asking when the answer came to her in claw stripes and teeth.

She'd fallen in the field because she hadn't been able to keep up with the werewolves, partially or fully changed. She'd been utterly wild—wilder than them— and she'd spread that wildness around like wildfire. It hadn't taken much for it to catch on the wolves, who were already on their way to feral. Not just the children anymore, although they'd been first and easier, their emotions stronger and bigger than their little bodies could hold. Sela's power had joined with hers to make the magic simmer and burst from heart to heart like gunpowder from ignition.

"Oh, what did you make me do, Sela? What did you make me part of?" Tara fell forward onto the grass, coughing against tears trying to throttle her. "How could you do that to me, to them?"

Sela stepped into the darkness to help Tara to her feet. She wiped Tara's face of tears and whatever else had smeared there. "When are you going to get it through your head that there's no good and bad in our world? That's for souls to worry about. You may be in human skin, but you have no soul. You're either angel or demon, and we all play our part."

Tara pushed Sela's hands away. "You're not playing any part. You're not following anyone's orders. You're torturing kids because you can, and for what?"

"I just missed you."

Although Sela appeared clean, there was so much more blood on her hands. Tara could see rivers of it if she looked closely enough.

"When we were together, we yearned to experience this plane as completely as they do. We yearned together, my heartstrings to yours, until I fell to meet them, and every moment without you hurt more than any minute without my wings. I was shut from where you were, from seeing you, from feeling every time your heart hurt. You think what these children do is just random violence? This is what being without you does to me. I had to bring you down somehow."

"No, you didn't." Tara tried to wipe her hands on cleaner places on her jeans. As corrupted as Sela was, it was Tara who couldn't get the blood off. "We were created to never be alone, but it was you who left me. You fell, thinking I would follow, while I was still content to observe. You forced my hand. You found something so terrible that it would hurt me from heaven, and you lured me to fall, not through temptation but torture."

Sela took Tara's stained hands in hers. "Wrath doesn't want to be stagnant. It wants to spread. And I wanted you down here for all the things you're clearly enjoying, too. Andrea may have been surprised by my kiss, but Noah certainly wasn't."

Underneath her tears, Tara's cheeks burned as Sela reminded her what Noah and Andrea had made her feel, sending it like electricity through her nerve-wired hands.

"I've watched how voraciously you eat. You used to paint whole swaths of our walls with images of feasts like teenagers put pictures of their crushes above their beds. And we used to peek into the rooms of honeymooners, of furtive lovers, of incubi and succubi, and wonder, wonder, with our sexless bodies, what it was like to be so driven by parts we never had. The other angels didn't understand why we were so obsessed with what they considered the messiest and most dangerous element of humanity, but we could almost feel it in a way they never could. That was our gift, as well as each other. But the other side of what we were able to feel is this, Tara. It's that what they make us feel, we give back threefold. That's the curse of the blessing. But when you're the demon, you don't suffer the curse anymore. You *are* the curse."

"I don't want to be the curse." Tara yanked her hands from Sela's. It didn't spare her the emotions, only the sensation of her skin crawling. "I don't want to cause this pain just so that I don't have to feel it anymore. How could you do this? How could you become a demon just because you didn't want to deal with the less pleasurable elements of being human? You could have endured your ten years, then been cold preserved stone against its storm."

"Ten years on earth and unknown years in stone? A drop of wine in the ocean and then the ocean itself?" Sela laughed. "No, thank you. Give me flesh. Give me form. Give me feeling. I still feel what they feel, but it doesn't overtake me like it does for you. I feel no more *pain*, Tara. You don't have to feel yours anymore."

"Some humans feel this their whole lives. I can bear ten years. If I could bear it longer, I would. Perhaps I will be granted that grace. But even if I'm not, I will have been blessed with what I was given," Tara said. "For convincing me to fall, I give you some measure of thanks, but not for what you did to convince me. As for service in stone, we're not supposed to *be* here, Sela.

They're not supposed to feel more than our presence. We're not supposed to take up their space. That's why we only get such a short time, and why we serve longer, where we won't clutter their world but can still protect it."

"Speak for yourself," Sela said. "I'm here. I'm in their world, living and laughing and loving, dancing on their streets. I'm feasting and fucking and I'm *supposed* to be here. *We're* supposed to be here. It's not such a terrible thing, to be the terrible thing prophesied. We can have the feast for twenty years, a hundred, a thousand, until the very end."

"At what price? Children in an inadequate asylum? Parents with hearts ripped from their chests? Lovers heartbroken? When we yearned for pleasures of flesh, we never imagined we could want those things at the expense of the people we enjoyed. For you to have it, you have to take it from someone else. That's what makes you the demon, not your pleasure but the pain you cause. The twin I knew would never have done that."

Sela stomped to her feet and crunched into the pebbled playground. "They don't deserve the feast! They can't appreciate it like we can."

"They don't know anything else." Tara staggered into the light and tried to ignore what it revealed. Her joints creaked and cracked as she struggled for balance in the uneven gravel. "They were born into the flesh. We love the food, but they need it so they don't die and are given its glory so that satisfying their needs is a pleasure. We love their bodies, but they need sex because they're not immortal. They continue through progeny, and they're given its glory so that satisfying their needs is a pleasure. They don't know the song of angels. They don't know the peace of a body with no needs. They don't know what it's like to have never been born and never die, just change composition in heaven or in hell. They know only flesh. We can become them, but they can never become us. We're given a chance to understand. You took that unique and exquisite gift and decided that you deserved more."

"We're angels, Tara. Of course we deserve more."

"We were made of light and they from dust, but light is no better than earth, immortality no better than mortality, fire no better than flesh. You fell for a very different reason than I did, if you believe they deserve to serve your whims rather than that you were made to serve."

Sela sat on a swing and pushed off to rock back and forth with a groan and a creak from the chains. "You think you're better than me? The only reason you're not in the company of your feral friends is because I will it so."

"I came down human. You're more powerful, and you've had more time with your power. But you're not better than me. You're part of me, and no matter our form, no matter our matter, we are equal." Tara stopped the swing before Sela could kick out to coax her swing higher. She grunted as Sela's knees hit her legs, but the pain was no better or worse than what she already felt. "Help me stop this, or else I fear this will end badly. Perhaps for all of us."

"It's done," Sela said. "And you were the one who did it."

"I don't remember, which means *you* did it. I can be guilty on your behalf, but you can't convince me that I am the source of this evil that you do."

"Evil? Is that what you think I am?"

"You cause suffering. You steal the feast and call it your own. You hoard pleasure and deal pain. That's evil, Sela." Tara stepped away from the swings, peering through the dark, but the park was empty now, as far as she could tell. "If you were a neutral demon, or even a good one, you would save the children you destroy. The suffering would have a purpose other than your entertainment, like the pestilence demons who cleanse even while they make unclean. You got what you wanted, Sela. I'm here, and I remember you. You can stop this chaos."

Sela spread her black wings behind her and flew backward out of the swing. Tara envied those glorious wings, rolled her shoulders in longing.

"This city invites chaos," Sela said. "It conjures it. I'm not the only Horseman who found their way to this place, and it's no coincidence I answered its call and that you fell for me here. I don't know if it's the end of the End of Days. I don't know if it's darkness or light that beckons. But there's *something* here. Are you sure that you still want to be human when it surfaces?"

"I fell for them, not for me," Tara said. "I'll stand with them. I'll die with them, if I must. That'll just get me to heaven faster. Would you like to reach hell faster, too? How long and how much labor do you think would be required before you to make it back to earth to enjoy all its fruits? Would you call that suffering?"

"Killing me would be killing yourself."

Staring at Sela was like staring into the most flattering mirror, which was why it hurt so to look at her, to see herself as she should be, satisfied and majestic, with the weight and grandeur of wings, if not enough of them — such a strange diminished form and yet beautiful and unmistakably her, recognizable as reflection when she remembered what she was supposed to look like.

"Get in my way again, Sela, and I will. If I can't kill you, I won't stop the others from trying. And if you refuse to clean up your mess, I need to do it for you." Tara edged around the playground, then let the darkness swallow her as she struggled to see through, to determine which direction to go.

"You can't stop them. Don't you walk away from me!"

Wings billowed above Tara, but she refused to look up. There was no point in entertaining demons by giving them the attention they required. An entire world to use as their playground, and they still couldn't admit what they needed, even to themselves. They thought themselves better than humans, but what would they be if they had nothing to torment?

"Did you really think I'd let you go?" Sela didn't need to shout to be heard. Tara heard her right in her ear, even though she still flew above.

Darkness wasn't the only thing that swallowed Tara. Cold fear sank deep into her fingertips and toes, chilling its way up her limbs to the center, where fire burned branding hot through her roiling gut. She didn't even know what she was so afraid of or mad at, but it churned like hell pits set aflame, worse with every step, as though she breathed it. As though she was falling again.

She stumbled to her knees, grasping her head. "Stop it. Stop it, Sela. The more you try to destroy me, the more you only destroy yourself."

"You're the one holding your head like it's going to explode."

Tara forced herself back to her feet, moving as fast as she could. General population might be the last place she needed to be, but it was also the last place that werewolves needed to be. She had to stop them. She had to warn everyone. She had to... She had to something, too hard to remember with a metal vise tightening, tightening, tightening around her skull, like someone trying to make orange juice the manual way.

Orange juice. Orange juice brought her to breakfast, which brought her to Noah, when they were both tired and achy but he smiled as she ate everything he put in front of her. Which brought her to breakfast tacos. Her stomach growled, but that at least distracted her as she remembered the tired bliss of the 'morning' after. Enough to find her feet again and stumble toward the river rush of racing thoughts and writhing emotions, more intense at night when darker thoughts took sway with the shadows.

"Damn it, Tara, stop running!"

"Stop holding me back. You're not going to make me love you by making me your weapon of mass destruction. I won't be part of this, and I swear, Sela, if you try to force me, you're the one whose throat I'll tear out."

She finally noticed little darts of movement in her periphery. More than that, she could *feel* them. They ran on all fours, but the feeling was the same as the other kids—a complete blank, except for that wild fearful anger that wanted nothing more than to lash out. Human children didn't have many tools to do so. They were easily influenced and easily quelled. Werewolf children were another monster. They knew better what damage they could wreak, even without coherent thought.

Tara tried to reach them, to make them think of cheesecake and arms around their shoulders, but they were too far and flitted in and out of her influence.

She was too slow, too weak. She couldn't stop this. There was no point to trying to stop what she had inadvertently set in motion.

She slowed down on the hill, even as howls rose from all directions, not aimed for her but away and to the sky. Now she could see them, silhouettes on the edge of the streetlights.

She would never see Noah or Andrea or Hannah or anyone again. Her world would be this darkness, this fear, her twin spinning above like a carrion eater until the end of End of Days. This was only the beginning, the first shot fired — a biochemical weapon. She should stay far away. She should let Sela take her, maybe kill her. She should stop right here, not go another step further.

She'd fallen to her knees again, her face buried in her arms on the grass, before she realized Sela had done it again, as insidious as whispers in her dreams — instead of fearful anger, mind-numbing despair.

"Stop this, Sela!" Tara pushed herself back up, with anger more organic than Sela's welling up behind her eyes. "If you want me to join you, why do you make me bow again and again? You want me to ascend to your pedestal, but you keep placing your boot on my neck."

Sela landed behind her. "Because you don't seem to understand that you can't stop what's coming. The wolves have scattered. There aren't enough hunters in the city to lasso the parks and hold them all in. One way or another, there will be blood, and so much fear."

What Tara had done to the wolves came back piecemeal, like the fall.

A headache so bad she thinks her brain is leaking out through her nose and eyes, and she tastes blood in the back of her mouth. She is held yet not safe, so afraid of falling even with the comforting sound of wings above.

She's released onto soft grass, close to the ground so that it doesn't hurt — except her head, of course. She screams into the darkness. It doesn't matter that she can't see. People and creatures dart all around her, shouting back, some angry, some scared, some attempting to be comforting, but she doesn't understand a word, and she strikes out at them. They strike back, not with teeth but with claws, careful, defensive, until the pressure in her head becomes too much from more and more and more and more being poured in, water into an ever-expanding balloon. Instead of exploding out with release, as with the kids in the station, it explodes out with everything that has been poured in, until she doesn't scream alone anymore.

One by one, those closest to her are struck with her fear, and they whip around and bite at each other, scratch at themselves. Then, so much more powerful than before, the contagion continues on to those a little bit farther, and farther, starting with the children's guard, then the children themselves, then the next pack as they come to their children's aid in response to their fearful, furious howls.

It pulses from her head again and again and again, an endless supply as she screams and scratches and pours the feelings out in a flood. There is no peace, no relief, no breaking of the dam, unless she is the dam. And as she floods the minds around her, it comes back, buffeting her mind until Sela doesn't even have to give her more. She drowns in her own returned emotions, plus the added ferocity of werewolves with nothing left to harness the beast.

Those wolf minds echoed in hers now — with anger and fear, yes, but also a deep and abiding hunger so long denied for the taste of meat they weren't allowed to have.

The werewolves were murderous, and if that, too, was contagious, the hunters would take on that same murderousness, impulses just as long denied. How much blood would be shed before the feelings had run their course, if someone didn't stop it? The playground children she hadn't been able to help immediately had still been having episodes a week later.

Meridian would suffer under the initial onslaught. It might not be able to survive the aftershocks.

Rather than continuing to run down toward the wolves creeping their massive, monstrous bodies toward the light, their growls rumbling like distant thunder, Tara spun around. Startled, Sela reeled back, then up. Her wings kept her hovering above the ground in front of Tara — the reflection Tara wished she could have, yes, except Tara knew all too well what lay beneath that endearing exterior. She could only read emotions, but looking into Sela was like reading whole thoughts, because Sela's were distortions of what they'd once shared.

"You want fear? You want anger? You deal them out so easily. Do you even remember what they really feel like anymore?"

Tara gathered all the violent feelings from the wolves around her like dozens of jute ropes in her arms, then passed them through herself to magnify, charging herself with the same emotions to give her the added momentum as she flung them directly at Sela.

Sela reeled again, spinning backward, off-balance, and unable to keep herself in the air. She collapsed to the ground, her wings crumpled beneath her.

"What you put in the world, you deserve to suffer yourself," Tara said through gritted teeth.

Because wasn't that her problem, too? She put out worry, she put out desire, and it came back to her threefold, so she sent it out at that threefold, and it came back to her threefold again. When she gave her peace to the kids, it had been like the first breath of real air with each passing second, threefold peace returned, until they were breathing together, their lungs expanding all the way instead of constricted by the fists of panic. She earned the peace that she shared. The least Sela owed was the pain she caused.

"How *dare*..." Sela righted herself, her teeth bared and golden eyes capturing the streetlights like fireflies in her irises.

"This is what you do to them. But what you do is worse, isn't it? Because you can still string two words together. How feral do you think I can make you if I really try?"

"You wouldn't. You wouldn't do that to me."

"You did it to me!" Tara shoved Sela's shoulders, sending her backpedaling before her wings could right her. "Twice! Why do you expect to remain untouched, sitting pretty atop your perch as though still just an observer? You did it to me because this is all about *you*. It was about you when you yearned. It was about you when you fell. It was about you when you changed. It was about you when you wanted me to fall to stop you. And it was about you when you tried to ingratiate yourself with the people I chose to help me. I'm not jealous, Sela. I'm furious. How could you do this to me and expect that I'd fall into your arms and never let go? Or was all you wanted just your reflection?"

Tara thrust more of the wolves' violent anger into Sela, who fell back and had to pull her wings into herself because she kept getting tangled in her own limbs. Or maybe she forgot she had them as she clawed her long nails at her arms and shoulders.

When Sela screamed, the wolves sent up a howl from all directions, near and far.

Tara lost her grip on the wolves' anger — and her own — at the startling percussive blast of gunfire, also from all directions. She whirled around, squinting into the night, just as the extra lights in the park — including the playground, basketball court, pavilion, and parking lots — shut off. The streetlights didn't, of course, but her vision wasn't good enough to see whether the bullets had caught the werewolves, whether bestial bodies were sprawled, fallen, or if the hunters had turned their guns on each other from emotional infection.

Either way, each gunshot was one that never should have had to happen.

"Look what you've done!" Tara plastered Sela to the ground, writhing and ripping at herself with all the anger Tara had for her.

But Tara couldn't keep her down like that, couldn't see in Sela the same snapping teeth and wide, wild, aimless eyes of the children from the alley. It wasn't that Sela was Tara's mirror image in turn. She simply couldn't stand doing to Sela what Sela had done to others. Tara found it neither entertaining nor amusing.

She pulled the emotions back. Leaving Sela there on the ground, Tara stumbled downhill toward the wolves.

"Tara! Tara!" Razorblades of lingering wildness rasped through Sela's cries.

Eight more gunshots sounded off through the night. They weren't as loud as Tara expected them to be, but perhaps hunters had developed the means to quiet their weapons through multiple shots.

"Don't shoot!" she shouted. "Don't shoot! Please! They're not responsible for what they're doing!"

She tried to find her peace again, like she had with the kids, but that had been in a small, contained, quiet room, one child at a time, most of them not in the midst of a violent outburst. Here, she was running down a hill, her heart galloping with both exertion and panic, the pain of bewildered wolves pinpricking through her as she tried to pluck the anger and fear from them. She could only dismantle pieces at a time, which was like trying to shred a shirt by pulling at loose strings. It confused them, but within that confusion, their instinct to run, fight, and freeze tangled their long limbs, leaving them vulnerable to more gunshots.

"Stop shooting! We need to help them!" Tara shouted again.

"Tara?" A large shadow, followed by a smaller shadow, sprinted across the street. "Is that you?"

The smaller shadow aimed a rifle at one of the wolves darting at them.

"No!" Tara tried to stop the gun by sheer force of will, but the wolf — at least five times larger than their local coyote counterparts — went down and fell still in the grass. The smaller shadow reloaded, then shot another wolf. Tara's panic at watching the wolves die right in front of her — because of Sela, but also because of *her* — didn't help the other wolves closest to her. Slaver foamed at their mouths, striking her with saliva as they tossed their heads side to side against their own spiking panic.

"Tara, is that you?" Noah called, the taller of the two shadows.

"You don't have to kill them! They were made violent. They're not breaking the rules."

"We know." Noah panted while Andrea covered him and Tara with her rifle, keeping an eye on the wolves stalking them, although Tara's distress appeared to conflict them into a certain amount of hesitation. "They're tranquilizer darts. Enough to bring down a mid-sized elephant, more than enough for an amped-up werewolf. Some of us have tranqs, others have sleeping powders and other spells. We're using what we can. We know Sela's doing this."

"She made me do it," Tara said. "She made *me* do it."

"She's still doing it," Andrea replied through clenched teeth. Her hands shook so hard that the gun rattled.

"It's more contagious than before." Tara grabbed Noah's forearms. "The fear and the anger. She gave it to me, I gave it to the wolves, and the wolves passed it to other wolves. Fuck, it's getting to Andrea. *It's getting to Andrea.*"

"And it's getting to me, but it's okay. Andrea, I need the gun."

"Why do you get the gun if we're both losing it?" Andrea's voice had risen about half an octave, and she was clenching the gun too hard — fortunately not on the trigger.

"Because I've got anger management under my belt, and you won't even meditate. Give me the gun."

Andrea swung the bore toward Noah. "I'll give it to you, you absolute man-slut. Really? Really? You can have anyone you want, but I finally find a nice girl who doesn't leave too many lipstick stains, and you sleep with her first?"

Noah knocked the bore aside, the square of his jaw more defined as he fought to keep his temper. "I can have anyone? I have the same exact problems with women you have. The only difference is that you have kids, and I never had the pleasure. I had no fucking idea you were interested in Tara, much less that you were having sex with her evil twin thinking it was her at the same fucking time I was. How was I supposed to know? How were either of us supposed to know? Is it really me you're mad at?"

"Yes!" Andrea swung the rifle like a bat and caught Noah on the side of his head.

Noah went staggering in one direction while Andrea aimed the tranquilizer at him. He was less than half the size of the werewolves. Even with contagious rage pulsing through him, that amount of tranquilizer could kill him.

"No!" Tara couldn't find her inner calm so she grabbed the panic instead and sent it into Andrea enough to shudder the gun out of her hands.

A scream throttled into a whimper as Andrea fell to her knees, gasping for breath against the clenching in her gut and lungs.

Tara snatched the gun for herself and aimed it at a wolf who took advantage of the disarmed and quite noisy humans. Now that she knew it wasn't designed to kill, she didn't hesitate to shoot. But when she turned toward another approaching wolf, she realized that she didn't know how to reload.

"I don't ask much from you, Dunn," Andrea snapped, "but I didn't think not groping our investigative subject was too much to ask."

"Could say the same for you."

"I had the demon first. What's your excuse?"

"Just because she's not a demon doesn't mean she's not powerful. You weren't even there when she hit our department with a sex bomb. Andrea, come on. We can talk about this when wolves aren't about to decide our retirement plan for us."

A solid punch sent Noah falling almost comically backward. Even in the darkness, his expression was stunned. As he fell, he twisted and landed hard on his cheek. Andrea jumped on him, punching whatever she could reach while Noah covered his face with his arms and tucked his legs up to protect his balls.

"Black, you are sorely testing my patience," he said through gritted teeth.

Tara sent her continuing panic and distress toward the wolves closest to them. Two of them stopped right where they were and cowered, whining as though they were being struck by Andrea instead of Noah. The third veered off, yelping.

Andrea flew through the air as Noah launched her off him with both legs. She landed on her back, the breath knocked out of her.

Noah pushed himself upright, but as soon as Andrea caught her breath, she clambered back up and ran at him with a bloodthirsty scream, reaching for her off-duty weapon. Noah reached for his service weapon. They aimed their guns — their real guns, safeties off — straight at each other.

"You're friends!" Tara shouted, pointing the empty tranq gun at both of them, for all the good it could do anyone. "You're practically family. You've been working together for ten years. You're not angry at each other. You're angry, and you're looking for the reason, so you landed on the first thing that made you upset."

"Upset? Upset? Do you have any idea what it was like to be kissing you, to be... And then you tell me you don't understand why? Do you have any idea how much that hurt, bitch?" Andrea turned the gun toward her. "I introduced you to my *daughter*."

Tara dropped the gun and held up her hands. She'd seen that enough when she'd been an angel, but she also didn't want Andrea to think for a second that Tara would shoot her back. "Because I was a friend who needed help. Because you're a good friend and a good person. Both of you are. I'm not the only one you've helped by bringing them back to your own homes. And, Andrea, I wasn't mad. I was there with you, like I was with him. I only stopped because you surprised me by saying we'd already done those things. I didn't stop because I didn't want to do those things."

"That's right. You hadn't done those things with me because you were fucking *him*." Andrea pointed the gun back at Noah.

"Would you decide who you're going to point that at?" Noah snapped. "I didn't take her away from you. I didn't know. She didn't know. You didn't know. This isn't any of our faults."

"I don't know. It looks an awful lot like one of your faults."

Sela laughed behind Tara, sending a shiver of icy fear through her again that shuddered out to Andrea and Noah, widening their eyes to the whites and trembling their hands as they continued to aim at each other.

Sela landed close enough for the breeze from her wings to ruffle Tara's shirt and hair. "This is even better than I'd envisioned. I thought there'd be a massacre with lots of biting. I didn't know I was going to get a ragtag team of hunters fighting the wolves or this nice little soap opera."

"You can stop this. You have the experience and the power," Tara said. "Please don't make them do this."

"We're not making them do anything. If they're angry enough to point loaded guns at each other, that's on them."

"They weren't angry enough for that before we gave it to them," Tara said. "*Please.*"

"Yeah, but don't you want to see what they do now?" Sela whispered in her ear. "Which one wins the girl?"

Tara whipped around and caught Sela's face with her elbow. Sela cried out, covering her eye, open-mouthed in shock.

"If one shoots the other, you think I'll be able to look at them ever again? If someone dies, no one wins *anything*. Don't you understand that? Everyone loses if one suffers, if one dies. Someone's already died because of you. You should move on now, demon, while you can. Another city. Another state. Anywhere but here. Are you going to stop this?"

"Do you want me to leave, or do you want me to save them?" Sela said, still holding her eye, which was dripping—not blood, just tears from force of impact.

"Both! You brought me down here to change into what you are, to be sisters once again. Was it ever part of the plan that you would disgust me? Was it part of the plan that hurting them hurts me? Is causing *me* pain fun for you, too? Does it please you? Is this a good storyline for your favorite soap opera?"

She tried to stay angry but her words thickened as her sinuses reacted to the tears — hers of grief — building behind her eyes to spill salt over her cheeks and down her throat. She tried to stay angry, but Andrea and Noah, the best of partners and friends — enough for Noah to be Uncle Noah to Hannah — were still pointing guns at each other over how Sela had made them feel about her.

Tears poured from Tara's eyes like a water feature. Everything inside told her to squeeze her eyes shut, but she didn't want to *not* see Noah and Andrea, didn't want to close her eyes only to open them and learn which one she'd lost. She tried to keep talking, to say what she meant, to say what she felt, but words weren't enough.

Everyone's anger and pain still assaulted her from every side amid Sela's faltering amusement and just *everything* hurting, emotionally and physically. And Tara didn't know how to fix it, because she had neither the power nor the control she needed with everyone so far away and her own despair keeping her from saving the people right in front of her.

Tara wept with the sadness of a million days and nights that her many, many angel eyes had watered with the mourning of the grief-stricken — another color in the vast array of human emotion she'd experienced a distant secondhand. Now here she was, with pulsing and pounding in heart and lungs and guts and spleen, and she was still experiencing it secondhand, as fresh and untouched as though it were her own. But she also had her own, the product of a human brain with human hormones and human experience — the whole point of falling, the only real reason to leave heaven.

In the station, she had wept for the children's pain and panic, overwhelmed by her novel confusion. This was deeper, richer, because it *was* her own, and arose like a wellspring, neither artificial nor secondhand. She knew that many people tended to cry in private, but she didn't know why, didn't want to hide what she felt when it was a gift to feel at all.

Andrea lowered her gun, her face wet and lips trembling. "What... What are we doing? Why do I... Oh my God, Noah."

Noah dropped his hands, too, then holstered his gun. "I swear I didn't know. Neither of us did. I wouldn't hurt you, Andrea. I'm not that petty."

"I know. I know you wouldn't. This was just a freak coincidence, and I *knew* that, I knew you wouldn't, but I was sure... I thought you were laughing at me, the both of you... God, I feel so fucking humiliated." Andrea dropped to her knees and left her gun in the grass as she covered her face with her hands and wept.

Noah sniffed and wiped his nose with his sleeve. His face wasn't as shiny, but the shine it did have was more than just sweat. "There's nothing for you to be ashamed of. You know I knew about you liking women, right? I let it stay quiet because it was none of my business, but I know you too well, Andrea. We're like family. I'm the one who should be ashamed."

"What do you have to be ashamed of? You weren't the first one to point your gun."

"Neither of us should have been with Tara in the first place, but I was the one who was with Tara first and the most. It was irresponsible and unprofessional and unethical and... And it was my choice. You had Sela because she was playing her little game."

"No, no, I get it." Andrea gestured to her face with a laugh through her ugly crying. "She was the subject of a supernatural investigation, but once we knew she was an angel, it was just a matter of figuring out how to finish the paperwork. It wasn't you. But I really should have known better."

"You were with her tonight, really with *her*. Sounds like you knew better just fine. And at least it wasn't during work hours. She was struggling and *I* was irresponsible," Noah said. "Geez, I haven't cried like this since the goddamn divorce."

Seemed Tara's grief was threaded through with a generous helping of guilt, but that didn't stop her from weeping — made it worse, in fact — as Noah and Andrea held each other up in an embrace as though someone close to them had died. Lonely and even more ashamed of herself, Tara knelt ten feet away with Sela still behind her. If Sela was trying to send something else through Tara, there wasn't any room for it. Tara's grief was a whole tsunami that seemed to come from nowhere and spread everywhere.

The wolves creeping around them lowered themselves to the ground with their noses on their paws, making their large bodies as small as they could, with eyes wide and ears tucked back in placation, tail firmly between legs. Some of them had even transformed back into human form, their feelings too complex for a wolf to hold, because a wolf couldn't understand guilt.

They poured their tears into the earth with Noah, Andrea, and Tara while hunters slowly approached and proceeded to hit the wall of Tara's grief, which sent them stumbling to their knees. For all their self-righteousness, hunters had too much guilt to mine and grief aplenty, and it fed hers even more.

She'd helped cause this destruction. Now she was the direct cause of their sorrow and shame rising to the surface like toxic foam. Tara sobbed all the harder, as though if she poured out enough tears and cries, she could ultimately extract that toxin. But the well was bountiful and bottomless.

"No, no, no, no, no…"

Tara twisted around to face Sela, almost afraid what she would see.

Sela had spread her wings again, but they were strangely flat, draped over her back and the ground as though she didn't have enough strength to lift them on her own. She, too, wept, her eyes glowing gold as she held up her arm.

The arm was turning gray. Porous. Hard.

"No. No, that's cheating. I'm not ashamed. I'm not. God, someone stop it. Tara, what are you doing?"

Tara didn't respond. Sela had been selfish from the very beginning in a way that Tara couldn't understand, but Tara wasn't doing this to her on purpose. It was a direct consequence of what Sela had done to Tara first. In that sense, Sela deserved every square inch of her distress.

Tara wasn't sure Sela had properly earned salvation if the guilt had been triggered by someone else. Still, a Sela bound to stone would be much less of a threat. As much as Tara wanted to cling to the Sela she remembered before their respective falls, her twin had made her own choices, as though nothing at all could touch her back.

"No. Stop it. I'm not done. I'm not finished. Goddammit, stop!"

"I'm not doing it," Tara said. "It's your own regret."

"No!" Sela shoved herself to her feet with her stiffening arms and forced her heavy wings to spread. "Goddamn you, Tara!"

"That's what you tried to do to me. It was bad enough you compelled me to fall for you instead of in my own time. I'd get out of Meridian if I were you. You never know where stone is going to root you here, and I have grief and guilt enough for two to ground you permanently."

Sela bared teeth sharp as the wolves', no longer looking anything like Tara. But as gray climbed up her arms to her shoulders, she fled, using the downward incline of the hill to give her speed before catching air and flying as fast away from Tara's shared guilt as she could.

Even so, Tara wondered if it would be worth listening for reports of a fallen statue, or even just broken stone on the sidewalk.

Chapter Sixteen

Tara bowed forward again and sobbed along with wolves and hunters alike. She'd lost a twin all over again, and now she knew what she'd lost her to.

Hands on her shoulders and arms drew her up. Noah gathered her into the warmth of his jacket. "It's okay. I don't know if it's over, but it's okay. She's gone. The anger and violence are gone. Look."

She stared over his shoulder at naked werewolves in human form speaking through tears to the hunters. Despite the fact they still wept, they were calm in comparison to what they had been, not a trace of violence left, because that hadn't been from Tara in the first place, whereas she'd come by the sadness honestly. Other wolves and hunters were dragging all the unconscious wolves together for the rest of the packs to tend to.

"And that's you, sweetheart. This is because of you."

"Everything is because of me," Tara said. "Sela…Andrea…you…these people… If I'd remembered in time…"

Noah stroked her back. "That's not on you. That's on her. She played us all."

"She's still out there."

Andrea came up behind her and rested her hands and cheek against Tara's back. Noah accommodated her without effort.

"But now we know what she looks like," Andrea said. "And the ways she doesn't look like you. And the hunters know to watch for her now. They'll tell other hunters. She won't be safe here."

"No one is safe with her still out there," Tara said.

"This world was never safe," Noah replied. "That's the price we pay for living. This has been a rough week for you, but it's just another week for us. Our routine is regularly interrupted by new threats, some new terrible thing rising or falling on our streets."

"If she comes back, we'll deal with it," Andrea said. "But although I've seen demons flee before plenty of times, I've never seen one flee quite that scared. And *that* is because of you. What the hell'd you do?"

Tara's grief wasn't subsiding, but the crying finally was. Now that she could sniff more back, she noted that everyone else's crying had settled into a gentler flow, too, down to a trickle. More talking. Even a little laughter, an embarrassed effort to break the emotional intensity and tension. Floodwaters receding.

"I was so upset, so sad at how much everyone hurt and how I'd contributed to this chaos and couldn't reverse it, guilty for the part I played in their pain. That guilt was just as contagious to Sela as to everyone else. Demons can repent, if they understand what they've done and feel remorse. That's how gargoyles are born. Even though the guilt she felt came from me, it draws from what's already there, as your fight showed. There must have been enough there for the stone to start taking hold before she'd truly repented on her own. She flew away, away from the guilt I made her feel. I don't know if she can reverse the transfiguration or if the change itself is irreversible once it starts. I don't know what to hope for more — that she escapes as far from Meridian as she can or that she's bound in stone. Do both of those make me a bad person?"

"She's your family," Andrea said. "That makes you human. God, are you okay? You're covered in blood."

"I don't think it's mine. The werewolves were violent, but as it took them over, they directed it away from me."

"Even so, we should get you checked out. I hate to say it, but if you got bit, you need to know now rather than later." Andrea stroked Tara's messy, dirty hair.

On the way to the cars, Andrea and Noah kept holding her as well as they could without knotting their limbs and falling into the dirt. Noah nodded to some of the other hunters in silent gratitude, and Andrea briefly checked to make sure that the werewolves were all right.

The hunters must have already explained that Tara had been a tool of Sela's whimsy rather than the direct cause of the destruction wrought, because Tara felt no animosity from them. Just commiseration. And relief.

* * * *

Andrea picked up Hannah on the way home in her own car, but Noah brought Tara to Andrea's home as well instead of his own, not least because her main bathroom was bigger and nicer than his. It wasn't the first time he'd come to Andrea's home with blood on his clothes, although his was clearly transfer.

Hannah was far more concerned about Tara's state. Andrea reassured Hannah that they were going to take care of Tara, but if she could prepare some French bread pizza for when they were all done in the shower, she'd really appreciate it. Noah grabbed extra clothes from the back of his car. After his shower, the house smelled like pepperoni grease, which would hit the absolute spot after all the damn crying they'd done — and after whatever had happened to Tara when they hadn't been there.

Noah hated that there was a whole stretch of time that Tara had been scared, angry, and violent, and she'd been completely alone. He was still angry with himself, and guilty, as he had been in the park, that they'd let her get abducted like that, that he'd done things with Sela that he'd meant to do with Tara, that he'd done anything at all with Tara, as fucking amazing as it had been.

He'd stayed in the shower longer because of it. His feelings were his own. Tara didn't need his to compound hers, and vice versa. But once he was out, he made sure he'd achieved a tentative peace with what he could change and what he couldn't — *hello, anger management training* — so that he wouldn't take his frustrations out on her. Or on Andrea.

He didn't know how he felt about Andrea right now, given how both he and Andrea seemed to have found themselves in the most mortifying inadvertent love triangle. He and Andrea had never been in competition before, nor had their social or sex lives mingled much, not least because they'd both been married when he'd first met her.

He didn't want to step on anyone's toes. At the same time, he couldn't conceive of a world in which he didn't hold Tara like he had in the park. He didn't need sex from her, but fuck, he didn't think he'd ever convince himself not to want her.

Yet Andrea had been ready to shoot him for her, so he had to conclude that she felt the same way, and around Tara, hiding one's feelings wasn't an option.

Which left them in this awkward position, and a frustratingly necessary need to talk about it eventually. Soon. Tonight. Probably after Hannah went to bed.

Hannah was putting the French bread pizza on plates for everyone when Noah came out. They kept the plates in the oven under low heat until Tara and Andrea came out, too. Tara had borrowed some of Andrea's loose house clothes and wasn't wearing a bra. Noah expected no more or less after everything she'd been through. Andrea—in house clothes, too, and without even the basic makeup she tended to wear— looked just as tired as Tara looked and Noah felt.

"Thanks, baby girl," Andrea said as Hannah took the pizza out of the oven again and arranged the plates on the kitchen island.

"Was it really that bad?" Hannah asked. "I knew something was wrong when you left me with Miranda, but..."

"Yeah. Yeah, it was a bad night, Han. But not *that* bad," Andrea added when she noticed Noah's surreptitious check for visible bites on Tara. "No, she's physically fine. Just claw marks and nail marks. Turns out she's just a fast healer in general. Didn't get bitten. Didn't even need bandages."

"I seem to have been given the blessing to heal faster physically when I can't mentally," Tara said, picking at her pizza. It was the only time Noah had ever seen her play with food, not dig in so fast that she could be a teenager with a growth spurt. "Or maybe I...take after my family. I wouldn't know." She seemed to have just registered that Hannah was there and didn't know what she was, so Tara left it open for Andrea to tell Hannah what was going on. When she didn't, Tara stared back down at her food again, stabbing it to death with her fork.

"I can't believe I have to tell you this, but you should really eat. And drink. That whole glass of water. Or three. We all should," Noah said. "After all the tears, we're probably dehydrated."

Tara nodded and forced herself to drink half her water glass before tackling the pizza. Once she started, enthusiasm slowly returned, some color returned to her pale cheeks, and the dark circles under her eyes seemed less dire.

"Okay, you're right. This helped. And not just because it's delicious. Thank you, Hannah. I appreciate you helping take care of me tonight."

"I take care of Mom all the time," Hannah said.

Andrea tilted her head in wry acknowledgment. "To be fair, you turned twenty at four. I love you, Hannah-bean, but don't you think it's time for bed? You look like you want to be in pajamas."

"Is Tara going to be here in the morning?" Hannah glanced between Tara and her mother.

"She might sleep through the morning after everything that happened tonight, but yeah, she's sleeping over, if that's what you're asking."

"We had plans for this weekend, didn't we?" Tara's smile didn't require as much effort as it would have before the pizza and water, which Andrea topped off. "I wouldn't miss it."

"Okay. Love you, Mom." She put her plate in the dishwasher, then came around the island again to give her mother a hug and kiss. "Night, Tara."

Tara accepted a hug from her and kissed her hair. "Good night, Hannah. Sweet dreams."

"I'm sorry you're hurting."

"Thank you. I'm feeling much better."

"It feels like you are." Hannah gave her an extra squeeze, then headed upstairs to her room.

"Yes, I don't deserve her and don't know how on earth I made someone so good and pure," Andrea said. "I'd ask if anyone wants a beer, but maybe that's a bad idea."

It was tempting for Noah, too, but he was also technically on shift. He could justify being there, since Tara was still part of his job, at least for a little while longer, until they finalized her file with the end of the mystery of the feral children.

"I think that would delay what we have to deal with here," Noah said. "May I suggest that we be completely upfront and honest? Our feelings are already utterly transparent. No secrets. We've already shared more than we thought we ever would, and although it doesn't happen often, it wouldn't be the first time we confided on something this personal."

Andrea never discussed her dating life, but he'd been right there for every divorce and custody rant, and for the hearings when he could. He'd been there when she'd overindulged at a hunter bar and couldn't figure out how to get a rideshare. And she'd been there during his divorce and when he'd had a stalker. Ten years they'd been doing this together. Their working relationship had lasted longer than both of their marriages.

"So, what?" Andrea said. "Are we doing another less formal custody hearing? Does Mommy or Daddy get week-old Tara? This is a mess. We spend so much of our lives together that we're not supposed to overlap here. This was never supposed to be an issue between us."

"And if you'd stuck with men, that wouldn't have been a problem." Noah held up a hand. "Not a dig. Just a fact. Once you added women into your dating pool, we had more of a chance to cross the streams. Not with Cam Brumley, of course, but Tara's an ambidextrous batter at plate."

"Wow. A sports metaphor to avoid saying 'bi' or 'pansexual'. Could you be any more straight and male?" Andrea said. "And how the hell'd you know about Cam?"

"Andrea, there are a lot of surreptitious women in the world. Cam is not one of them."

"Well, Cam and I aren't dating. We just…hook up now and then. She has a girlfriend."

Noah raised an eyebrow.

"They're fine about it, and she knew she was a rebound."

"But Tara isn't?"

"It's partially because she's emotionally contagious, but I've never felt with anyone else what I feel with her. Are you going to tell me the same thing?"

He nodded.

"So…" Andrea crossed her arms on the island, hunched over like her whole house pressed on her shoulders. "We both care. We both like her. We both probably shouldn't, but here we are. We're invested. What do we do now?"

Noah turned to Tara, who stared at her knotted fingers in her lap. "Andrea had more time with Sela than you, but Sela was pretending to be you, and you did have some time with Andrea of your own. Was that enough to tell us what *you* want?"

Tara finally looked up now that they'd stopped talking about her instead of to her. "I haven't even been conscious for a week. I don't know what I want. I only know what I feel."

"And what do you feel?" Andrea asked, a little chagrined.

"I didn't come here for this, specifically, but I put myself in the path of both of you," Tara said. "I like how you both make me feel. If it were up to me, I wouldn't have to choose. Everyone knows how I enjoy a feast. Maybe my appetites will change, but maybe they won't, and I have room in me right now for the both of you. If neither of you has room for the other, we can come up with something else. Or I can look elsewhere so that neither suffers from what the other receives."

Noah and Andrea struggled to meet each other's eyes, but they managed. This really wasn't their usual subject of discussion, and Noah was having trouble letting himself imagine Andrea kissing Tara without getting a little turned on and seeing Andrea in a light he'd never wanted to see her in, since he had to work with her.

She'd been partially dressed in front of him before, but it had always been strictly business, practical clothes, practical partial nudity, given that their job wasn't always the cleanest, and they didn't always have the luxury of privacy. He was a warm-blooded man and Andrea was pretty — sometimes despite her best efforts to downplay her looks — so he couldn't claim he'd never had passing thoughts, but the more he'd gotten to know her, the less the thoughts occurred to him. He had so many other outlets with fewer complications.

He had no way of knowing if she'd ever had passing thoughts about him. She'd always played that sort of thing close to the chest. The fact she was visibly upset about Tara meant that what she felt was more than shallow selfishness, which didn't surprise Noah at all, because he'd arrived at the same place over the same short period of time.

Not love, perhaps, but also not something as simple as infatuation, despite the amazing sex. He'd never thought he'd fall for a fallen angel, because the only ones he'd ever met had gone demon. But every time he looked at Tara, whether she was sad or happy or hungry or horny, he wanted to hold her and fall with her, and every time he thought about how hard she'd hit the earth, he knew she'd done it to be with them. To help them. To save them.

He felt helpless in the sweetest, scariest way when he was with her. And given Andrea's vulnerability, he suspected she might feel the same.

"My shifts and Andrea's mostly align, but not always, and you'll eventually have a day-shift life," Noah said slowly. "At least odds suggest so."

"I was thinking about asking Dr. Kim if he had a position for someone without a medical degree to help people at Mattea," Tara said, still not quite looking at either of them. "Maybe I can eventually become a nurse. But it's important for both of you to know now that angels have an expiration date as humans —

usually ten years, give or take. We're given a taste, rarely more. Then we're relegated to stone far longer than a lifetime. With these feelings that you…we have, that we share, that we're sharing right now, it may not seem long enough. Or maybe it'll seem too long if something goes wrong or I turn friend against friend."

"Longer than some people get." Noah hadn't been thinking diamonds. He'd be happy just waking up with her in his arms.

"You won't be able to hide your feelings, even if I won't always know why you feel them," Tara said. "I'll create feelings. You'll question if feelings are yours or mine. Maybe you're questioning that now, because I'm fond of both of you and hated to see you hurt."

"It hurt us to see you hurt, too," Noah said. "Just because we see terrible things all the time doesn't make it easier. And speaking for myself, I think about you even when you're not with me. I know that hasn't been a lot, but it's enough."

Andrea angled away from both of them. "I was with Sela first, but she was so good at being you that, to me, it fit seamlessly with our time at the Wheel. It really feels like I'm losing my mind, Tara. I want you so much. Not just *want* want. I want you in the morning when our breath stinks and you've stolen all the blankets and look so peaceful before you wake up. I have more blankets."

"Sounds like we want the same things," Noah said. "So where does that leave us, Andrea?"

Andrea rested her hand on Tara's shoulder, rubbing lightly. "Are you upset still from tonight? You don't normally look like this, like you want to make yourself even smaller or disappear altogether. Do we just need to let you get some sleep instead of deciding your entire ten-year future at once?"

"No. I mean, yes, I'm still overwhelmed and this is a lot and not at all what I was looking or hoping for nor pursuing. I wanted to *feel* things. Well, I've felt a lot of things I hadn't set out to feel, but right now, I'm really just trying not to feel what you're feeling or letting out what I'm feeling."

Andrea pressed her lips lightly where Tara's hair brushed her neck. "While I appreciate you holding back around my daughter, she's gone to bed, and she goes to sleep fast. So if you need to let go because you're still not comfortable with controlling it, you should. I want you to be comfortable here."

"Are you sure?" Tara asked Andrea, but she glanced at Noah, too. Muddier hazel eyes, more green than gold. More human. "I don't want to compromise your relationship with each other just because I'm hungry and don't know enough to choose."

"I want to know how you feel," Andrea replied.

Noah nodded in agreement.

He knew the second she let whatever shield she'd built crumble, because both he and Andrea groaned. Andrea pressed herself against Tara's back more fully, and her kiss became more intimate than tender, a wet slide over Tara's neck that did something new to Noah's arousal as Tara arched her neck back to rest her head on Andrea's shoulder in encouragement. Andrea curled her fingers in Tara's drying wild hair to hold her there. The T-shirt Tara wore was loose, but the angle of her body showed how her nipples were tight and pressed against the fabric.

"It's stronger when you do it than her," Andrea moaned against Tara's skin before taking it between her teeth.

"That's because I'm feeling Noah as well as you and myself." Tara beckoned for him to come around the island.

He'd held himself apart so Tara would know he didn't just want her for her body and Andrea wouldn't feel threatened. Now he rounded the island to take Tara's hand, which she used to draw him toward her on the barstool and between her legs.

He loomed over her, hovering his lips above hers, almost afraid to taste her again and find out just how much both he and Andrea wanted her at the same time, but she was impossible to resist when her arousal wove in and around him like a sea snake. Strong, like Andrea had said, and raw with unbridled sincerity. His pants were too tight and the crux between her legs was warm as he brought himself more fully against her to meet her kiss.

Noah sent his moan into her, Andrea joined hers with his, and Tara added hers in response, crisscrossed vibrations that Noah felt under his fingertips on her cheek. Andrea slid her hand between them to stroke over Tara's breast over her shirt. Then she dipped the other hand down between Tara's thighs with a brazen caress that had Tara arching, deepening the kiss with Noah as though she wanted to swallow him.

Andrea's knuckles nudged against his cock through his pants. At first, she was tentative, but Tara rocked into her touch. Her resultant desire was an electric jolt down to his quickened erection with every rock. The harder he became, the more Tara whimpered and the harsher Andrea's breathing.

"Fuck, how am I going to come already?" Andrea whispered. "Jesus, Noah, is that you?"

"Yeah, that's how it works with us. It's amazing, but it has its issues."

"Among which may be that we're going to disturb Hannah if we stay out here. Damn, I thought I was too loud when we...when Sela... Anyway..." Andrea chanced a shared glance over Tara's shoulder with him. "Bedroom?"

They'd seen each other aroused before, from when they were around sex demons, but never so close that he got a good look at those big brown eyes darkened by shadow and desire, her lips flushed and wet and her beauty as fresh-scrubbed and tousled as Tara's, but with more knowledge in the shift of her tongue behind her parted teeth.

Noah leaned in and gently pressed his lips to his partner's. He still didn't know how he felt about the whys and wherefores of what he was doing, how this was going to change things — sex usually did — but even though they were here because of Tara, they wouldn't be able to escape each other when they were with her together. If they couldn't touch each other without it being too uncomfortable or even revolting, this was going to go downhill fast, especially if Andrea wasn't as bi as Noah had assumed.

While Andrea continued to play with Tara's nipple through her shirt, she turned the hand between Tara's thighs over to cup his erection instead — hesitant, then bold. Tara moved between them with an almost serpentine sway, reaching around their waists to pull both of them closer to her, to each other.

Both Andrea and Noah groaned with his pleasure at her strokes.

Panting, Andrea pulled away, then pressed her forehead against his. "That *is* you. That is so damn *weird*. But a girl could get addicted to that. It's not that it's better, it's just so goddamn fast. And *focused*. Like the effect of a vibrator without actually using one. Oh God. Oh *God*." As she stroked over him more firmly and faster, he felt himself getting too close, which of course brought both Tara and Andrea to the same edge, a chorus of exclamations between the three of them.

He was more used to his own libido and its reaction time. Reluctant though he was, he stepped back from the quickening strokes and drew Tara off the barstool to follow him.

He didn't need to have slept with Andrea to know where her bedroom was. Before they entered, Andrea took Tara's hand and crossed that threshold with her first. Noah was all too willing to let Andrea take the lead. Not only had she not actually been with Tara like this before, it was her house, her room, her bed, and he was far from jealous or angry to watch Andrea spin Tara around and pull her down to kiss her.

Andrea had to stand on her toes, and Tara tangled her long, lanky limbs around Andrea, stroking over her more substantial curviness with the same relish as she consumed food. They were in house clothes instead of sexy lingerie, but the sight of their hands on each other, bodies flush and moving to each other's rhythm was something that Noah had literally never seen in real life before. It seemed like an elaborate execution of a fantasy he'd always had but hadn't dared express. He didn't know whether Andrea had ever seen herself in the same fantasy, but she didn't seem to mind, if the pressure building in his barely alleviated erection was any indication.

Much as his cock was desperate for some kind of contact—hand, mouth, fabric, anything—he resisted touching himself for as long as he could so that he could feel their pleasure rising in him rather than just his own.

Both Andrea and Tara had commented on how narrow and intense his pleasure was, but he was equally addicted to Tara's, and by extension Andrea's. It rose like a whole lake of water threatening to spill over a dam rather than the focused but formidable power of a waterspout. It hit such unlikely places between his cock and head, lit things inside his skull that he associated with the pointed physical lust of a full-on crush, that heady mimicry of love, supplemented by what he suspected was its first seeds—for Tara, although Noah loved Andrea in his own way, or else they never would have survived as partners this long.

Even so, he hadn't anticipated how he would react to the sight of Tara pulling Andrea's shirt over her head, exposing breasts that he already knew from Christmas parties were excellent. There was such a long distance between imagining and seeing for oneself.

Nor could he have expected how sharp his arousal would be as Tara kissed down to one exposed breast, taking in Andrea's nipple with a generous tongue to weaken his knees there in the door frame. Sweat sprang from his forehead, scalp, back of his neck, small of his back, especially as Andrea gave in to Tara's feasting with an abandon he was definitely not used to with her. That kind of freedom out in Meridian was dangerous, but her bedroom was her sanctuary. She could afford to go boneless in Tara's arms, especially now that she knew for a fact that this was Tara.

Noah pushed off the wall to come at Tara from behind, taking the hem of her T-shirt and pulling it up to double-check that her birthmarks were in the right place. Andrea didn't mind the brief break from Tara's mouth making her already dark nipples as flushed as her lips.

Tara straightened and lifted her arms to let Noah pull the T-shirt from her, and Andrea bent down to lick up to her breasts before giving them similar treatment. Between the two of them, his own nipples were small and taut and driving him a special crazy he wasn't used to.

Andrea raised her head with a particularly lingering lick and reached around Tara to tug at his shirt. "Off."

She pulled Tara back down for a kiss, walking backward to the bed while Noah removed his shirt and left it on the floor with the others.

Andrea shoved down her sweatpants before she sat back on the bed. Knowing what Andrea looked like naked and how much he liked it was really going to change their work dynamic, especially around the occasional sex demon. Maybe that didn't have to be such a bad thing. Even so, it overwhelmed him, especially as Andrea drew the rest of Tara's clothes down her body so that when they fell into bed together, they tangled their limbs fully naked, moaning, kissing each other like they needed it for oxygen, and fuck, he wasn't going to make it, which was probably why they weren't, either.

"I'm sorry," he gasped. "I need to come. I need to get this over with."

Tara knelt above Andrea on hands and knees, which made her breasts seem fuller and displayed her pussy, the lips spread with her spread legs. Noah had to close his eyes, gritted his teeth almost hard enough for them to grind. He gripped the base of his cock to the point of pain to keep from coming in his pants again.

When he opened his eyes, Tara looked at him over her shoulder, still displaying herself like an animal in heat. With her, that wasn't such a bad comparison, even without a werewolf bite. Andrea tried to pull her down, but Tara gently pressed her wrists to the bed and pillow.

"I want us to feel you come," Tara said. "No condom this time. We're making a mess tonight."

"*Fuck.*" He'd brought condoms in his back pocket, but he hadn't exactly prepared for a threesome and all that might entail. He hoped Andrea had some spare.

Noah undid his trousers and removed his briefs with them. They were all naked together in the dark room, lit mostly by the automatic porchlight outside her French doors.

Tara settled back on her heels to let Andrea push herself up by her elbows, a little line of curiosity between her eyebrows.

Noah fought the urge to hide his erection behind the codpiece of his hand under Andrea's scrutiny. "When did *I* become the center of attention tonight?"

Tara slipped two fingers between her legs and stroked through the folds to her clit, making all three of them moan together and convincing his hand to at least move over his cock rather than covering it. Then she pushed her fingers inside, and he heard that she was wet. He stepped closer to the bed to watch her fingers disappear inside her.

Andrea fell back against the pillow, panting so hard that Noah was surprised she didn't pass out from hyperventilation.

"Make us come, Noah," Tara said softly, moving her fingers inside herself to a much slower rhythm than his hand on his erection. "We want you to come."

"I just want to go on record…unh…and say that under normal circumstances, I'm not this fast."

"Mm-hmm. Totally," Andrea said. But she smiled, then bit her lip hard as she raised her hips off the bed toward nothing as their shared desire gathered in his scrotum.

He wasn't going to last much longer. They all knew it.

"Oh my God. *Oh*...that's..." Andrea stuffed her arm in her mouth and bit down as Tara buried her face in a pillow to cry out and Noah stroked himself furiously through his groaning orgasm, their pleasure sweeping into Tara and back out so that he not only felt the sparklers of Tara's orgasm but Andrea's, and yes, this could all too easily become addictive, theirs different enough from his but enhancing it, too. Tara shivered and shook as she slithered her fingers from her pussy and rubbed over her clit to extend the orgasm for all of them.

"You're getting better at that," Noah said, relieved as the last drops of his orgasm spilled over his shaft. "Learning fast."

"I've seen most of these things before, you know." Tara tucked herself next to Andrea, playing with the weight of her breast. "It's just one thing to know and another to put into practice with a body so drastically different from the one I was in when I saw."

"So you've been a voyeur for what? Thousands and thousands of years?" Andrea punched her arm playfully. "Filthy angel."

"Shame is an emotion for this world, not mine," Tara said. "It's our duty to observe. It's not our duty to feel, but sometimes we do anyway."

Noah climbed onto the bed. "Sorry about the sheets." Thick splatter marks stained all over the side, impossible to avoid.

"That's what washing machines are for. Believe me." Andrea licked her lips and covered Tara's hand over her breast. "These are new sheets from this afternoon. Quick shot, but excellent stamina, Dunn."

Gentle mocking, but her gaze was soft and a little insecure as well.

"How do you women do this? You get off and just keep going and going, like the fucking battery. I don't know how I still have anything left in my balls after this afternoon, and yet… We need to manage this to keep from going on for hours. I don't think I can do that again."

"We don't usually do marathons twice in one day," Andrea said. "Tara's special, the dirty little voyeur. And speaking of batteries… You want him to feel a woman's orgasm, to feel mine, like we felt his?"

Andrea turned over in bed to reach inside her nightstand.

"You've got to be kidding," Noah said as she revealed an entire collection of vibrators and dildos.

"I've been divorced for two years and taking care of myself for longer. I don't kid about these things. Just don't report me to the authorities for having more than six, copper. I've no intension of distributing what's mine. Just…sharing." She came back around with a finger bullet vibe and a sleekly curved vibrator that looked more like modern art. "I can take care of a woman with just my sweet little self, of course, but I played with these with… I'd like to replace the memories, and a gentle tongue is so sweet after a good, hard, rumbly vibe."

"I was just impressed by your selection," Noah replied, too fascinated by the process to be overly concerned by the fact that he was in bed and discussing sex toys with his partner.

"Different days, different cravings. There's one that just kind of pulses around the clit and, oh, hello, kitty. That's a vanilla-candle-and face-mask indulgence. There's my tried-and-true wand, another rumbler. But these, my fallen angel with the strangest indulgences, are for you. I'm going to make you come so hard, we'll all collapse into a delicious heap until you're settled enough to beg for my mouth to bring you over again. You, Noah, sit over there against the headboard, and don't touch yourself unless it's to hold back."

That part Noah was used to. Both he and Andrea could bark orders at the other without indignance in response. It was usually for safety and efficiency and hadn't happened in bed before, but Noah trusted Andrea and was almost too excited to watch Tara fall apart without being as distracted by things she was doing to him in return.

Tara twisted toward him and guided his face to kiss him, desire a warm fire in his abdomen that didn't seem to need additional stoking until Andrea switched on the finger bullet to its lowest setting and trailed it up Tara's thigh to the patch of hair around her folds.

Both Noah and Tara jerked apart, each crying out.

"Don't worry," Andrea said, looking smug, even though she had to have felt that, too. "As long as we don't scream. Tara, do you mind getting on your hands and knees again? I think that'll work best. Just like that, angel."

Noah had never thought of Andrea as the pet-name type, but Tara seemed to like it, maybe because it distinguished her from the demon.

Andrea crawled out from under Tara, then kissed over her shoulder to the wing stump, which she lingered on like an injury. Tara flexed her back as though spreading the ghosts of wings. It still didn't appear to bother her.

"She have any trouble with you to start?" Andrea held up the dildo to elaborate.

Noah shook his head. "Not after the first. She should be fine."

Andrea brought the tip to his mouth. "We've come, so we should be nice and juicy, but get it wet anyway, just in case."

It wasn't his thing, but Tara watched keenly, her intrigue clenching in his abdomen as he let Andrea push it over his tongue. He imagined his cock in Tara's mouth — and he wanted it to be *her* mouth this time, like Andrea wanted to use her toys with the real Tara, not the facsimile. Saliva wasn't a problem as he watched Tara watch him, as her desire became his. Andrea, too, seemed rapt by the sight.

"Hotter than I thought it was going to be," Andrea said, breathless as she pulled the dildo from his mouth. "I'll bet watching us kiss wasn't as surprising."

"No." He was a little breathless, too.

"You enjoy that, angel?" Andrea kissed between Tara's wing stumps as she tucked her finger vibe between Tara's legs.

Tara reared up, surprised into a shudder that was almost an orgasm on its own.

"First time is always so sensitive if you haven't enjoyed vibration before or for a long time," Andrea murmured into the back of her neck. She pushed Tara back down with her kisses. "My first time in college, I came in seconds. That's why it's on the lowest setting.

I like something stronger, but I don't want you coming too fast. Now, correct me if it's not the same, but you're kind of sensitive to direct contact. You like it like *this*."

She brought the vibe a little more forward to press just above the clit.

Tara fell forward, her forehead on her forearms as she cried out again into the muffling pillow.

Noah, too, slumped backward, making fists in the sheets to keep from touching himself as his erection tightened to unbearable tension, desperate to snap.

Andrea pulled back a bit with the vibe to keep it torturous but too far for the contact that Tara's canting hips demanded. Instead, she brought the curved dildo vibe to Tara's pussy. It barely needed the added lubrication, pushed in with limited resistance with the same wet sound as Tara's fingers entering her. The dildo was slender except for the more bulbous head, designed for angle rather than girth.

"Oh fuck." Noah braced himself when he realized what Andrea was going to do.

"I'm pretty sure it was— Oh my God, yes, right there. Oh God, that feels good." Andrea nearly sobbed as she hit the spot inside with the curved dildo. Tara bore down and rocked with a wail.

Noah's erection was taut against his abdomen and left pre-cum smears as he flexed and fought not to just grab his cock and rub out the next climax. The whole point was that it wouldn't be his.

Andrea didn't let up. Once she found the spot, she was relentless, bringing tears to Noah's eyes for a whole new reason. Tara, too, nearly wept and even seemed to be trying to get away from the intensity of the pleasure that jolted through her like electricity, if what was going through Noah right now was any indication. Somehow, Andrea managed to keep her composure, though she bit her lip through each thrust designed to rub directly over the G-spot over and over and over. Then she brought her finger vibe back to Tara's clit.

Noah nearly broke the wooden headboard as he came without so much as a touch. Something spattered the sheets near Tara, and it wasn't him. He only hit himself and a portion of the wall above him.

Andrea almost seemed to be fucking Tara herself, half draped over her from her other side as she continued penetrating Tara with the dildo and teasing with the buzz of the finger vibe until the climax became utterly unbearable. Then she eased the vibe up to Tara's mound to keep her less directly stimulated while she slowed the inner massage with the dildo — no less insistent, but slowing, slowing, slowing, Tara pushing back to meet it, until Andrea drew it out with a whine of protest from both her and Tara.

Andrea turned off the finger vibe, and Tara took the dildo and tossed it behind her to climb over Andrea and kiss her hard, parting Andrea's legs with her bony knees. Then, to Noah's unending fascination, she kissed down Andrea's body to her folds and her pretty pink clit, more prominent than Tara's and looking just as delicious with her spread and glistening like that — even more so when Tara brought her mouth to it to apply what she'd learned so far, and learning more about what Andrea herself liked from her reactions. Andrea crossed her legs behind Tara's back and sank into a far more languid but no less powerful arousal.

Tara gripped Noah's leg and tugged at him without removing her mouth from Andrea's clit. She made her invitation perfectly plain by raising her hips and spreading her legs, too.

Noah left the bed to grab his condoms from his pockets. He didn't worry anymore that he only had three. There had been a box in Andrea's nightstand.

He put one on, with the pleasure of good head making him hard again. Then he climbed into bed behind Tara and pushed his way in without unnecessary preamble.

Even with the condom suppressing some of his sensation, both Tara and Andrea moaned, and he joined them with his own as he thrust in, finally giving in to his impulses and driven forward as much by Tara's pleasure for his pleasure and Andrea's pleasure for Tara's pleasure. It was all one and the same. They were bound together into the same uncanny rhythm until Andrea tightened her fist in Tara's hair to push her away and pull her closer at the same time, and Noah gripped Tara's hips to bury himself inside her as she stroked around her clit through their simultaneous climax once again.

"That is fucking ridiculous," Andrea said as she collapsed back on the pillows.

Tara crawled up to rest next to her in the valley between the pillows. Noah removed the condom, tossed it into the wastebasket next to the nightstand, then put his other condoms next to the alarm clock. He took the pillow on Tara's other side, tucked against Tara's back. Andrea turned over to face Tara. Together, they brought their warmth to her.

"I should distinguish myself from Sela somehow," Tara muttered, stroking Andrea's arm with her fingertips and Noah's leg with her toes. "Maybe a tattoo. Or I should cut my hair, color it. I don't know.

All those things can be copied if she knows about it. But I don't want the marks on my back to be the only things that make me look different from her, if hunters are looking for her."

"They know about the birthmarks, though," Noah said, combing through her hair. "And they know not to kill a fallen angel who hasn't chosen to throw in her lot with demons. They didn't help save you tonight only to go killing you by accident."

"She might not come back. Might not risk it." Tara sounded distant, like she was already drifting to sleep while speaking. Noah gentled his touch in her hair even more, hypnotic.

"We can hope," Andrea said. She closed her eyes, arm around Tara's waist. "For now, we rest."

* * * *

At four in the morning, Noah's phone rang, jolting them awake. The porchlight outside had since gone off, and Noah had to depend on the glow of his phone screen to find it in his discarded trousers.

He spoke softly as he gathered his clothes and tried to put them on one-handed. When the conversation ended, clothes were much easier to put on.

"I have to go," he said softly to the glint of eyes near the pillows. "Playing hooky on shift, aren't I? Worth it, but there's something I need to take care of."

"Need help?" Andrea asked. "I'm not offering, of course. I've worked enough during my weekend."

Noah smiled, even though Andrea wouldn't be able to see. "No. Just the usual kind of weird. Reports of occult youth activity in the industrial park. Probably nothing, but I should go check it out. You two get some sleep and have a nice weekend. I have to recover and…you know, replenish. Have fun with Hannah. I'll see you Sunday night."

"Love you," Tara murmured, half- or maybe three-quarters asleep.

Noah didn't know if she'd meant to say it or if she really meant it, but he massaged her foot lightly. "Love you, too, angel."

Sign up for our newsletter and find out about all our romance book releases, eBook sales and promotions, sneak peeks and FREE romance books!

Meridian: Tooth & Claw
Aurelia T. Evans

Excerpt

The line out from Sordid didn't curve around the corner, but it was still ten o'clock before Rose made it to the front. However, once there, the bouncer immediately pulled back the velvet rope to let her in.

Becoming a vampire didn't make a person much more beautiful but for smoother, firmer skin and the healthiest of hair and nails, which continued to grow after undeath. However, vampires did tend to change humans who fit their ideal of beauty. They preferred not to forge deeper connections with humans, only the vampires they became, and given their long lives in the dark, they almost always chose for a lovely view.

She wouldn't have been the only lovely view in line for the historic downtown speakeasy, but the way she displayed that view certainly didn't hurt—nor the way that the bouncer's neck scars stretched up from under his shirt collar as he turned.

Rose's gold heels were thin and high, but she didn't struggle on the steps down into the building's basement. Despite the dim red-tinged light—a staple for bars and clubs, but also a courtesy for Sordid's more nocturnal patrons—she could see the whole room clearly from its entrance.

She wasn't old enough to have attended speakeasies in their heyday, but she'd visited a number of dance and novelty clubs around Meridian since arriving a week ago, and already she liked Sordid better than most. A band at the front played low and slow, if not soft, with a torch singer whose voice was so sultry, Rose wondered if her blood would taste of smoke.

In dance clubs, there was freedom in losing oneself to the music, to a rhythm so strong she thought her heart might be beating again, but it could also be so much flashing lights and sounds that she couldn't hear herself think even when she wanted to. Here, the bass provided a gentler pulse, the upright piano tingled emotion over her skin, while the singer's smoky alto thrummed something deeper, but she could also hear her own thoughts, and other people didn't have to shout to be heard. Sordid was not a place to discourage whispers or first or second thoughts. As the lights were dimmer for night eyes, the music was more tolerable for those with keen ears. Her senses all seemed to let out a sigh of relief as she stepped into the speakeasy.

There were roughly a hundred to a hundred twenty-five people in the relatively small basement, which was the reason for the line, although it was difficult to get a good count due to privacy curtains in the booths and a hallway that would lead to private rooms.

The speakeasy was strict about no money changing hands except between bouncer, bartender, or band. Everything else was barter, which was no different than any other venue that encouraged shallow carnality between its patrons.

She left the bar with a frosted glass of red to weave through the crowd.

One thing that set her apart from the rest was that she'd come alone. Most people in Sordid arrived in groups, from couples to packs, regardless of species. Safety in numbers, safety for curiosity, with members of one group or couple sometimes breaking away to join another, mingling on the dance floor like tentative watercolors to the hypnotic, evocative, seductive music coming from the stage.

Rose was tempted to ask if the woman was a siren but decided to simply leave a good tip at the stage edge. The singer, with meticulously crafted finger curls, glistening red lips, and a glittering black dress, glanced down over her ribbon microphone and locked dark eyes with Rose. Then her gaze drifted down. Rose stood still, allowing the singer take her time over the slinky liquid dress the color of pewter, loose enough that the thin straps threatened to fall away from her full breasts at the slightest provocation if Rose didn't know how to hold herself, or how to be perfectly, predatorially still. In Sordid, there was no reason to pretend she was anything but what she was.

She'd moved down to Texas because she'd wanted to finally enjoy solitude, and space, and rooftops, and beautiful windows that never slanted sunlight onto her bed but still brought day into her world. Yet she'd only been in Meridian alone for a week and already felt…lonely. A little over twenty years as human, a little over sixty as a vampire, she didn't think she'd ever been completely alone.

As a vampire of a vaunted and tight-knit family house, she hadn't been able to really choose her own company since she'd died—until she'd packed up all her beautiful things and signed away her right by blood to remain or return without going through the same channels as any outsider.

She didn't think she'd ever return.

That didn't mean there weren't things about her decision that were difficult, even a little frightening, although she was usually the creature in the dark that people feared.

The delicate titanium cuff on her ear and the oath in new ink around her wrist, however, indicated to those who knew what they meant that she was safer than most. And Sordid was an Alliance business. Not a demon club, where humans were either victims, servants, slaves, or hunters trying to prove they were badass and unafraid. The Alliance was an agreement between vampires, werewolves, and hunters in Meridian that none would hunt the species of the others. Urban werewolf packs could run freely through city parks after dark, aiding the coyotes and bobcats in controlling the rodent, rabbit, and deer populations. Vampires could live peacefully off butcher blood and voluntary donors with a promise not to kill or turn. Hunters could focus their efforts on hybrids more inclined toward carnage.

The Alliance wasn't universally beloved, even among those who'd agreed to it, as evidenced by the occasional glower between the three camps coexisting within Sordid's walls. Sometimes mistakes were made or someone tried to use the Alliance to get away with murder. But the last twelve years had been a largely successful experiment, which was why Rose had moved to a completely different city in a completely different state, all by herself for the first time in decades.

And looking for someone who might make this freedom all the sweeter.

The torch singer was sweet indeed, and the shift of her body and cant of her hips suggested she thought the same about Rose in her evening gown, her inked oath and former family crest, her Art Deco diamond and emerald pendant—a gift from her sire long ago, chosen because of the way her cleavage framed it. The lower the singer sang, the more Rose wanted to draw her down to the dance floor and against her body so she could swallow the vibrations.

Rose sipped from her drink, unblinking, enjoying the music both close to the instruments and coming from the speakers and the waves of desire emanating from the singer, rising in something reminiscent of heat low in Rose's abdomen.

Large, hot hands smoothed over her shoulders, threatening the straps so carefully placed to keep herself as decent as a woman needed to be in a place like this. The man imposed but did not expose, trailed his palms down her arms before he pressed gently behind her.

"Beautiful woman like you shouldn't be alone." A subtle growl in the voice shivered like the singer's alto over and under Rose's skin. There was something so very alive in the stranger's heat and scent, heightened by the animal musk entwined with it. "I can see that you can take care of yourself, but you wouldn't have to with me."

Rose was tall in her heels, and the man still had to angle his head to rest his cheek on her shorn scalp, where his stubble was rougher than hers. She briefly leaned back in his hold, relishing his scent—all the vitality of a human and all the virility of a werewolf, pouring from every pore and responding to the pheromones from hers. Perfumiers of her family house made colognes from both to sell to those who could afford not to ask the price.

He dragged his lips over her scalp and whispered in her ear, "Meet me there." He pointed to a booth currently occupied by another werewolf-vampire pair, both wearing titanium cuffs on their ears as well. The vampire was buried deep in the werewolf's shoulder. "I'm going to get myself a stiff drink, and you can get a *real* drink from me. Someone like you doesn't have to be alone for long."

Rose shrugged his hands off her arms, then stepped away from his furnace body. She didn't mind the ambient chill. "I already have a drink."

The werewolf's low rumbling growl of desire harshened. Rose didn't resent his upset. Werewolves were not renowned for their ability to conceal how they felt. Between human expression and werewolf volatility, emotions made themselves plain one way or another. Despite his disappointment, though, he drew away from her to seek satiation elsewhere.

It would not be unusual in Sordid to be approached out of interest for her bite. The vampire's thrall—a combination of mysticism, which vampires could control, and pheromone, which they could not—was addictive on both sides of any encounter, casual or long-term. There were vampire clubs in Meridian, like the Slaughterhouse, designed to reel humans in like fish, but Sordid advertised itself through word of mouth as a place where people could satisfy the desire for a safer bite—one where they were guaranteed to make it through the night. There would inevitably be both the curious and the experienced from all factions allowed in the speakeasy.

As the band finished their set and headed to the bar for a break, stereotypically trance-like goth music filtered through the speakers—still not so loud that it would drown out conversation, whispers, the squeak of vinyl and soft moans, louder cries coming from behind closed doors. The speakeasy knew its patrons and what they came for, couldn't conceal the metallic tang of warmed blood on tap next to beer from local breweries, nor the raw or lightly cooked meat that they provided from the kitchen. Most of the attendees were dressed in the gothic mode, much like the family many an evening within their sprawling house.

Expectations were clear — not to mention detailed on their website and on a poster outside the building. It was a place for humans to safely visit, but it was *for* the vampires and werewolves, whether they embraced their costumes or not. As long as it wasn't some cheap Halloween ensemble, humans donning elements of vampire culture was considered both flattery and a certain amount of permission or invitation. The cultural expression was all a bit reductive — Rose had many more clothes than formalwear or gothic style — but sartorial expression was part of the ritual, like wearing Sunday best to church. She respected the effort and clearly made some of her own, as she had during feasts and parties in her own family house.

She joined the band at the bar with her drink and settled on a barstool a few seats away, waiting to see if the torch singer had merely been playing to her audience or was genuinely interested.

Twenty years ago, she would have simply switched on the thrall and had the singer right there against the bar, leaving her faint or dead. There was an abundance of gutters here in Meridian in which to throw bodies. Her new butcher had his own crematorium.

The singer glanced over her shoulder and met Rose's eyes. Then she slipped off her seat to bring her glass of prosecco over with her while the bassist and pianist grinned and returned to their discussion.

As the singer joined Rose on the next stool, she brushed her fingers over Rose's arm and leaned in. Rose was ready to kiss those lips, to smear the singer's red lipstick over her own makeup-free mouth like blood.

The singer shifted to the side to murmur in Rose's ear like the wolf. "No visible scars, but I flow freely in other places." She took Rose's hand and drew it under the slit in her skirt. She stopped Rose's fingers on her inner thigh, where smooth knots of scars suggested she'd had teeth there many times before.

Rose kept her sigh to herself, but her lust went cold, like swimming through warm waters and hitting a pocket of fresh spring chill. She stroked over the scars with her nails, then pressed a kiss just under the singer's jaw, yearning for the pulse underneath and mourning the moan that arose. The singer's pleasure was just as pleasant as her music. Rose wished she could explore that more, perhaps in one of the private rooms. But she stroked the singer's cheek as she withdrew from her neck, from her thigh.

For a moment, the singer was stricken, but like the wolf, she accepted Rose's refusal with grace, despite confusion and frustration visible in the furrows beneath her finger curls.

Rose drank deeply from her glass, then left the bar again.

Searching.

Maybe this wasn't the place to find what she was looking for. Sordid was a venue where humans and werewolves wanted to get bitten by a vampire, where humans and vampires wanted sex with a less inhibited werewolf, where they all wanted to walk on the edge of a forest fire without getting burned. At its less aesthetic heart, it was a safe space for chasers.

Rose had had enough of that over the decades. So many humans had chased her into early graves. Werewolves had followed her into their own servitude.

But here she was, weary of arson and looking instead for a cozy little fire in a hearth.

She didn't think either the wolf or the singer would have trouble finding what they wanted, though, among the crowd of steadily introduced new blood as pairings and groups left the speakeasy — mutually satisfied or with the promise of a more private evening in softer, larger beds.

Rose's gaze finally fell on a cluster of werewolves gathered around a table piled with the chaos of cleared and partially cleared plates and assorted glasses of beer, wine, and bourbon.

As becoming a vampire smoothed and firmed skin, becoming a werewolf increased tone and tightness of muscle, bulky or lean as body type demanded, and they burned hotter than humans, which especially appealed to her sensitive sense of smell — sensitive everything, from heat-sensing that bordered on reptilian to the almost-taste of wolf musk emanating in a denser mist around them. Not to mention the scent of carefully prepared raw meat, designed for such patrons but also to keep health inspectors happy.

Among the friends gathered around the table, men and women met her eyes, angled toward her, and she knew she could hold out a hand and one or more might come with her. For an hour. For a few. There was knowledge in their consideration, in their quickening hearts, broadening desire, the intrigue of their attraction.

She stopped in front of the boy occupied with his plate of beef tartare. Stood in front of him until he noticed — or showed that he noticed. The larger cuff on his ear pushed through his long hair. When he looked up, the curtain of his hair fell away from his face. She expected it to be as casually scruffy as his hair was healthy and wild, loose around his shoulders and reaching halfway down his chest. But he was clean-shaven, with only a shadow of stubble from the end of the day. His hair was brown in low light but gleamed with enough gold that sun likely made him blond — not that she could easily see that for herself. His eyes, too, seemed sun-bleached, piercingly blue, unsettlingly guileless.

Time would tell if those pale eyes, widening pupils, and wild hair could be trusted. In Rose's experience, beauty itself was suspicious, including her own. Many sharp things were wrapped in silk. But she liked what she saw. And there was no mistaking he did, too. Men had more trouble hiding that from her, werewolves even more so. That made them easier to manipulate, if she chose, but also less guileful by default.

The boy — everyone younger than her was 'boy', and as a vampire, she struggled to gauge ages, especially among the hyper-healthy werewolf population — lifted his plate of beef tartare to her like an offering. "Would you like some? I don't know if you can have it or not, but…"

Rose used her nail to gather a few pieces of beef. She didn't need anything other than blood, but she could appreciate animal protein as well as sugar. About the only foods she couldn't enjoy like she had so long ago that they seemed like dreams were vegetables and plain bread, although she adored chocolate cake.

She took the meat into her mouth and hummed around the bland shallots and hit of salt. Raw meat was better than cooked for her, too. She took his fork and gathered a larger bite, fought the urge to slither her tongue around the metal. She left the rest for his more voracious appetite, though she craved myoglobin.

A flush blooming over the boy's cheeks deepened the color in his lips. "So you *can* have things other than blood."

Now she wondered how young he really was, in the sense of how recently he'd been changed. All she knew was that, because he was here at all, he was old enough for her purposes.

"I like savory and sweet. What do you think runs through blood?" All blood tasted more or less the same to humans — that much she remembered — but vampire tongues discerned a thousand differences in the balance of what blood spread through a body to maintain it, from vitamins and minerals to fat, protein, and glucose. There was a mystical element to vampirism, of course. Nothing without a heartbeat should be able to live, move, breathe, speak, fuck, and yet they did. But in other ways, they were just as biologically grounded as the werewolves.

She stole a slice of salmon from the sashimi plate and rested it on her tongue before drawing it in. Buttery, slick, rich, a little sweet, tender to bite.

In return for his hospitality, she held her drink out to him.

"Blood?" he asked.

"Does it smell like blood?"

A wolf could drink it if it were. He'd even enjoy it. He leaned in and put his lips where she'd put hers. When she glimpsed his dark tongue, she tipped the glass to give him a taste. He smiled even as he swallowed.

"Sangria. Why choose cold around here when you can have hot?" he asked.

She took another drink. Macerated fruit mixed with red wine made her feel like a fruit bat trophy wife, but she loved it anyway. After just a week in Texas, she'd discovered sangria swirl margaritas and known she was going to have a problem, even though her body processed alcohol such that it had only the mildest psychotropic effect.

She set her mostly finished glass on the table. She took the boy's hand instead, smiling when he shivered from her cold, wet skin. "Is that what you want me to do?"

"I asked you first."

"Dance with me?"

"Yes, ma'am."

"Boy, I know I moved south, but if you 'ma'am' me again, this evening's gonna end before it begins."

A charming grin stretched across his face. Fine folds suggested he was older than she'd initially thought. She still couldn't pinpoint a decade.

Rose stepped back until he had no choice but to stand to follow her. Standing took longer than expected. Everything about him was lankier than it appeared slouched back in his chair. His tunic-like shirt over fitted jeans accentuated the length of him, everything just a little too long.

Everything? part of her wondered, but that didn't distract her as much as the way he seemed to burst from his own clothes, shirt sleeves rolled up to keep from showing how his arms were too long for them, his jeans ripped from artistry rather than wear. His shoes were fashionable, buffed, and large.

She backed through the tables to the dance floor without having to look behind her. Either people got out of her way, she sensed their closeness, or she saw them through the werewolf's eyes — in their reflection or his concern.

On the dance floor, Rose guided his hand to her waist. He got the hint and joined it with his other, but he was still a gentleman, with space between their hips as they swayed to the rhythm of the pre-recorded music. Rose thought that was adorable, approaching perfect, and had to convince herself not to get her hopes up.

Even if he wasn't exactly what she was looking for, though, she'd already decided to give him the night, nice young man that he was.

"You're new around here," the wolf said.

"If that isn't just a line, how would you know?"

"I've never seen you in Sordid before. I would have noticed. I'm not cheesy enough to say you're the prettiest woman to walk through that door, but you're certainly striking. Also, your Alliance ink still smells wet."

He blushed again, but she drew an inch closer and smiled for him without letting her fangs slide down, although she caught him searching for them.

"Fresh. I mean it smells fresh," he said.

"Don't you mean ripe?" She sidled close enough now for her hips to brush against his.

He didn't pull away, just adjusted his arms to hold her better and encourage her to press closer, and she did. His natural heat wrapped around her like a good blanket in summer.

"I am new here," she finally replied. "To Sordid. To the city. I've been getting to know the nightlife. It's better than where I came from."

"It's not quite Vegas or New York, cities that never sleep. Meridian sleeps at least a few hours a night, but it has more stamina any other Texas city. Maybe because it's younger. Or maybe because the monsters don't stick to the shadows like they do most every other place."

"You consider yourself a monster?" Cuff and oath aside, she wasn't interested in someone who would moralize her all the way to a Catholic confessional for something that had been done to her against her will sixty years ago.

She accepted her responsibility for most of the decisions she'd made since, but the fact was that she wasn't human anymore, wasn't subject to the same rules and laws. Just because she could eat meat and chocolate cake didn't mean she could live on anything other than blood. Not every city had sanguine butchers who happened to serve the vampire community without asking awkward questions about what they needed all that pig's blood for. And every vampire knew that human or hybrid blood was better by multiple factors. It made the undead feel alive.

"Only in the traditional 'Universal Horror' sense," the wolf replied. "I've been told I look quite mild-mannered."

"Are you as laidback as you seem?"

He gave her that charming crooked grin again. He had dog teeth, unironically — both canines, which made him appear more like a vampire than her to the untrained eye. Long arms, long torso, long legs, long teeth. She'd bet he sprawled in chaotic directions on a bed.

"I guess you could say I'm slow to anger. I don't Hulk out into the werewolf or anything. But I've still got the wolf in me. Everyone does, even the ones who aren't tied to the moon. I might be more nervous with you if I were less in tune with mine."

Rose was entranced by how he didn't look away from her now, although he'd barely let himself look before she'd chosen him. If she hadn't known that werewolves had no intrinsic thrall beyond the animalistic quality of their pheromone, she'd think he was trying to hypnotize her.

"Wouldn't that put you more on edge, knowing what you could do if you lost control?" she asked.

"You may look one shake away from naked, new girl, but anyone who isn't a fool knows a vampire is dangerous. I'm not afraid of you, though, because I trust your new ink, and because I trust my wolf to protect me. You can't turn me, and I can't turn you, but we can do damage to each other if we need to."

"You're not afraid I can make you do whatever I want, if I chose? You're not afraid I'm doing that right now?" she asked, her breasts heavy against his chest and threatening even more to fall out of alignment with the dress, to expose her to him and anyone else watching out of curiosity or envy.

"I think the fact we're dancing like goth prom instead of me on my knees or in one of those booths or rooms, and you're not mixing my blood in with your sangria, suggests you're keeping your thrall to yourself. Not that I'm against any of those things, if that's where you see tonight going."

"Is that all you want from me?" Not plaintive or petulant. That he wanted her was academic. She needed to know if he was like the others. "My bite in exchange for your blood?"

"To be honest, I just come here for the food."

Rose burst out laughing into his shoulder.

"They have a good raw meat menu. More seasoned than rat or squirrel. And I like their music, and the way people look to be here. Everything's so casual in the pack. It's nice to have an excuse to get dressed up." He swayed into the music with more emphasis. "If all we do is dance, I'd still be happy."

Her fangs slid out of their own volition, mimicking the stiffening of his erection struggling against his jeans, against her. She wrangled her thrall back to just pheromones, but not before he curled his fingers into her waist and hips and fought against a groan.

As the band headed back toward the stage, the pre-recorded music faded from the speakers. Rose and the boy stopped dancing.

She looked up at him and wondered if her gaze captivated him like his did to her. She knew what the rest of her looked like, but she hadn't seen her face in decades, so her memory of that was less clear. She remembered that her eyes were gray or blue, depending on the light, but she didn't know whether being a vampire had changed their quality, beyond the mercury reflection that moonlight flashed in the pupil. Werewolves flashed green.

"Have you ever been with a vampire before?"

"Do you mean have I ever danced with a vampire?" The teasing sparkle in his eyes had nothing to do with reflectivity. "I'll admit, dancing's all I've done."

"I won't ask if you've never had sex before." Whatever his age, he was old *enough*, and when werewolves got together, lived together, stripped down to nothing, they were as prone to indulge their sexual appetites as their more prosaic hungers. It was both vampires' and werewolves' natures to indulge — the nature of the beast, as it were.

"You looking for some young thing to corrupt?"

The torch singer resumed singing with her band again, which did nothing to curtail Rose's lust. The slither of her tongue between her fangs tantalized the nerves in and around them, made her imagine his tongue between her folds.

"Is this corruption?" Rose slid her hand down between them and, without hesitation, underneath the waist of his jeans. It was a tight fit, and she moved slowly to give him a chance to stop her. But he didn't, not when she crossed the line, not when she found the hot shaft of his pulsing erection and wrapped her cold fingers around it—which did nothing to shrink or soften him. Quite the contrary.

And yes, *all* of him ran long.

A low growl mingled with his startled moan, hot exhalation against her bare scalp, which was when he discovered that her close-shorn hair was soft. In his moment of hedonism, he drew her even closer, canted his hips to thrust against her hand, and rubbed his cheek against her head. His neck was mere inches from her aching fangs, which begged to sink into him slow and fill herself with his heat, but she held back, even as she stroked him as well as she could in the small space provided.

"The preachers say what they say," he finally replied, when he could think well enough to string words together, "but they're just threatened. Threatened by pleasure that isn't transcendental, celestial. Threatened by bodies. By the mess. They'll make you feel guilty about anything and everything if they can, by the fact that you're just an animal who can think it's something better. But we *are* animals, and animals don't care. They just…ah…do as they please, as they're created to do, and pleasure is good and pain is bad, unless it's also good and… God, your hand is cold, how does it even…?"

With her free hand, she guided his—with its long fingers—up from her waist to her breast, barely covered by the dress strap, then not, as she eased him underneath to cup her. She admired the way his hand looked while molded to her curve, then raised her head again. His pupils were dilated, and he panted, tongue wet behind sharper teeth, flushed lips licked.

"Would you like to come home with me tonight?"

"Is that a trick quest—?" The growl infiltrated his voice, deepening it, and to the shudder of the torch singer's vibrato, Rose tilted her head to capture the last of the growl and cut his reply short.

There was nothing she could do about her pheromones, nor the effect of her fangs with direct contact, but at this point, the boy mostly knew what he was getting into. She wrapped her free arm around his neck to draw herself up on her toes and surge her breast into his hand. He squeezed, although not hard, teasing her taut nipple with his thumb and the webbing next to it.

She teased him just as much, making him gasp when she used her nails—just nails, not claws—to smooth his pre-cum over the head and shaft. Her hand burned from the heat he created.

And the rest of her threatened to go up in flames from how quickly he showed that he was *not* inexperienced with his kiss. Whatever meat he'd consumed earlier had done nothing to deter this different but just as carnal hunger, only heightened by the caress of her fangs against his lips, his tongue, which met hers, before he succumbed to her.

They'd lost track of where they were on the dance floor. Rose slammed back against a table, which was fortunately bolted to the floor. The people at that table laughed instead of shouting with indignance. They grabbed their glasses before the impact could topple them over. Which was good, because Rose tightened her grip on both neck and cock and whirled the boy around to shove him against the table instead.

He broke from the kiss, gasping. Rose abruptly released his erection so that he wouldn't come — or if he did, so her hand wouldn't get too messy yet. She trailed her touch back up over his tunic shirt and stopped where his heart beat faster than the bass.

He caught her nipple between fingers, pinching a little harder, but mostly he tried to control himself — not a wolf's natural state, but neither man nor beast would want to finish too soon.

Not that a werewolf was as limited as a man, and her thrall could extend the endurance of the quickest shot.

She admired his self-control, though, and his naked desire for her as he stared at her lips, her teeth, her eyes, her breasts — one bare now, the other barely covered and threatening to escape from the tenuous strap.

"My name is Rose, puppy. What's yours?"

He was still breathless when he replied, "Simon. But you can call me 'puppy' or anything you fucking like. *Fuck.*"

She stepped back, her hand over his heart pinning him against the table still. With the other, she readjusted her dress, although what had been seen could not be unseen. She didn't much mind. Living so long half-demon meant that so many people had seen her without clothes, and many of them would live much longer knowing the sight. As long as it was her choice.

She curled her finger to beckon him as she started for the door. "Follow me."

"Anywhere."

About the Author

Aurelia T. Evans is an up-and-coming erotica author with a penchant for horror and the supernatural.

She's the twisted mind behind the werewolf/shifter Sanctuary trilogy, demonic circus series Arcanium, and vampire serial Bloodbound. She's also had short stories featured in various erotic anthologies.

Aurelia presently lives in Dallas, Texas (although she doesn't ride horses or wear hats). She loves cats and enjoys baking as much as she dislikes cooking. She's a walker, not a runner, and she writes outside as often as possible.

Aurelia loves to hear from readers. You can find her contact information, website details and author profile page at https://www.firstforromance.com

ENTWINED PUBLISHING